FORGET ME NOT

Q.B. TYLER

Copyright © 2019 by Q.B. Tyler

All rights reserved.

ISBN: 9781692131043

No part of this publication may be reproduced, distributed, or transmitted in any form or by any means, including photocopying, recording, or other electronic or mechanical methods, without the prior written permission of the publisher, except in the case of brief quotations embodied in critical reviews and certain other noncommercial uses permitted by copyright law.

This is a work of fiction. Names, characters, businesses, places, events, and incidents are either the products of the author's imagination and used in a fictitious manner. Any resemblance to actual persons, living or dead, or actual events is purely coincidental.

Cover Design: NET Hook & Line Designs
Editing: Kristen Portillo—Your Editing Lounge
Interior Formatting: Stacey Blake—Champagne Book Design
Proofreading: Leslie Middleton

PLAYLIST

Somebody That I Used to Know—*Gotye*

Everybody Knows—*John Legend*

Video Games—*Lana Del Rey*

Breathe 2 AM—*Anna Nalick*

Unbreak My Heart—*Toni Braxton*

Someone Like You—*Adele*

Come Home—*One Republic*

Speeding Cars—*Imogen Heap*

Run To You—*Whitney Houston*

It Will Rain—*Bruno Mars*

How Can You Mend A Broken Heart? —*Al Green*

It's All Coming Back To Me Now—*Celine Dion*

Drunk in Love—*Beyoncé*

What do you do when the love of your life *forgets*?

Not the good times.

Not the love.

Not the passion.

But the *pain* and *heartbreak* and *betrayal*.

He doesn't remember that he broke my heart.

But I do.

He doesn't remember the darkest parts of our marriage.

He doesn't remember that six months ago, I said goodbye.

What do you do when the love of your life remembers your marriage *but not your divorce?*

For the women who fought like hell for their happily ever after…

and for the ones still fighting.

FORGET ME *Not*

PROLOGUE

Olivia
Present Day

FOUR ZERO SIX
Four zero seven
Four zero eight...

The sound of my heels against the linoleum flooring is all that floods my ears as I walk down what appears to be a never-ending hallway.

I pass the rooms one by one trying my best not to look inside. Trying my best to avoid eye contact with all of the families that are waiting anxiously in the intensive care unit to know the fate of their loved ones. I'm not good with tragedy or death or sickness. I'm not good with hospitals; they give me a sense of uneasiness I've never been able to shake. I've been here ten minutes and I already feel the anxiety crawling up my throat and threatening to expel from me in the form of bile or tears. The agonizing fear had taken ahold of me the second I received the phone call and slowly unfurled in my chest the entire way to the hospital.

"Mrs. Clarke, are you in any position to drive yourself to the hospital? Perhaps you should arrange for transportation? ...Mrs. Clarke? Mrs. Clarke?"

I'd let the phone fall from my fingertips, and it crashed and skid across the freshly mopped marble floors of my kitchen. The breath fell from my lips in quick bursts as I imagined a life without the man I'd known for the past nine years. The one I'd been happy with for over ninety percent of them.

Four zero nine.

I stare at the numbers next to the door, holding my breath as I attempt to make my way through the open door when a familiar face comes into view.

"Liv." The sense of familiarity washes over me, giving me a sense of comfort as he walks towards me and shuts the large door behind him. I try my best to see inside before he closes the door, but he pushes me back slowly and guides me to a small bench in the hallway. "Did you drive here?"

"N—no." I stammer out as I shake my head. "I wasn't sure I could. How…" I swallow down the tears. God knows my eyes have cried over this man hundreds of times, but now wouldn't be one of those times. He was fine. He had to be fine, and thus I wasn't about to cry for him now. Not when he'd eviscerated my heart earlier this year. He wasn't allowed to spend another minute holding my tear ducts hostage. My lip trembles, refuting my thoughts and I swallow down the tears. "Wren," I whisper the name of my husband's best friend, Wren Hamilton, who also happens to be the best neurosurgeon in the city. "What…what's going on?"

He puts his hand over mine, and I watch his eyebrows furrow as he rubs his hand over my bare ring finger. "He loves you so much, Liv. He's such a wreck without you."

I look up from where our hands are joined, where his warm hands cover mine that feel frozen solid. Despite the comfort, I slide my hands from underneath his and just like that the tears have dissipated. "Yeah, I'll bet. I didn't come here to rehash the details of my failing marriage, Wren; I came here because I was told Bennett was in an accident." I turn my gaze towards the door and speak my greatest fear into existence. "He's not going to die, right? Because..." I clear my throat, trying to dislodge the ball of emotions that has filled the space from speaking those words aloud. "He can't die." I bite my bottom lip just as tears well in my eyes. I'm afraid to blink, knowing it will cause one to cascade down my cheek.

"He's alive, Liv, but he's unconscious. He was in a car accident and suffered quite a bit of head trauma. Traumatic brain injuries are quite normal in the severity of his accident, but there are some things I need to keep an eye on." He pulls his stethoscope from around his neck and holds it in one hand as he leans over and rests his forearms on his thighs. "He's banged up, Olivia, but he'll live. If that's even what you would say he's been doing the last six months..." he trails off and I roll my eyes at his obvious attempt to make me sympathetic to our situation.

"Okay, now is really not the time." I brush my hands down my black pencil skirt and cross my arms over my chest. *I'm so not in the mood for this. Is this an ambush about the divorce? Hell, is Bennett really even in there?* I let the morbid thought float through my mind once before shaking my head, knowing that Wren would never do something deceitful like that. He's actually a good guy, *the best*, and I know he's just being Bennett's best friend, but he's *my* friend too.

"Then when is the time, huh? You won't talk to me or Lys," he barks referring to his wife and my best friend as he stands up and begins to pace the floor in front of me. "Whatever is going on with him physically, will heal. I'll see to that. But his heart won't heal that easily." His eyes transform into haunted and exhausted orbs with a hint of resentment. Like it's my fault that all of this is happening. As if it's *my* fault that we're going through this.

"He cheated on me, Wren. I didn't *do* anything."

"I don't completely agree with that." He puts a hand up in attempts to silence me. "But I agree his offense outweighs yours. Liv, it was a mistake and he's been begging you for your forgiveness!"

"And? He fucked some woman. A woman he's STILL fucking!"

"He doesn't want her, Olivia! It's...complicated," he snaps as he puts his hands on his hips. His dark blue scrubs are harsh against his pale skin, but bring out the color of his eyes, especially now as they're so dark and angry, they're almost navy.

"Bullshit, don't hand me that. He's still sleeping with her, Wren. He's still with *her*."

He sits back down next to me. "He only wants *you*."

"Wren, you need to let this go. Bennett and I are over," I whisper as I put my hand on top of his, as if he's the one in need of comfort. I look down at our hands again and note the contrast I'm very familiar with. My honey brown skin against his pale. Although my soon to be ex-husband was much tanner, with an olive complexion, just the visual causes a flutter of nostalgia.

It's 2019, so being in an interracial relationship isn't something that causes much, if any negative attention, except when my husband was hit on and women just assumed I wasn't his wife.

Or when I was forced to interact with my mother-in-law. *But no, of course she's not racist, because "Jennifer Porter has been my best friend since college."*

It didn't bother me, and Bennett kept her far away from me much of the time, not to mention his devotion to me was unwavering. He loved me deeply, irrevocably almost painfully. The "threats" to our marriage, if you could even call them that, were shot down without another glance. It was obvious he only had eyes for me and wore his ring proudly.

He was that way from the beginning. He pursued me for months and convinced me to date him. Showing up at my job, sending me flowers, and finding me almost anywhere as if he had a tracker on me. I would have been a little creeped out if it weren't for the fact that his best friend was dating mine.

Even still, it was a little creepy.

It took all of two dates for me to fall, *deeply*. And though I tried to play hard to get, I was his from the moment he pressed his lips to mine on that bridge in Central Park. And the way he proceeded to court me the next few months, showed he was mine too.

We were engaged within a year and married the following. We were that level of happy that people hated. Outwardly our marriage was perfect and on the inside, it was just as beautiful. We had passion and love and trust and I was completely devoted to Bennett Clarke.

Life was perfect.

Until everything came crashing down.

CHAPTER
One

Olivia
Nine Years Ago

"I THOUGHT THAT WAS YOU." I LOOK UP JUST IN TIME TO SEE Bennett *something* take the seat across from me at my very small table at the coffee shop just off campus. My textbooks litter the space in front of me as I'm studying for finals and my laptop is perched precariously in my lap. I pull my headphones from my ears, wondering in what world my appearance gives the impression that I have time for chit-chat even if the man is unbelievably gorgeous.

Piercing green eyes with flecks of honey trace my face. Eyes full of promises—though I'm not sure what they are yet. Effortlessly dressed in a full navy suit that looks like it cost more than three months of my rent, this man oozes sex and style and a masculinity that makes my heart race. He's not wearing a tie and his top button is undone revealing just a hint of chest hair that I never realized is such a turn-on until this very moment.

"Umm…Bennett right?" I narrow my gaze slightly, trying to recall the last name of my best friend's new boyfriend's friend.

My best friend, Alyssa March, is a biology major and somehow had gotten mixed up with this very young, very cute Doctor, Wren Hamilton, at this hospital that she volunteered at to collect the hours she needed for med school. It was all so very *Grey's Anatomy*.

I'd met Bennett in passing one night when Alyssa and I had gone out after class, and said dreamy and very possessive Doctor paid us a visit to make sure we were "behaving." I rolled my eyes at the sentiment and asked her what it was like having another parent disguised as a boyfriend and she giggled back that she loved it and made some *Daddy* joke.

Bennett, who'd followed in tow, introduced himself and proceeded to stare at me for the remainder of the time, his eyes burning into me over his whiskey like he was a lion and I was his prey and he was plotting his next move. I knew I looked good that night, in my favorite black dress that hugged my curves as my sleek straight hair cascaded down my back, but the way he went back and forth between undressing me with his eyes and sabotaging any conversation with a guy who tried to talk to me, I'd briefly wondered if he liked *more* than the way I looked.

"You wound me, Olivia Warren." He smiles and I don't miss the fact that his smile is quite literally perfect. Straight white teeth and a dimple on only one side underneath one layer of stubble. He nods at my computer and the array of books surrounding me. "What are you studying?" He takes a sip from the paper cup and I try to ignore the way his throat moves or the way his Adam's apple wobbles as he swallows.

Don't look at his mouth, Liv.

I tuck a long curled hair behind my ear, a telltale sign that I'm nervous, and try to avoid his gaze. "You can just call me Liv. That's what everyone calls me."

"Well, what if I don't want to just be like *everyone*. Then what should I call you?" He smiles again with a hint of cockiness, but more playfulness, and I'm grateful I'm sitting down, or else my knees would probably buckle.

"Ummm..." I look away from his green eyes. Green gorgeous eyes that look emerald. I'd never seen eyes that color and mixed with his tanned complexion, he looked like the "Greek God" women went on about in romance novels.

I was going to bomb this exam if I didn't get my shit together.

"Statistical Analysis," I say finally.

"That's what I should call you?" he jokes.

I roll my eyes, but I can't stop the uptick of my lips at his corny attempt to be funny. "That's what I'm studying and I have a final in like two hours." I blink my eyes several times as if to say, *sooo bye?*

He puts his hands up in defeat before running a hand through his thick dark hair. "Fine, I'll let you be." He pulls his card out from his inside pocket and hands it to me. "Maybe when you're done, you'll call me and we can celebrate you being finished?"

I lick my bottom lip and realize my mouth has gotten very dry. I reach for the coffee in front of me and take a long sip. "I don't know if tonight will work," I tell him as I pray that this blow off will deter him from pursuing me further. It's not that I'm not attracted to him, or that he'd done anything wrong. I just don't date much, and I don't need the possibility of this clouding my head while I take the most taxing final of my college career.

He smiles and nods his head as if he hears the implication loud and clear. "You're graduating this weekend, like Alyssa?" *Or not?*

"Yep." I run my fingers over the indents of the precise block letters stamped on his card. I run my gaze over it and catch his full name.

BENNETT CLARKE

"I'll see you this weekend then," he says and my eyes shoot up to meet his. *Wait, what?* He winks and then he's gone, leaving me alone with my very confusing thoughts and the smell of the sexiest man alive swirling around me.

By the grace of God, I made it through the test because I spent about half of my exam wondering what he meant by his ominous statement.

Is he coming to the graduation? To be supportive of Wren?

He asked you out on a date and gave you his cell phone number, and you think he's coming to be supportive of Wren?

I ponder this all the way home when I spot the pink roses sitting in front of my door. I pick them up as I walk into the apartment I share with Alyssa, pressing my nose into the pale pink flowers. I'm just about to call out for her, as I assume they're from Wren, when I see my name very carefully written on the card.

Olivia,
I hope your exam went well.
Congratulations on being finished with college.
I hope you'll give me a call sometime.
BC

Present Day

I'm brought from my thoughts by someone approaching, and before I even look up, my heart sinks and I dig my nails into my palm as I steel myself for my mother-in-law. "Wrenny!"

"You called her?" I groan, under my breath as I stand up and wait for her to criticize everything about me. Heaven forbid I stay seated. Dressed to the nines, as usual, Caroline Clarke glides down the hallway. Her brown hair is cut into a sleek bob and I know there's not a hair out of place. Bennett's mother exuded style and confidence and is undeniably chic. I always thought she reminded me of Audrey Hepburn in *Breakfast at Tiffany's*. If she didn't drive me completely insane, I'd actually love to raid her closet.

"Mrs. C." He smiles and gives her a polite nod.

She doesn't acknowledge my presence when she stops in front of us and fixes her eyes on Wren. "What happened to my baby? Is he alright, can I see him?" Her voice is surprisingly calm, though I'm sure she's just building up to the full-blown hysteria.

"I was just discussing that with Liv. He's suffered some head trauma, more specifically a subdural hematoma, which is a brain bleed." I immediately prepare myself for the performance that Caroline Clarke is gearing up to give. It will be unprecedented, I'm sure. Her hand finds her chest and then her mouth and then her chest again. Her heavily made up green eyes are wide and unblinking as they move to room four zero nine. "Very common in car accidents, nothing to be alarmed about, we're just going to keep him for a few days."

"I…" She sniffles. "I want to see my child. *Right now*." She points at the ground, and I give him a look that says, *see what you did?*

"Olivia, I don't know what that look is for, but I'm here now, so you can go. I know you may not care, but I certainly do," she says snidely.

"I care," I tell her. "I was still married to him for almost seven years."

"Shame, all that time wasted."

"Enough, Caroline." Wren speaks up and I know that he's typically the peacekeeper and usually polite, so I'm surprised at his comment, although I know that he's very familiar with our relationship.

"Wren, dear, try to understand my perspective. She left my poor son *after* she failed to give him any children." She pulls out a compact and dabs at her eyes before sliding it back inside her Chanel bag. Her eyes flit to mine and for a second, I see a bit of regret over her choice of words beneath her green eyes that match Bennett's, but just as quick as I see it, it's gone and I'm left with the usual contempt she has for me.

"God, you're hateful," I whisper. "I am sorry your son fell for me." And it's true. I'm sorry. It certainly would have saved me six months of what was quite possibly the worst pain I've ever felt. "Really, I'm sorry, but we are over. So, you're getting your wish." I nod at her.

"That's not what Bennett wants," Wren growls. "And frankly, Caroline, he'd be about ready to throw you out of here for speaking to Liv that way, so cool it." He rubs at his jaw and shakes his head. "You've become impossible since Mr. C died, and it's awful and sad and I know you're hurting, but lay off."

"Don't be rude, Wren." She glowers at him like he's a child, but Wren stands his own.

"Oh, hello pot, I'm kettle, pleased to meet you." He raises an eyebrow at her as if to scold her right back. "I'm going to take Olivia in to see her husband because that's what Ben would want."

She huffs and rubs her hands down her vintage Dior black dress and sits on the bench. "I'll wait here. If you could bring me some water though, that would be wonderful. Preferably a Perrier?"

I let out a sigh as I follow Wren into the dim, stuffy room. The shades are drawn, and it's nearing dusk in September, which means it'll be dark within thirty minutes. The soft hum of the monitors is the only sound in the room other than my heels clicking against the floor as I move closer to his bedside. There's a bandage wrapped around his head, a few cuts and bruises on his cheeks, but for the most part, his face is unscathed. I note a nasty burn on his neck, assumedly from his seatbelt and I wince as I run my fingertips over the skin. Various cuts and bruises scatter his arms, and I'm grateful that he doesn't have any broken bones. "Oh, Clarke." Immediately, my brain recognizes the nickname and the fact that I haven't called him that in months. When we were dating, I called him that, and it just stuck even though I now share his last name.

Well not for much longer.

"We thought we needed to intubate him, but he's breathing fine on his own. He's going to be okay, Liv." I feel Wren's hand on my shoulder. "I'm going to go deal with the ice queen out there and give you a minute."

I wait until I hear the soft click of the door shutting before I succumb to the tears I've been holding in and let them slide silently down my cheeks. "I'm so angry at you," I whisper, grateful to have this time to speak what I'm feeling without his reply. "But you're not allowed to die." I look towards the monitors that are beeping monotonously. "You're not allowed to..." I let out a breath. "Well you left me already but as angry as I am, I don't want you to die. I want you to be happy," I add and that's taken months of self-reflection and meditation and the most expensive therapist in the tri-state area for me to get to this moment.

I want you to be happy.

Even if it's not with me.

A commotion outside the door has my mother-in-law pushing through the door and Wren shooting me a look. "You cannot be in here if you are going to act like this," Wren tells her. "I will have you removed."

"It's fine." I wipe my eyes and nose and move slowly towards the door when I hear my name whispered so faintly. Under normal circumstances, I may not have heard it, but my ears, my body, my heart are so trained to hear this name, I could probably hear it even if he only thinks it.

"*Livi.*"

CHAPTER Two

Olivia

THE GOOSEBUMPS RISE ALL OVER MY ARMS AND LEGS INSTANTLY, that one word, chilling me to the bone but also setting me ablaze. He always called me Livi. It was his thing, and it made me feel special that he called me something no one else did.

I swallow hard, turning slowly and meeting those familiar green eyes that I hadn't seen since our last mediation over a week ago. I can't stop the smile that pulls at my lips to see that he's awake and more importantly, alive. Or possibly because he's staring at me with those eyes I know all too well. A gaze so intense, it's like he's almost afraid to blink for fear that I'll disappear.

"Oh my God, Benny!" Our moment is interrupted by his mother, *of course*. And I blink away from him, to watch as his mother bombards his space and all but throws her body on top of his. "My sweetheart, you're okay! You're alive! I was so worried." She pulls back and holds his face, doing her best to turn his gaze towards her, but they're still locked on me. I nervously look at Wren, hoping that he'll say something to break the tension, but he just alternates from staring at Bennett and me.

Well, someone speak? Besides the wicked witch of the Upper East Side that is.

"Why are you all the way over there?" He nods at me. I can see the hurt in his eyes and hear it in his question. He winces slightly as he turns his hand palm up, assumedly so I'll hold it and I move a little closer to not make the situation more tense.

I guess the man did just come out of a coma, I suppose I could hold his hand.

I slide my hand into his and instantly feel that spark that's never seemed to wane between us. His hand is large and warm wrapped around mine as his thumb rubs my knuckles gently. I drop my gaze to where our hands are adjoined.

How is it that something so simple can have me feeling like the walls are closing in?

I suddenly feel too hot and the energy swirling around me is almost stifling. Even though my heart is broken, and my brain comprehends this, my hormones are raging and my sex pulses slightly. It's like my heart and sex are at war with each other over which could beat faster, and right now, my heart is losing *badly*.

"What the hell happened?" He looks at me, his eyes tracing me over. "You weren't with me." It sounds like a statement of relief, but also a question.

I shake my head. "I—I don't know exactly what happened. Wren may have a better explanation."

"Right. Car accident," Wren chimes in, "and we can go over all the details of what this means for you because you did give us quite a scare, but for now I need you to look into this light for me." He brushes past me, but Bennett refuses to let go of my hand.

His gaze is still fixed on me, despite Wren flashing a small flashlight into his eyes and tension zips through my body as his green stare into my brown. I feel like I'm starting to get light headed by how little I'm breathing. I let out a breath and try to pull my hand from his when he grips it tighter, his eyebrows furrowing deeper. "I need a moment with Olivia."

"Ben—" his mother starts and his gaze snaps to hers angrily.

"Mother, I'm fine. You can see that. I just need a moment alone with my girl."

Caroline's eyes flit to me, and for a second, I peer over my shoulder, wondering if his girlfriend has somehow manifested.

I'd kill her.

He can't mean me? He must be out of it.

"Wren," he says with as much conviction as he can muster, "two minutes."

Wren nods, as he grabs his chart and takes one final glance at the monitor before ushering Caroline out of the room much to her protest. "Two minutes, and then we need to run some tests, so don't get comfortable."

"Not likely," Bennett grumbles and lets his eyes flutter closed. "Fuck." He sighs. "Everything fucking hurts." His eyes open slowly and he smiles again when he meets my gaze. He tugs me gently and the quick movement sends a lightning bolt zipping down my spine. "Are you alright?" He asks as he runs his hand up my arm and massaging my forearm gently.

What the fuck?

"You were in a car accident, and you're asking *me* if I'm alright?" I smile despite my discomfort over his touch and he chuckles slightly before wincing.

He lifts his chin slightly. "Give me a kiss."

"What?" *Did I hear him correctly?*

He looks down at himself and then at me, cocking an eyebrow in that sexy way that used to make me wet instantly. "I was in a car accident, and I guess a coma? Come give me a fucking kiss, Olivia. I'm rather surprised you didn't attack me the second I woke up. But that's why I got rid of my mother." He licks his lips, and I watch the muscle I used to be very familiar with in fascination until I remember what he's asking.

I finally pull out of his grasp and my expression morphs into irritation. "You know what? I'm not doing this with you right now. I'm happy you're okay. But I'm not going to let you manipulate me any more than you already have." I shake my head and run a hand through my mahogany waves. "It can't *always* be about you, Bennett."

"Wait, what the fuck?" His face looks like I've slapped him, and maybe I should have left off that last part. *I mean he is hurt. But I refuse to let him suck me into this based on sympathy.* "Who's manipulating anyone? Because I want my wife to kiss me?" He glares at me and I notice his jaw ticking meaning he's gritting his teeth. I used to say his jaw was so sharp it could cut through glass and right now it looks like it's ready to cut through me.

"Don't call me that," I say as forcefully as I can, though I fear it comes out more like a plea.

"Call you what? My wife? What would you prefer I call you?" The agitation radiates off of him in waves and I'm instantly affected. It's how it's always been. His reactions and his body language have the power to control my moods. It's why just his smile could make me feel like I'm on top of the world, and when we're fighting, *which was rare when we were married*, I could feel like I was literally underneath it. The same went for him, which is why I know he's so agitated.

But why is he agitated over...this?

"I haven't been your wife in quite some time, Bennett, can you not do this?"

His eyes widen and narrow in anger. "You take that back. How dare you say that to me." His voice is low and filled with fury and washes over me, sending shivers down my spine.

I press a hand to my forehead, trying to rub away the stress lines that are forming. "Bennett, why are you acting like this?"

"Acting like what, and what the fuck is up with you calling

me Bennett?" I can tell his patience is wearing thin and I'm not trying to poke the bear, but I'm exhausted and officially over this back and forth.

"Like you don't..." I freeze, my mind slowly running through every TV show, movie, and book that involves head trauma. "Ummm..." I bite my bottom lip and clear my throat steeling myself for the question about to fall from my lips. "What day is it?"

"I don't know? Tuesday? Livi, you're acting strange as hell and in case you couldn't guess, I'm kind of not in the mood." He rolls his eyes and throws his head back against his pillow.

"Year." I choke out.

"What?"

"What year is it?" I ask softly and realize I'm now holding my breath as I wait for his answer.

He looks around the room before settling back on me and I wonder if he's figuring out where I'm going with this line of questioning because he takes a few moments before he replies. "Are you serious right now? It's 2017, what are you getting at?"

It feels like the wind has been knocked out of me. The blood rushes to my ears and I take a step back, as I try my best to catch my breath. My hands begin to shake and before I can think, I'm bent over as I take slow breaths in and out. I'm vaguely aware of him saying my name, telling me to breathe, and calling for Wren but I block it out.

Two years.

He doesn't remember two years.

Two years ago, Bennett and I were happy.

Two years ago, Bennett and I had been married for five years and we were still very much in the honeymoon phase. We couldn't be in a room without being on top of each other. Our sex life couldn't be more passionate and carnal and we were talking about taking our family from two to three.

When hands find my shoulders and help me to stand up straight, I see Wren's eyes fixed on me. "I think you're having a panic attack." He holds a bag up to my face and I shake my head before I turn to the bedridden man who looks as if he's about to rip out his IVs to get to me.

"Baby, you're scaring the shit out of me, what's going on?" Bennett's eyes are wide, his nostrils flaring and he's flexing his hands every few seconds, a sign he wants to touch me but *can't*.

Wren's eyes slowly move to his, probably in question of hearing the term of endearment he called me before turning his gaze back to me. "Uh-huh!" I answer his unspoken question.

"Am…am I missing something?" He pushes his glasses to the top of his head, confusion written all over his face, and I shake my head in response.

Are you back together? I can practically hear him asking.

"No."

He turns to Bennett and pulls his flashlight out again. "B, what's going on, man?"

"You tell me? I'm fine, but Livi looks like she's about to lose it. Stop fussing over me, I'm fine. What's going on with her?" He tries to look at me again. "Come over here."

I ignore his command, even though somewhere deep inside, my body wants to listen. He still knows how to make my body respond to his voice and I hate the traitorous feeling. "Wren, can I talk to you outside?"

"Outside? What for? If this is a joke, I am far from amused." Bennett groans rubbing a scraped up hand through his luscious chestnut hair. Wren and I are silent as we watch him slide his left hand out of his hair and stare at it for a second. "Hey, hand me my ring, will you? It feels so strange not having it on." He rubs the finger. "I'm kind of surprised I don't see the indent of it."

I look at Wren, my eyes widening as if to say, *you see!* "Okay, alright, B, humor me for a second alright?" He crosses his arms and stares at him. "Just need to do a couple things. Name. Birthday. Where do you live?"

He rolls his eyes. "Bennett Clarke. March 23, 1980. In SoHo. I have a very expensive, overpriced three bedroom apartment that I share with my wife Olivia Clarke, are you happy?" He meets my gaze and gives me a small smile, though it fades when I'm sure he sees the look of pure horror on my face.

"Alright." He nods and turns towards me. "So, we'll run a couple tests. An MRI and potentially a CAT scan. Everything's going to be fine. This is normal. It'll probably restore over the next few hours. Confusion is very common in these situations."

"Confusion?" Bennett snorts. "I'm not confused. Livi, did I make any of that up?" I don't know what to say as he looks me over and I suddenly feel the overwhelming need to sit down. "Fuck. Wren, get her some water."

I shake my head. "I—I'm fine."

"You need to drink some water," he commands, and I feel a sense of nostalgia wash over me hearing his words. *He was always telling me to drink more water.* "Wren, get her some. If she passes out, I'll kick your ass. Fuck all of this." He waves at the monitors and the wires hooked up to him.

There's a chair to the right of his bed, and before I can think I'm lowering myself onto the hard uncomfortable cushion, feeling the weight of the day physically pressing down on my shoulders. Wren hands me a glass of water and I take a slow tentative sip because I'm not sure I won't be sick at any second. "Good girl." I hear Bennett using *that* voice and it instantly breathes life into me.

The voice he uses when I'm sick and he's taking care of me. The voice he uses when he's taking care of me *that way.*

Fuck fuck fuck.

He's fucking with me.

This is all a dream.

There's no way he thinks we're still married.

That we're still happy.

I look up at him and he nods, telling me to drink more and despite not wanting to obey him, I comply. He lets out a sigh and shakes his head. "You drive me crazy, Mrs. Clarke."

Hearing him call me that makes the dam burst, and suddenly the tears are flying down my face. I don't look up but I hear him moving and Wren trying to keep him on the bed. "Let me fucking go, Wren. Why is she crying? Why is she so fucking upset? What the fuck is going on? Someone better start talking right now."

One of the machines begins to beep rapidly. My lip trembles as Wren tries to appease him. "Your blood pressure is skyrocketing, you need to calm the fuck down, B."

"Don't tell me to calm the fuck down. Look at Olivia! No one is telling me anything and you know what seeing her upset does to me."

I squeeze my eyes together even harder. *Stop talking. Stop talking. Stop talking.*

"Please just stop, Bennett." I cry. "Stop." I stand up on shaky legs and prepare to tell him the truth, just so that he'll stop pushing down all of the carefully constructed walls I'd put up in the past six months. "We're getting a divorce. We're...we're not together." I bite my bottom lip as his face morphs from confusion to sadness to anger to confusion again all within the span of a second. And then he's laughing. *Hard.*

And it reminds me I haven't heard him laugh like this in a while. A true hearty laugh that used to make my heart smile. "Oh my God, laughing hurts like a bitch, but I can't help it." He pinches the bridge of his nose and wipes his eyes. "That was cute, honey. But when I'm better, I'm taking you the fuck over my knee for using the *d* word."

Wren looks at me. "Well, I think you've got it from here. This isn't usually how we handle it, but I'm going to let you field it. I'm calling for a consult. I'll be back in ten, try not to kill him before then." He nods at me before he's gone.

"Livi…" Bennett's voice is low, just above a whisper. I look at him, preparing to explain to him just what he's missed in two years all while trying to keep it together. "Am I dying? Is that…is that why you're so upset?"

My heart squeezes and pulses at the thought of living in a world where Bennett Clarke doesn't exist. *I want him happy, even if it isn't with me.* That mantra I repeat at the start of every day just to get me through it means he *has* to be alive. "No! No, you're not dying. It was just a car accident. But…but it looks like you've suffered some memory loss, but Wren said it's normal. And you're going to be fine." I sniffle as I look towards the window. The automatic lights have flickered on, as the room was almost dark and I turn on the light just over his bed illuminating the room even more.

It's then, under brighter lighting I notice the bags under his eyes and the slight graying by his temples. "How…how much time am I missing?"

I hesitate, wondering what to say; if I should lie or just come right out with it. I go with the latter. "Two years," I say softly, unsure of how he's going to take it.

"What the hell? Two years? And…" His eyes immediately move to my hands, the hands I have by my sides. He zeroes in on my left hand and assumedly my bare ring finger. "No fucking way."

"Bennett…"

His eyes pry away from my hand and find mine. They aren't

angry or filled with rage, but sadness and despair. "You...you left me?"

Yes. "Not exactly."

"I'd never leave you, so that means you left me. When? How? Why?" The tears are in his eyes and he doesn't even try to stop them from slowly trickling down his face. "I love you...did you stop loving me?"

"No." I shake my head, tucking a hair behind my ear. "I'll probably never stop loving you." I've never said that to him, not in the six months we've been going through the separation and divorce. I probably shouldn't have said it now under these circumstances, but my heart feels like it's been ripped open. I feel raw and exposed and Bennett is pushing himself into my soul again. I can feel it.

Be strong. He's going to remember. Don't let him back in. He still broke your heart.

"You broke my heart, Bennett."

"No...I would never." He shakes his head, disregarding the words. "I would never break your heart. I promised you that on our wedding night. And I never go back on my word when it comes to you." He speaks these words of finality and my hands begin to shake.

"You did."

Chapter Three

Olivia

"Did I...? I didn't..." His face falls, as he tries to pose the question, I know he's thinking. *Did I cheat on you?*

I nod slowly, the tears swimming in my lids, and I know the second I blink they'll trickle down my cheek. I twist my mouth and look away from him, trying to keep the tears at bay when I hear him whisper my name again. "Baby, look at me." His voice sounds as pained as I know mine will be the second I open my mouth.

"I'm not..." I start, my gaze fixed on the floor. I stare at my shoes, black open toe pumps that were a part of my *I'm getting divorced* shopping spree.

"Olivia." He speaks again and when I look up his eyes are filled with devastation. "I am so sorry. I don't know how or... why...but there's no excuse. I don't know what would have possessed me to do that."

I do, I think and I push the rationalization down and back into the box in the corner of my mind that I'd labeled *do not open*.

The box full of rationalizations that I'm not so innocent in this.

I didn't cheat on him though.

No, you just let him think he was in this marriage by himself.

I squeeze my eyes together, trying to quiet the voices in my head and when I open them he's staring at me. "Your hair is a little shorter and more curly," he says. "But you look beautiful. You've always been beautiful." His voice washes over me like a warm spring rain, heating my chilled bones instantly.

My hair was still past my shoulders, though only barely, and I wore it more wavy or curly now as opposed to sleek and straight like when we met. Two years ago, my hair was longer, although not by much, which made my heart flutter with just how much he noticed everything. But that's how he was. He was the husband that noticed the haircut or the new clothes, or when my nails were a different color. He was the husband who could sense my period without looking at a calendar because my breasts looked bigger.

"Thank you."

"Wait, two years?" He scratches his jaw and narrows his gaze in question. "That must mean...I mean we must have...do we have any children?"

The lump in my throat almost feels painful as I attempt to swallow and shake my head slowly. "No." My lip trembles as my stomach flips, my heart sinks, and I feel the need to sit down again as I remember each time I peed on that stick. Each doctor's appointment. Each moment of euphoria learning that I was pregnant. And then the low after I learned that I no longer was.

Both times.

"Livi..."

I take a deep breath and wipe my eyes. "This has probably been a lot of information for you to take in at once. We don't have to do all of this now." I back away slowly. I need to get away from him. I need to get away from his penetrating gaze and his sweet words and whispered *Livis*. This is the man I'd fallen for and if I wasn't careful, I'd fall again.

I can't.

I won't.

I'm just about to open the door when Caroline comes through it again and walks by me as if I'm not standing there. "Wren said we need to run some tests? Oh, sweetheart, I hear you're having a hard time remembering?"

"Livi filled in some of the details, but yes."

"Speaking of...Olivia, your *boyfriend* is outside," Caroline says snidely and I don't even try to stop the anger from flashing over my face. *Always stirring the fucking pot.*

I wince as Bennett's eyes flash to mine. "Her fucking what?"

"He's not...he's not my boyfriend. He's a friend." A friend who may or may not make me feel better while going through this painful divorce.

"What the fuck kind of friend?" Bennett demands, his eyes filled with fury. His full lips are curled into a scowl and his eyebrows are slanted in anguish.

"Oh, Bennett, stop. You didn't expect her to never move on, did you?" Caroline shakes her head at him as she fluffs the pillows behind him.

My eyes flash to hers in surprise of her defense, and I notice that Bennett's face has softened and is looking at her equally shocked before turning back to me in question. "No, that's new," I say, answering his unspoken question of whether his mother and I have become amicable in the past two years.

"You have...a boyfriend?" he asks me.

"He's not my boyfriend. We are still married." I press my lips together in a straight line. "You have a girlfriend." I chuckle, though the words feel like a knife just pierced my heart.

He narrows his gaze before nodding towards his mother as if to say, *can you not in front of my mother?*

"Your mother knows. They're like besties." The smile on my

face matches my saccharine tone and I watch as his eyes snap to hers.

"What?"

"She's a very nice girl and she's been so worried about you…" she starts.

"WHAT?" he roars. "You've been giving my wife a hard time since the day you met her, and you've accepted my…for lack of a better word, mistress?" he snaps. "I don't want to see her. Tell her it's over." He lets his head fall back and scratches his beard. "Since you two are so close."

"Bennett…" his mother starts.

"I don't want her here, and if she shows up, I'm calling security. I mean it, Mother. I don't know what would possess me to cheat on Olivia, but I don't want her here and I don't want her around my wife."

"Oh, she's afraid of me." I give them both my most smug grin. "Don't worry about that."

"Yes, she assaulted her!" Caroline points at me.

"I did not assault her. Don't be so dramatic, Caroline." I look at Bennett, who looks more amused than anything despite the circumstances. "I did key her car, but, if I assaulted her, she'd know it." I shoot a pointed glare at his mother before turning back to Bennett. "You paid for the damage to her car, so, no harm no foul in my opinion."

Bennett's face falls at my brief story and shakes his head. "I'm so sorry you've been dealing with this shit."

"Can I at least tell her you're okay?" Caroline asks.

"Do whatever the hell you want, Mother. If she shows up here, she will be disappointed. As I said, tell her it's over."

"Caroline, maybe just explain that he's having some trouble remembering and now just isn't a good time." I shake my head, not wanting to cause any issues between Bennett and his plaything.

Even if I do hate her.

"Not hate." I can hear my therapist's voice in my head, scolding me for the harshness of the word.

"Why are you so okay with this?" Bennett commands and I can hear the unspoken questions. *Why are you okay with me having a girlfriend? Why aren't you upset? Why aren't you fighting for us?*

"Trust me, I'm not. But…she gives you something I can't, and I think you care for her on some level." I bite my bottom lip.

"There's no way I feel for her what I feel for you." My brain, my heart, my soul, nothing misses the fact that he's speaking in the present tense but I try to ignore it.

"I believe that." I nod. "But she's helping you get through… this."

"Is that what the asshole out there is doing for you?" He nods towards the door and I swallow as I think about the man in the waiting room. *I did not ask for him to come, why is he here?*

"Alright, that's enough of the lovefest," Wren says as he comes back in with two other Doctors in tow. "We're going to go down to run some tests, and then we can continue getting acquainted when you get back. How does that sound?" The sarcasm drips from his voice, especially as I know he caught the tail end of this conversation, but Bennett just stares at me.

"Are you staying?"

"Umm…" I start.

"There's no need for her to stay, Bennett. I'm here. If she needs to leave, I won't be going anywhere," his mother interjects.

He doesn't even look at her. "Are you staying?" he repeats. The pleading look in his eyes implores me to stay. To never leave his side again.

Fuck, this is too much.

I look at the four other people in the room all staring at me, waiting for my response. "Yeah, I can…I can stay."

He nods and I can see the relief in his eyes and his body language. "Can you do me a favor?" He asks, his eyes trained on me. "Can you get rid of him? I'd rather not see him when they wheel me out of here."

I bite down on my bottom lip and nod, preventing myself from mentioning that they've met before.

It was far from pretty.

I make my way out of the room, pressing a hand to my chest as I close the door behind me. It's been a very taxing forty-five minutes and I feel like the air is fresher, less complicated outside of this room. I take a deep breath.

"Liv," I hear my name, and I look up to see David Jacobs sitting on the bench outside of Bennett's room.

David is kind and sweet and treats me like the very broken princess I am. He was a gentleman from the very first time he saw me crying into my hands and a box of Krispy Kreme's in Central Park. He'd sat down next to me and slid a flask across the bench. We became friends instantly.

We'd been intimate, yes. But it was few and far between, always ended with me sobbing uncontrollably, and never in an orgasm for either of us. To be honest, I'm not sure why he still keeps me around. He's gorgeous in a different way from Bennett. Blonde hair versus Bennett's dark brown. Blue eyes versus his green. Closer to my height versus Bennett who towers over me at six foot five. He works for a non-profit organization, unlike Bennett who works for a real estate firm that basically rules New York.

He's the opposite of my husband in every way.

I have a love-hate relationship with the sentiment.

He stands and begins walking towards me. I pull him down

one hallway and another that ran perpendicular so that we'd be out of sight when they wheel Bennett towards the elevators. "What are you doing here?"

"You texted me—"

"Yes, but I didn't ask you to come," I whisper. I didn't mean to sound ungrateful when all he wanted was to be there for me, but I couldn't handle David being here on top of everything going on with Bennett who I was legally still married to.

"I know, but I just wanted to be here for you. Are you hungry? Have you eaten anything?" He brushes my hair behind my shoulder and cups my cheeks gently before he attempts to kiss me, but I back away slightly.

"David, this isn't the time or place. My mother-in-law is running around like a woman on a mission, and Bennett just woke up and I'm sorry…" I shake my head. "It's just too much."

"Okay, okay. I'm sorry," he whispers as he pulls me into a hug. I reluctantly allow it because I think I need it. I press my face into his chest and cry for the inability to catch a break. I'm exhausted. Mentally, physically, emotionally. A divorce will make you feel like you've just gone to war and I'm more than ready to wave the white flag of defeat.

I want it over.

I just want peace.

I feel his lips against the top of my head as the tears fall down my face. "I promise, I'll call you later. I just can't deal with all of this with you here." My voice is muffled against his chest.

I can't handle this with Bennett's state and my reaction to said state.

What did this all even mean? Was I still in love with him?

Yes.

Enough to give us another chance?

No.

Eventually, he'll remember everything and when he does, I can't be in this headspace because he'll break me down. Despite his girlfriend, I know he wants me back just as Wren had said.

My eyes fly open and I squeeze David harder. I need him. I need him to help me stay strong. To not fall back into the trap of Bennett Clarke. If I'm not careful, I'll fall back into old habits. I have to remember that.

He may not remember the past, but I do.

Even as I think the thoughts, I don't believe them.

No one could save me from Bennett.

My heart. My mind. My soul.

All of it still belonged to him.

CHAPTER
Four

Olivia

No more than thirty minutes later, I hear the ding of the elevator just over my right shoulder and my head jerks up immediately as Bennett comes back into view. Green eyes find mine and he gives me a small smile and I try to ignore the familiar feelings welling in the pit of my stomach. "Miss me, did you?" He winks and I fight the urge to roll my eyes to hide what I'm actually feeling. Standing, I follow them inside as Wren gets him settled.

"I've sent the images off to the radiologist, but I haven't seen anything abnormal. We can see signs of amnesia now on MRIs, but it won't give specifics such as the severity of the memory loss." He pushes his glasses up higher on the bridge of his nose and scratches his jaw. "I want to keep you here overnight." He looks at Bennett and then at me and I nod.

I look at Bennett who, for the first time, isn't staring at me like I might break or disappear or flee from the room. "What does all this mean? I mean will I regain my memory?" he asks.

"It's hard to say at this point. Amnesia comes in all different forms and there's no real way to cure it. A lot of doctors urge routine and familiarizing yourself with your old life to trigger old memories. But as far as a medicine to reverse the damage, unfortunately we aren't that advanced yet."

"So, it's possible I may never remember...the time I'm missing?" Bennett asks and to the untrained ear, it may sound like he's upset or worried about that, but I know Bennett like the freckle on the back of my hand and the one on his that matches. *He's hoping he doesn't remember.* He's hoping that he doesn't have to face the harsh truth that we aren't together. That he broke my heart. Right now, the thoughts are unfathomable to him and he wants to stay there. In the place of ignorance and confusion because it really is bliss.

"I can't say for sure, man. But we are going to do everything we can to get some answers. The MRI results will take a few hours, but we should still be able to get you out of here tomorrow unless there's something troubling on the scan. I don't want to hold you hostage."

The sound of beeping interrupts and Wren looks down at his pager. "Shit it's a 911, I've got to run, but I'll be back as soon as I can, alright?"

He's gone in an instant leaving me and Bennett in this room that feels like it gets smaller every time we're inside. I pull my jacket tighter around me and rub my arms up and down. "You get rid of your boyfriend?"

"Bennett..."

He scrubs his face with both hands and groans. "And stop with the Bennett, it's freaking me out. I don't think you ever call me Bennett unless I'm in trouble." I don't say anything because calling him Clarke feels too *intimate.* He sighs in defeat. "I don't expect you to stay, I'm sure you're exhausted."

"Well I was thinking I was going to leave, but I'll wait until you fall asleep..." I start. *But do I want to leave him alone in the hospital?* "Or maybe I could stay..." I whisper as I look around the small room. I do have some work I need to do, but I suppose I could send the emails from my phone.

Despite the fact that my husband makes more than enough money so I don't have to work, I didn't spend four years in college for an MRS degree. I wanted to work. I enjoy working even if I don't have to.

"I'd love if you stayed, but...I always want to be near you. I'm selfish like that." I purse my lips and look nervously at the ground as I try to come up with something to say. The knee jerk reaction is to agree that he's been selfish, but this definitely wasn't the time to go down that road. "Don't be nervous, baby."

I snap my gaze up to look at him. "Stop with the baby," I grit out.

He winces and nods slowly. "Sorry, force of habit." I sigh, suddenly feeling like shit for scolding him. It isn't his fault he doesn't remember. That his body has shut down and forced him to forget what's going on between us. It's almost as if he's developed amnesia as a way to escape the pain. All he knows is that he loves me and that we're happy. He doesn't know *this* Olivia and Bennett. "Do we...I mean I assume we aren't living together?"

"No. I live in our apartment. You moved out." I tell him, trying my best to keep my voice even.

A flicker of disappointment washes over his face. "I see. Where do I live?"

"Upper East Side. It's closer to your job anyway." I shrug.

"Am I still with SPR?"

I nod.

Sloane Prime Realty is one of the biggest real estate firms in Manhattan—hell, in all New York—and he's been one of the highest paid realtors ever since a handful of socialites worked with him. Twenty-somethings with Mommy and Daddy's money flocked to him because he was young, outgoing and *hot*. The girls were in love and the guys related to him because he was what they aspired to be. Thirty-something and rich. They flooded Instagram with their posts thanking him for finding them THE BESTTTT APARTMENT EVER!! And thus, Bennett Clarke became the most coveted realtor in all of New York.

"What about you?" he asks. "What have you been up to?"

"The same." I shrug. "Though I've been promoted in the past two years. I'm an editorial production director now." A smile crosses my face as I think about the job that I worked my ass off to get.

"That's amazing, congratulations." He beams. "Still with *Conde Nast*?"

"Yep," I tell him. My finance degree had somehow led me to a life of glamour and working for the most prominent fashion magazine in the world.

"I'm proud of you, Livi. I knew you'd take the world by storm."

I'm proud of you. Those four words used to have the power to turn me into a horny mess, and even now, my sex throbs under his praise. Words of affirmation were my love language and Bennett spoke it fluently.

"Thank you."

"Have I missed anything else…? Besides…?" He shifts uncomfortably and looks at me to fill in the blanks.

"Wren and Lys got married," I tell him.

"Really? When?"

"About a year ago." I think about their long courtship and engagement versus Bennett and my whirlwind one.

"Shit." He chuckles. "Did I at least bang the maid of honor in a coat closet?" I narrow my gaze and his widen. "If it was you! Was it you? Shit, Lys doesn't have a sister, does she?"

"It was me." I roll my eyes. "And yes, we did." I blush at the memory of Bennett's hands roaming all over my burgundy bridesmaid's dress. Lifting the long chiffon material up around my waist and sliding his hand in my panties and rubbing my wet slit as he whispered dirty words in my ear.

"You're blushing." He smirks. "You're remembering it."

I'm broken from my sexy trip down memory lane by his words and instantly I'm annoyed that I let it show all over my face that I was reliving it. "I'm leaving," I tell him.

"No no no!" He chuckles just as I turn around. "I'm sorry, I'm kidding. Cut me some slack here, Livi. The last memory I have of us is fucking you in the shower this morning, yesterday morning…whenever the fuck I showered last." He rubs his hands over his face. It's not like I can pinpoint which time he means. When things were good between us, Bennett and I showered together more times than we showered separately. "I'm not going to lie, the idea of us not being together really fucking sucks."

Who are you telling?

"This wasn't all my doing, Bennett."

"I know, I know. I just…*fuck*." He lets out a sigh and his head falls back. "I hate that I did this to us." I don't say anything even though there's so much more to the story. Yes, he cheated, but there was a catalyst. A catalyst that I helped form. I'm not giving an excuse for his behavior because I'm still angry and gutted and pissed beyond belief. But I did push him away.

I pushed him away when I needed him.

I pushed him away when *he needed me*.

I did give up.

On him.

On myself.

On us.

Looking back, I can see how hard he fought. Looking back, I can see how one slip up could have happened. He'd slipped up once. One time.

It was a random isolated incident. A girl at a bar. A man drunk and alone and hurting over the fact that his wife had shut him out over the struggles in their marriage.

He'd confessed the next morning.

I'd walked out that afternoon.

Somehow after that, the girl and he had formed a friendship or a *fuckship* or whatever.

Maybe said friendship wouldn't have formed if I hadn't told him I wouldn't forgive him. If I told him I wanted to work things out, maybe we wouldn't be here.

But I couldn't forgive him.

Or maybe I could, but I'd never forget. And living with him *and* the memory of him fucking someone else wasn't something I was prepared to do while the wounds were so fresh.

So, I said I wanted out.

I run a hand through my hair, pulling my wavy tresses over one shoulder as I sit back down in the chair next to him.

"You used to play with your hair when you wanted my attention."

"Excuse me?" I look up at him.

"When you were anxious and needed me, you'd twist your hair around your finger, or run your hands through it." He gives me a sad smile. "I assume it doesn't quite mean the same now."

"No, it does not." Although, I didn't have a whole lot of control over when I fussed with my hair. It was a subconscious tick I did when I was nervous or bored or...*flirting*.

Fuck.

I can't wrap my brain around what's happening. I drop my fingers from my hair and fold them in my lap.

Things are awkward at best between us and I'm straddling the line of feeling bad and annoyed over the fact that he doesn't remember.

He's the old Bennett, but I'm not the old Olivia.

He'd broken her in the wake of his betrayal and I had no intention of being her ever again. I wanted to love again. I wanted to move on, and I couldn't if I let Bennett suck me back in again, no matter the circumstances.

I had to be strong.

My thoughts are interrupted by Caroline floating into the room with a *Starbucks* cup in her hand. This is one of the nicer hospitals in New York, but it wasn't one that had that particular coffee shop inside. "Did you... leave?" I ask.

"You didn't expect me to order a latte from *here*, did you?" She scrunches her nose. "There was a Starbucks just down the street. Unfortunately, I had to go get it myself." She rolls her eyes.

Never in a million years, did I expect her to ask if I wanted something, but I'm also shocked that she left the hospital while her son was getting an MRI. I know I'm doing a horrible job at hiding the judgment on my face, and it's confirmed when I hear a chuckle from the bed.

"Olivia's right Mother, you couldn't even bring *me* something?" He puts on his best pout and puts a hand over his chest dramatically.

My eyes flash to his angrily. "I did *not* say that."

"Your face did." He smirks at me.

"Oh sweetheart, do you want something? Olivia, do you mind? I think it was starting to rain when I came in."

I flex my hand into a fist and shoot him a look, that thankfully after all this time he still understands.

Get rid of her.

"Okay, Mom. Enough. I'm exhausted, I think I'm going to try and get some sleep. It's been quite a fucking day."

"Of course, sweetheart." She looks towards me. "Are you

going to stay? Someone should stay with him, I think? I can—" she starts.

"No." Bennett interrupts. "Just go, I'll be fine. You both can go. Wren's here if I need anything."

"Hmmm." Caroline presses a red nail to her lips and then her nose that I'm fairly certain doesn't look quite the same as the last time I saw her. "Are you sure?"

"Absolutely." My eyes trace over his face as he stares her down, and once again, I notice the bags underneath his eyes and how glazed his usually piercing green eyes look.

"Okay, well get some sleep, darling." She leans forward and presses a kiss to his forehead. "Olivia, I imagine I'll see you tomorrow?"

I fight the urge to curse my bad luck at the idea of spending yet another day in a confined space with Caroline Clarke. I go for sarcasm. "I guess." I elongate the first word and smile at her, my body almost rejecting the function. *I've heard of mother-in-laws from hell, but I honestly felt like nothing could compare to what I had to deal with.*

She gives me a fake smile and shoots me two air kisses before she's gone, making me feel like I need a drink. I'm staring after her, my eyes narrowed into slits and my lips twisted into a snarl when I hear his voice again. "All this time and still nothing?"

My head snaps towards him. "That woman hates me, Bennett. It was different when we were together; I still wanted her approval. I still wanted her to like me. I don't give a fuck now. Now I might strangle her."

"She doesn't hate you. She's just…difficult."

Seriously? "Difficult? Bennett—"

"Wrong word. Sorry." He puts his hands up in defeat. "I don't want to argue with you." He lets out a sigh and his eyes flutter closed. "I am sorry about all this. You really can go, if you need to. I don't expect you to stay here all night."

I look towards the uncomfortable chair. "I...I can stay until you fall asleep." I pull my charger out of my purse and scan the room for an outlet. I spot one and plug my iPhone in, before setting it gently on the floor. It's nearing 10 PM, and based on how tired I know he is, he'll be out in no time.

"Thank you," I hear him whisper as soon as I sit down.

"For what?"

"Being here. Coming when they called you despite...what's going on between us. Staying all day. I'm sure you had other things to do. I'm sorry if I fucked up your day." His voice is sincere just as it always is when he apologizes. Especially when it came to me.

I blink my eyes at him. "Not important." I clear my throat, wanting to clarify. "I just mean... I wanted to make sure you were okay. That was more important."

He nods and looks to the space right next to me. "I think my stuff is in there. Do you mind grabbing my phone for me?"

"Oh, right. Yes." I reach for the clear plastic bag and pull it into my lap, searching for his phone amidst his clothes and personal items when my hand finds a thin chain. I've never known Bennett to wear any kind of jewelry so I frown when I tug on it to reveal a simple silver chain.

"Is that mine? That can't be..." He chuckles, probably thinking the same thing I am about the necklace when I reach the other end. I blink my eyes several times as a ring I'd know anywhere is attached.

"It's your ring." I clear my throat, trying to remove the emotion as best I can as I realize that my soon to be ex-husband has been wearing his wedding ring on a chain around his neck for God knows how long.

"I see," he says quietly. "Where...where are yours?"

"You have them."

"I do?"

"Yes, I gave them back. It didn't seem right for me to keep them...I mean...I know women usually do, but they just reminded me of you and us and...I was more hurt than angry by all of this. Keeping my rings and what...selling them for money? That wouldn't have made me feel better." I shake my head. "Besides they were too beautiful. I'd never be able to sell them or melt them into something else," I ramble.

He nods. "Are yours in there too?"

I roll my eyes at the thought that he'd be that sentimental to carry my rings along with his and continue searching through the bag when I find his cellphone and his wallet, a black Louis Vuitton bi-fold I'd gotten him for his birthday three years ago.

"Here's your wallet. Do you want to make sure everything's in there?" I hand him his phone and he shakes his head.

"You'd probably know better than me. Do you have any idea what my passcode is?" For the longest time, it was our anniversary, but maybe he changed it in light of recent events. I shake my head, and he sighs before setting it to sleep. "Well, I guess I won't be getting into my phone anytime soon."

With shaky hands I open his wallet, noting all of the credit cards. I had access to most of these still, and a few of them even had numbers that matched the ones in mine. I spot his license, a bit of cash, but other than that nothing out of the ordinary. I knew he used to keep an emergency credit card behind the rest, so I check to make sure it's still there when I feel something else resting against it. Before I even pull it out, I know what it is, and my heart sinks feeling the familiar object against my fingertips. I pull it out slowly and stare at the black wrapper with the gold writing.

"I don't know the Bennett that keeps condoms in his wallet," I whisper. I mean, I suppose at one point I may have known that man, but I'm fairly certain Bennett and I used condoms only twice before we had *the talk* and decided that we'd only be sleeping with each other and they weren't needed.

I can feel his eyes on me and when I look up his green irises are studying me. "It bothers you…"

I clear my throat and shake my head, sliding the condom back into his wallet. "No. I mean, good for you for being…safe," I respond weakly. "You're sleeping with someone else, Bennett." I brush it off, although the words slither up my spine and into my brain.

It bothers you.

He winces and hands me his phone and his fingers skate over mine in the process causing my skin to tingle in the wake of his fingertips. I fight the urge to catch a glimpse at his lock screen, briefly wondering if it's still the same picture of him and me from years ago. Bennett was a creature of habit, and for the entirety of our relationship, it had been a picture from our first trip together. The picture had made it through two iPhones and a short lived affair with a Samsung before his most recent iPhone.

Most New Yorker's first trips together as a couple are to the Hampton's or maybe Canada to Niagara Falls. But Bennett Clarke proved that he only knew how to do things *big*. Just two months after we'd been dating, Bennett and I hopped a 747 to Fiji and spent six straight days in carnal fucking bliss. The picture in question that had been his lock screen was one of the few brief moments we'd put on clothes. We'd gone to dinner and had someone take our picture right on the beach as the sun set behind us. I was gloriously sun kissed, slightly drunk—both literally and in love with the man next to me. He'd grabbed my ass and whispered *I love you* in my ear for the first time, just as the picture was taken.

I'd gasped out of surprise and shock and lust all the while he had smiled at the camera like he hadn't just sealed our fates.

I slide his phone onto the adjacent table so that he can reach it if he wants to take another crack at his code before rummaging through the rest of the bag. "Anything else in there?" He cocks his head to the side and gestures towards the bag.

I shake my head. "Just your clothes and your keys." I blink my eyes several times as I just now remember he must have been driving. "Shit, where's your car?" He gives me a look as if to say *how the hell should I know?* "Right, of course. But we should look into that. I'm kind of surprised you were driving."

"Do I not drive often?"

"You live four blocks from work. Not usually," I explain, "but maybe you were showing a house outside of the city."

"It's infuriating," he says after a few moments of silence. "Having to be told about my life. Having *you* tell me about things I can't remember." He's staring straight ahead at the blank wall in his hospital room as he lets his eyes shut. "You want to know what I do remember? I remember you. You in a yellow dress. It hugged your curves like it was made just for your body. God, you always looked great in yellow. It made you fucking glow. It cinched at the waist and went out slightly and you had on black heels that tied around your ankles. You'd worn your hair up because it was hot as fuck out and just before you left the house, I'd laughed and told you that you looked like a bumblebee. You flipped me off and smiled before kissing me as if you'd never see me again. That's how we always kissed, like it was somehow a promise of what was to come and also as if it was our last."

His eyes open and dart to mine, and I know I'm probably a mess, what with not breathing the entire time he spoke and now suddenly letting out the breath that I desperately needed in my lungs.

"I...I remember that."

"That's the last thing I remember." He gives me a sad smile before reaching up behind him to shut off the light, leaving only the emergency lights on and giving the room an ashy glow. "I guess it was our last for me."

CHAPTER
Five

Olivia

A HAND STROKING MY SHOULDER GENTLY PULLS ME OUT OF sleep and the first thing I feel is a searing pain in my neck. My hand immediately goes to the space and I wince at the stiffness.

"Why are you sleeping here in the first place?" I hear whispered in a high-pitched judgmental tone I'd know anywhere.

I blink to see my best friend, Alyssa Hamilton, standing in front of me in pale blue scrubs under a tan Burberry peacoat. Her jet black hair is pulled into a bun at the top of her head, and her pale skin is free of makeup minus a few coats of mascara. She cocks an eyebrow at me and my eyes float to Bennett behind her who is still sleeping soundly.

"I asked a question. Why are you here?" I briefly wonder what time it is, so I reach for my phone that's still plugged in and note that it's just after 4 AM. I stand, stretching my exhausted, aching body and usher her out of the room so that we don't wake Bennett. Although, being in the room with him was probably the only thing keeping her from yelling at me for staying all night.

"Lys..." I trail off, wondering what *she* could be scolding me about. "Wait a minute, I called you almost five hours ago, and you're *just* showing up? And you call yourself my best friend," I remind her as I cross my hands over my chest.

"I was in back to back surgeries, and it's not like he died." She scoffs. "It couldn't be that easy." Her brown eyes narrow and she gives me a pointed glare.

"Lys!"

"Relax, I'm kidding. Besides Wren gave me the rundown." Despite the start of Wren and Alyssa's relationship which consisted of late night screwing in the on-call rooms of this very hospital, Alyssa worked at a different one across town to keep the temptation at bay. "Amnesia is common."

"He thinks we're together, Liv."

"So I heard. Is that why you're here, sitting at his bedside like a good little wife? Where's the wicked witch of the Upper East Side?" Her hands find her hips as her eyes dart down the hallway, waiting for Caroline to manifest.

"She left." I ignore her comment about why *I'm* here.

"Shocker." She snorts. "That doesn't exactly answer my question about you, though. Why are you here?"

"Who else would be here? His father's dead, he's an only child, and his family is pretty small. His mother called his uncle and aunt in Brooklyn, but to your point, he's fine, so I guess they didn't feel the need to come. I didn't want to leave him alone. He's freaked out."

"And? We're supposed to be angry at him, remember? Cheating? Girlfriend? Divorce?" She holds her fingers up to tick off each of his infractions.

The sting of those words feel like a thousand knives piercing my heart. *He has a girlfriend. The very one he cheated on me with.* "He still wears his ring, Alyssa."

"What?"

"His ring. He wears it around his neck." I take a step back

and begin to pace in front of the door. "That has to mean something, right?" The thoughts I'd had since I felt that familiar ring in my palm come flying out of my mouth before I can catch them.

"I..." she starts before she freezes. "No. I'm running on like four hours of sleep, I'm not going down this road of *he loves me, he loves me not.*" She tucks a fallen strand of hair behind her ear and shakes her head.

Annoyance blooms in my chest. "We know he loves me," I snap at her.

"And *you* said that wasn't enough and made me swear to you that I would hold you accountable to that." She points at me.

"Did I mention you're doing a hell of a job?"

"Which is what you wanted! Why are you acting like this? Does this...change anything?" Her question is identical to the one my subconscious has been asking for hours. *This changes nothing!*

"I didn't say that! I'm just saying, it's startling that he's still wearing his ring while he's running around New York with that tramp," I grumble as I stomp towards the bench and sit down. Anger beats down on me as I think about Bennett with *her*.

The sound of the elevator makes me look up just as Wren rounds the corner. I almost want to avert my eyes, because Wren and Alyssa are...like me and Bennett once upon a time. Affectionate and passionate and unashamedly so. "I came as soon as I saw your page." He barely has the words out before she's in his arms and they're locked in a heated kiss. I look away, attempting to give them the privacy they don't care much about having when I hear them speak.

"I've missed you today," I hear her say and then the sound of another kiss.

"It's been a crazy fucking day, as you can imagine."

"Right, he thinks they're together? It's already fucking with her head."

I realize this is probably a time for me to chime in, so I stand and make my way over to them. "It is not!"

"Yes, it has, and if it's not, I give it 'til the first time he calls you *Livi*."

A flutter ripples through my stomach as I remember the way my nickname rolled off his tongue, the way it used to. "Oh, he already did."

"God, no wonder you're asleep at his bedside. He's already sucking you back in!" Alyssa exclaims.

"He is not! But I was with him for almost nine years and we've been apart for six months. I'm allowed to still have feelings for him, Alyssa. You have no idea what I'm feeling. And now, he's hurt and he doesn't remember anything. He's looking at me how he used to look at me. You should have seen the look on his face when I told him we weren't together. When I told him he cheated on me. I've seen him devastated. And this is right up there with losing his dad." I shake my head at my best friend who I know means well, but frankly coupled with my extreme physical and emotional exhaustion is irritating the shit out of me. "I'm not taking him back or thinking everything's fine just because he can't remember. I'm not so delusional to think we can just pretend it never happened because he doesn't have any memory of it, but I'm allowed to feel confused, Alyssa. Stop judging me over it."

She takes a step back, her demeanor drastically shifting before my very eyes. *Fuck, now she's upset.* "I'm not judging you, Olivia. But he broke your heart and I had a front row seat to it. I would never judge you, but I'm not going to sugarcoat anything with you either."

Wren hangs back, listening intently but not intervening.

He's in a tough situation being best friends with my estranged husband and married to my best friend. Sometimes I want to wrap him in a hug and apologize for the fact that he's very much caught in the middle.

"Listen, it's late," he interrupts, as he sees Alyssa shutting down. He wraps her in his arms and presses a kiss to her temple. "Baby, you're running on no sleep and so am I. I have rounds in two hours though, so I'm going to just grab a nap in the on-call room."

"You're not even coming home with me?" Alyssa turns in his arms and a pout finds her lips. The exhaustion must be weighing on her too because I note her eyes become glossy.

"I just...I need to be here for this." He nods towards the door. "He's like...my brother." I feel my lips turning up in a smile over Wren's ability to always want to do *good* by everyone.

"Wren..."

"Lys, I know how you feel about him, believe me, I do, but not only is this my job, but he's family. So, I'm going to go take a nap in the on-call room. You're welcome to join me." He presses a kiss to her lips and gives her a side smile. "You know which one."

She puts her hands on her hips as he walks away. "Leave the door unlocked," she calls after him and a giggle falls from my lips as Wren holds a thumbs up over his head. She turns to me and her eyes float to Bennett's room. "So, you're staying?"

"Yeah, just until...I don't know, he can go home. Or he's more settled. I would hate for him to be here all alone, confused and hurt. And yeah, Lys, I love him. I'm angry and hurt but those feelings haven't gone away yet. I'm trying, though. I swear." I bite my bottom lip. "I just wish it didn't hurt so much." Fresh tears swim in my eyes as the pain of all the loss I've suffered in the past two years comes barreling towards me. It hits me like a tidal wave, pulling me under and knocking the air from my lungs, when suddenly I feel relief—my lifesaver in the rocky waters of my life.

Alyssa's arms wrap around me and she squeezes. "I know, Liv, I know," she murmurs. "I can't even imagine what you've been through." She pulls back and rests her hands on my shoulder before cocking her head to the side. "You're the strongest person I know."

"Hardly." I snort.

"You are, and I'm sorry I was insensitive before. I just want you to be happy."

"Me too. But it seems to be a foreign concept to me lately."

"You will be again. I don't care if I have to drag you there kicking and screaming. We'll get you there."

"Thanks, Lys." I look down the hallway and give her a smile. "Now go get laid."

CHAPTER
Six

Olivia

THE NEXT TIME I OPEN MY EYES, LIGHT IS STREAMING THROUGH the tiny window in the corner. We are high enough, that the buildings aren't completely blocking the sun, allowing me a view of blue skies. The tightness in my neck is even worse and I can already feel my skin screaming for not taking my makeup off the night before. My eyes feel dry and weak, so I blink them several more times trying to create moisture when I hear his voice, quiet and sensual floating all around me.

"You stayed." I pull my head away from my fist that it had been resting against for most of the night and meet Bennett's gaze. I see the guilt in his eyes, as if he was the direct cause of my discomfort. "That chair does not look comfortable."

I flex my hand that feels numb and the tingles shoot up my arm as I shake it out slowly. "It's okay. How did you sleep?"

A small smile finds his lips. "Do you ever complain about anything?" He shakes his head. "I still remember that awful fucking hotel we had to get last minute when we were driving to Connecticut to go skiing."

I remember it too. The snow was coming down so bad, that the roads were undrivable, so Bennett and I pulled into a small hotel that looked like a setting from a horror movie. It was small, it didn't smell particularly welcoming, and it looked even worse. I wasn't pleased, but we had a bottle of whiskey and each other so I was perfectly content in that tiny hotel room. I scrubbed the bathroom from top to bottom, and we spent the night fucking in the shower because nothing about the bed screamed *get naked here*.

Again, the trip down memory lane comes at me hard and fast and my heart thumps in my chest as I recall the happier times. I had spent much of the six months recalling all of the bad times, disallowing myself from remembering anything happy or good because I didn't want to think I'd potentially made a mistake. "I—" I start, my heart has completely taken over, shutting my brain off momentarily. I'm prepared to engage in his memory, recalling how he'd walked a mile in the snow the next morning to find us coffee that wasn't complete trash before I even woke up. That's why I never complained, because *he* always made things so easy for me. He never wanted me to experience discomfort. The words are on the tip of my tongue when the door swings open.

"Bennett!" The tone is shrill and it's not only ear-splitting, but I feel like the split in my heart further deepens as I see *her* moving through the door quick as lightning. "Oh my God, Bennett." She rushes to his bedside and puts her hands on his chest and it's like a bad car wreck I can't pull my gaze from. Her blonde hair is curled and styled perfectly, but her face is completely void of makeup giving her a fresh faced glow. *She still looks flawless. Did she actually wake up like that? Bitch.*

Thoughts of how perfect they look together flood my brain and my insecurities begin to take form, loud and aggressively. *They look better together than we ever did.* They looked like Barbie and Ken.

Perfect. Gorgeous. All American.

I wipe under my eyes and smooth my dark curls back, hoping that I don't look too crazy having just woken up not too long ago.

Of course, I would run into my husband's girlfriend while I'm unshowered and looking like God knows what.

The movement must catch her attention because she turns towards me. To her credit, when her eyes find mine, she pulls away from him like he's on fire and swallows hard.

I stand, preparing to give them some privacy, even though I know it's the last thing Bennett wants, when his voice floods the room. "Who the fuck are you? And who do you think you are barging into my room like that?" His eyes pull away from her to me. "Sit," he growls, though beneath the command, I can hear the plea. *Don't go, please.*

"Bennett…" she starts. "I know that you're struggling with your memory, your mom called…" she says nervously, her hands completely dropping as she fidgets.

"I told her to inform you *not* to come. So, either she neglected to tell you that, in which case I'm sorry that you wasted your time, or she did tell you and you chose to ignore it, in which case I am not at all sorry for what I'm about to say to you. Get the fuck out." Her mouth drops open before she sinks her teeth into her lower lip. Her teeth are just as perfect as mine, and I briefly wonder if her lip biting does the same thing to Bennett as mine does.

"Bennett…" I start. And I'm not sure what I'm trying to say. It's somewhere between, let *me* go, and tell *her* to go.

"Livi, don't start. Maybe you've come to terms with this, but I have not and all I see is one of the reasons we're not together."

Tears swim in her blue eyes as she takes a step back and her gaze finds mine, for what, I'm not sure. *Help? Sympathy?* She can't possibly be asking me for that. I look away, and I notice her shoulders deflate in my periphery.

"You and Olivia aren't together, Bennett."

"I'm well aware of that, not that it's any of your fucking business what goes on between me and my *wife*."

I hear a sigh leave her lips as her cheeks turn pink. "I thought seeing me would…"

"Help? Well, your hypothesis backfired. All you've done is successfully piss me off." I turn my gaze back to them. I've known Bennett for a long time, so I can see how irritated he is. She, on the other hand, has known him for less than a year, which means she's probably not getting the hint.

She runs a hand through her hair and cocks her head to the side making me wonder if this is how she gets her way with my husband. "Why are you being like this…? This isn't you."

"I'm being like this because you thought you could show up here and ambush me, when I'm sure my mother *at the very least* informed you that Olivia was here."

"She…didn't." She shakes her head nervously before her eyes flit to mine again.

"Well, now you know, so maybe it's best that you go. And in case it wasn't obvious, it's over," he growls.

"What?" Her eyes widen to the size of saucers as her gaze shifts back and forth between me and Bennett.

"Surely you couldn't think that you and I were going anywhere. Even if I wasn't in this position," he says as he points to his hospital bed, "our relationship had an expiration date. No one marries their fucking rebound or fling, give me a break." He grits out and even I wince at the harshness of his statement. "I'm still wearing my wedding ring, and Olivia is still the background of my goddamn cellphone, you knew what this was."

My heart skips a beat at the mention of the picture I was thinking of last night. *So, it's still there?*

My head spins at his revelation and I let out a breath. I need out of this room. His words and her presence is just too much for me, especially this early in the morning. "Bennett, I'm just going to step outside to—"

"Don't," he growls at me and my eyes widen.

"No, *you* don't. I don't have to sit here and listen to you argue with your fucking girlfriend."

"She's not my—"

"She was!" I bark and I'm out of the room before he can respond.

I don't need this, even if he is in the process of breaking up with her, seeing her face made me irate and while a part of me squealed with glee over the fact that he was ending it with her, it didn't stop the voice inside of me that told me that eventually he would regret it once he had his memory back.

I'm alone with my thoughts for all of two minutes when the sound of the door closing interrupts my racing mind. I look up to find Amanda, tears streaming down her face.

"He's...he's never talked to me like that before."

"Should I... feel bad?" I cross my arms defensively.

She swallows hard and looks around the empty hallway. *Maybe for witnesses.* And I can see that she's struggling with what to say. "No...I...he told me he loved me. Before this. That he'd never met anyone like me. He wanted to get married."

The words are like a shock to my entire system. A harsh, painful shock that I wasn't expecting. "He's still married to me," I grit out.

"When...when you were officially divorced, we talked about it. *Us* moving forward"

Bullshit, I think. *But is it?* My mind questions. "Why are you telling me all of this? What's the point?"

"I love him." She has the decency, *if I can even call it that*, to look contrite when the words leave her lips.

Inhale. Count to ten. Exhale, my therapist's voice speaks calmly in my ear. I listen. "I didn't take him from you." I don't mean for the words to come out harshly but I hear the bite in my tone.

She bites her lip and looks down away from the icy gaze I know to be shooting from my eyes. "I know, I just…I don't know *this* Bennett."

Of course, you don't. This Bennett belongs to me.

I don't say anything because I don't want her to know how much she still makes me crazy. She knows where we stand, and going off on her *again* won't do anything but give her power. The art of indifference. It's something I've learned as I've gone through this process. Control your emotions. The less you show, the less power you relinquish. I blink a few times as if to say *anything else?*

She doesn't say anything and I'm preparing to make my exit when the door opens again and Bennett is standing in it. "My dismissal wasn't so that you could come out here and harass my wife," he bites out and I note that he's still hooked up to his IV but that he's dragged the pole from his bedside.

Amanda's eyes sweep to his. "You're being an asshole."

"Then it should be easy for you to get over me." His lips form a sneer, and I watch her crack completely in front of me, as if she's finally succumbing to the humiliation of this breakup. She lowers her head and moves down the hallway. I follow her with my eyes until she's out of sight before I turn to Bennett who looks completely defeated. He doesn't say anything before he turns his back and goes back inside his room, giving me a glimpse of his bare ass despite him trying to keep his hospital gown closed with one hand. I can't stop the feelings of lust coursing through me seeing that perfectly sculpted ass that I used to be very familiar with. Fantasies of gripping it, digging my nails into the skin as he plowed into me flash through my mind. God created perfection when he created Bennett Clarke's ass, I'll give him that. I follow behind him and stand in the doorway, unsure if I want to enter or leave.

Don't think about his ass, Olivia.

"You were kind of rude to her." There's not much emotion to my voice and I'm not even sure why I felt the need to comment. It's just a statement.

"Don't start, Olivia," he growls as he makes his way back into bed. "I'm fucking pissed at her."

"Just her? Because it's not all her fault. You were the one that was married. *You* cheated on me. She didn't." I hate her, but I'm not one of those women that misdirects the blame. Bennett cheated on me, she, on the other hand, didn't have any loyalty to me. She and I didn't take vows.

Yes, I hate her on the superficial, *"she's not even that pretty, how could he go from me to her"* that I fixated on when Alyssa and I drank too much tequila. But the hurt came from Bennett. The pain, the betrayal, that was all at my husband's hands. Not his mistress'.

"I'm pissed at myself too, is that what you want to hear? I chose to take that anger out on her, sue me." He rubs his forehead before letting his hand fall. "I hate myself for doing this to us, but she had no business showing up here."

"Fair. But..." I contemplate not sharing what she told me. *Fuck it.* "She said you love her."

"Bullshit."

My eyes widen at the thought of him not believing what I said. "When have I ever lied to you?"

"I didn't say you lied. It's bullshit that I said I loved her," he explains.

"How would you know?" I snap and hurt flickers over his face.

I expect him to snap back at me, but his shoulders deflate and the apology sits on the tip of my tongue. "That was unnecessary."

I'm about to apologize when Wren walks through the door. He looks surprised to see me. "Morning, sunshines. Did you... stay the whole night? Or did you leave?" He nods at me and I shake my head.

"I...I stayed."

Wren doesn't even try to hide the smile from creeping onto his face. "Is that so?" He's almost giddy and I roll my eyes at his ongoing *Get Bennett and Olivia Back Together* campaign.

"I need some coffee." My tone is even, almost deadpan and Bennett chuckles despite the tension between us before Wren walked in.

"Still not a morning person, huh?" he asks.

"There's a coffee cart down the hall and to the left," Wren tells me. "They just opened for the day."

I nod. "Do you want anything?" I ask Bennett. "Can he have anything?" I ask Wren, remembering his condition and Wren shakes his head.

"Not from there. A nurse will bring him something in a bit." He pulls the clipboard from the foot of Bennett's bed and begins to flip through it.

"Take my wallet," Bennett says and I scrunch my nose at his need to always take care of me.

"What?"

"You never have cash on you and I do," he says as if it's the most obvious answer.

"It's 2019, they take cards," I argue as a way to say, *I don't need you.*

"Actually, they don't," Wren adds, "but the one downstairs does."

"I'll go to the one downstairs, then," I tell him before I'm out of the room without another word.

I don't need Bennett thinking I need him to take care of me. Call me stubborn, but I don't need to be thinking it either.

I've been gone ten minutes, but it's obvious the air inside Bennett's room has shifted when I return. It's tense, like I could slice through it with a knife. My eyes shift back and forth between Bennett and Wren as I try to figure out what it is they're keeping from me. "What?"

"She's not going to go for it," Bennett says. His tone is sad and I avoid his piercing green eyes that are full of anguish as I turn my gaze to Wren.

"I'm not going to go for what?"

Wren shifts back and forth guiltily before he pulls his glasses from his face and stares at me.

"Ben, shouldn't be alone right now and I think for now... Bennett needs to move back in with you."

"Excuse me?" I choke out. My skin prickles at the idea and I can't pinpoint what exact emotion my body is responding to.

"Normalcy, Liv. He needs it and it helps with memory restoration."

He cannot be serious. We're going through a divorce! How is living together "normalcy?" "Living with me isn't his current normalcy. He lives alone or with ..."

"He doesn't. You don't." He reassures Bennett, who's looking at me with a look of terror at the idea of living with his girlfriend.

"It doesn't mean that living with me is his best option. What about Caroline?" I ask in reference to my insufferable mother-in-law.

"Absolutely not," Bennett snaps. "I'll go insane." He looks at me with his signature look that used to make me melt and give in to whatever he wanted. His face softens, his green eyes are full of sincerity and love. His full lips form a straight line and he looks up at me through thick full lashes.

"You've got to be kidding me with this." I shake my head, the idea of counting to ten long forgotten. "No way. You two aren't going to bully me into this just because you're team Liv and Bennett," I say pointing at Wren, "and *you* don't remember anything." I point at Bennett. "You can't just move back in and disrupt my life. I have a say in this too and this isn't fair to me." The tears well in my eyes more due to anger than sadness. I blink, and one falls down my cheek instantly. I wipe it away and take a step back preparing to make my exit before I completely break down.

"Please don't cry, Livi." Bennett shakes his head, and I turn around upon hearing that name as sobs bubble in my throat. "Wren, I'll come up with something else." I hear his dejected voice just as the door slams behind me.

I've been pacing for no more than five seconds when Wren interrupts my thoughts just as I get to "six." "Olivia," he barks out and my eyes snap to his.

"Fuck off," I growl. "Why would you even put that idea out there?"

"Because it's not just about you Olivia!" he shouts.

"It's never been about me! When the fuck has it been about me? When he fucked someone else? When he moved out?" I'm so angry I can't even think straight let alone focus on my breathing or worry about counting to ten.

"You threw him out! And don't start that shit with me. You

know he's still crazy about you. He's apologized a million times. He'd die for you to give him another chance. How long are you going to punish you *both* for?" He pauses and narrows his gaze before placing his hands on his hips. "You know you still love him." His voice lowers to a whisper.

I fix my mouth to rebut his comment when he puts a hand up so he can continue. "Right now? The man in there—that's the man you fell in love with and it scares the shit out of you. It scares you that you need him as much as he needs you."

"I don't need him or this. I have a life and a—"

"A what?" he interjects. "A boyfriend you're using to get over Ben?" His blue eyes narrow in concern, but underneath, I see the judgment lurking.

"You can't make me feel bad for moving on. He has a—"

"A girlfriend he dumped this morning?" I want to scream at being interrupted again. "Yeah, I happened to see her leaving looking like someone ran over her dog. Can't say I'm sad to see her go. She sucked."

"Wow, not the point," I grit out. *Like I give a fuck that he doesn't like Amanda? My husband did and that was enough.*

Ex-husband, my mind clarifies and my heart squeezes in my chest in response.

"And no, I can't make you feel bad for moving on. But I *can* make you feel bad for being insensitive right now. He needs you, Olivia. You're the only person he trusts."

The feeling isn't mutual.

"He trusts you," I inform him.

"He cannot come stay with me and Alyssa, Liv. Lys will murder him in his sleep, and we're also trying to have a baby which means when we're not at the hospital, I'm inside of her."

"Can you not?" I groan as I try hard not to picture the visual he's painted.

"I'm serious, Olivia." He crosses his arms over his chest and his eyes are scolding, which isn't something I expect from Wren who is perhaps the least confrontational person on the planet. "He needs you."

CHAPTER
Seven

Olivia

I SLAM THE DOOR OF MY AUDI Q3 SHUT, MY LIPS IN THE PERMANENT scowl they've been in since yesterday when I'd begrudgingly agreed to let Bennett move in *temporarily*. I'd even enlisted Alyssa to help me shut it down, but I hadn't banked on Wren wearing her down in a way I couldn't.

Fucking marriage.

I make my way around the car and see Bennett trying to pull himself upright, out of his wheelchair, and leaning on Wren for support. I know he's still a little banged up, and Wren said he'd still feel some aches and pains from the accident. When he sees me, he lets go of Wren immediately and gives me a smile. I notice that his facial hair has grown out a bit more, making his beard thicker than usual and I clench at remembering what it felt like between my legs when he let it grow out.

I blink several times as if I try to convince my brain that we are *not* affected by his perfect one hundred watt smile or the hair that surrounds it.

Or the abs that I could practically make out through his white t-shirt.

Fuck.

His smile falters when he sees the look I'm giving, and I

wonder if my unfazed look is coming off as something else entirely. I look away from his face and down his body, seeing him in normal wear instead of the hospital gown.

Caroline had brought some clothes yesterday for him to wear home from the hospital, and my mind immediately curses her for what she chose. I try my best to keep my eyes away from his pelvis, but the gray sweatpants he's wearing makes my eyes go there almost immediately before sliding up the rest of his frame. A white t-shirt sits underneath his leather jacket and if I didn't know any better, I'd say Caroline picked these clothes on purpose, knowing that it has the power to turn me on instantly. Visions of dry humping him in my bed while he was wearing *only* gray sweatpants come at me in full force and instinctively I press my thighs together, trying to dull the ache between my legs brought on by the memory. I remember the way his strong arms would move me back and forth against his cock as a way to get both of us off and my mouth waters. When I meet his gaze again, his eyes are dark and hungry, like he can read my mind and vividly see the dirty images playing on a loop.

"You good, man?" Wren asks, effectively breaking our eye contact. I clear my throat and look away from them before turning back towards my car. "Liv!"

I turn back around and give him a look as he slides two clear bags that have Bennett's clothes from the accident as well as the medicine he needs to be taking into the backseat of my car. "What?"

"Now you remember what he needs to take and when?" Wren says as he pulls one of the orange pill bottles out of the bag.

I roll my eyes. "I do have two degrees, Wren. I can read."

"As can I," Bennett quips from behind him before he slides into my passenger seat.

"I can't believe I agreed to this," I whisper. I didn't stay at the hospital last night. I went home and dwelled on the stupidity of my decision to let Bennett stay with me.

Sure, I was being selfless by pushing my own feelings aside—and helpful and whatever else—but I wasn't over Bennett. Not by a long shot. And now I was letting him back into my home, *our* home, and my heart. My heart that hadn't felt full since the last night he slept there.

Is this the path to reconciliation?

Do I even want to reconcile?

I'm still so angry but do my feelings for him trump my anger?

I'd give anything for him to remember. At least, he'd know where we stood.

Hell, so would I.

When I got home last night, I'd had one too many glasses of wine and then left a very dramatic voicemail on my therapist's answering machine.

And my mother's.

And now neither will stop calling me.

Or David for that matter.

I really need to call him back.

Wren motions me a few steps away from my car, just in case Bennett has the window open, to be a bit more out of earshot. "It's not going to be that bad, Liv. It should only be for a few weeks to a month," Wren says, interrupting my laundry list of people I'm currently avoiding.

"And if he doesn't regain his memory?" I rub my hand over my forehead before tucking a wavy strand behind my ear.

"Then we go from there. But at that point, he'll be strong enough and somewhat acclimated to his new normal that he can be on his own."

The wind picks up, chilling me down to my bones and I rub my arms to try and warm myself. "Fine."

"I'll try and stop by later and check on him, but I have to work late. Call me if you need anything. If you can't get me, you have the nurse's number, right?" He looks at me from over his glasses, and I can see something different entirely in his eyes. Maybe he's realizing that this is going to be harder on me than he thought.

"Yeah." I let out a breath.

"It's going to be okay, Liv, I promise."

"Yeah sure, Wren." I lean against the car and look up at my best friend's husband *and* my husband's best friend. "I'm scared he'll break me again," I blurt out and I can feel the tears in my eyes. I try my best to not let them fall, knowing that the pick-up lane of a hospital is not the place for this breakdown or breakthrough or whatever it is that's happening to me.

"Hey." His voice is strong and direct, and when I look up, his glasses have been pushed into his hair. "He *hates* himself for what he did to you." I go to say something when he puts a hand up. "I know you think I'd say anything to get you guys back together, but that *is* the truth, Liv. He made a mistake and he hates himself for it. He went back to her again after that night because she knew the situation. She let him be broken over you. Any other woman would have told him he had too much baggage, or he would have had to hide it from her. He got to be himself with her. He could be with her and *still* be in love with you. He was using her to try and get over you. Might I add, he was failing."

My heart softens slightly at the thought, though it does nothing for my subconscious screaming *this is exactly what we're afraid of!* "Is that supposed to make me feel better?"

He huffs in what I assume to be annoyance. "It's supposed

to make you understand that he is always going to be in love with you."

"He cheated on me." *And I'm supposed to just ignore that?*

"People make mistakes, Olivia, and for someone who's made a few of her own, you're certainly on a high fucking horse."

Is he for real? "I didn't cheat on him."

"No, you just left him," he points out.

"I didn't leave him," I snap.

"You sure *he* knew that?" Wren retorts and I realize he doesn't mean in the literal sense.

"I'm not arguing with you about this. You can't compare how I decided to handle my miscarriages—yes *plural*—to him seeking solace in another woman's vagina!" I try to keep my voice even, but I can hear the hysteria forcing my voice a few octaves higher. My heart hammers against my ribcage as I feel my body reacting to my words. *Deep breaths, Olivia.*

"No, but he needed you and you wouldn't even look at him." He crosses his arms across his chest, the bottom half of his tattoo sleeve peeking out from his scrubs.

"Because I was depressed!"

"That's fair. But he begged you to see someone. *He* wanted to see someone, and you wouldn't go."

I shake my head and take a step back. "I'm not going to allow you to villainize me here. Did you tell him all of this?" I nod towards Bennett and he shakes his head.

He slides his hands into his pockets and looks down. "Of course not. He did ask why you didn't have children though."

"And what did you say?"

He meets my gaze. "That he needed to talk to you about that."

"Great." I groan as I anticipate a long ride home if he's going to ask me a million questions.

"I told him to give you some space about it, and not to bombard you with questions. I'm sure he's pieced some things together."

I turn around and take a step towards the driver's seat before turning back around to face Wren. "You know it's a real fucking shame when it becomes the mother's fault over how she handles a miscarriage. *Miscarriages.*" I give him my back again when I hear his voice.

"You're not the only one that suffered a loss, Olivia. And the fact that you *still* can't see that makes you have to shoulder some of the blame as to why your marriage is the way that it is."

Chapter Eight

Olivia

Wren's words ring through my head as I pull away from the hospital. I pull my sunglasses over my eyes as a way to shield my emotions from Bennett, who I can feel studying me from the other side of the car. "Are you okay?" he asks and I nod once.

"I'm fine. Are you hungry?"

"I ate at the hospital."

"So that's a yes?"

He chuckles. "I can eat, but I don't want to disrupt your day."

"It's fine, they know I'll be working from home for the rest of the week."

"Is… is that okay?"

"Yep. I've also called SPR and told them what's going on."

"What did Jeff say?"

"Well…nothing because Jeff doesn't work for SPR," I tell him and I can sense his jaw dropping in my periphery.

"Say what?"

"Well…you kind of took his job."

"You're shitting me. He…he was my mentor."

"Yeah, well…" I shrug.

"What happened to me? Liv, what kind of asshole have I become?"

I laugh out loud at his apprehensive tone. "What do you mean *become*? You were an asshole two years ago, so I don't know why you're confused." He's silent and I chance a glance at him and he's staring out the window. "I'm kidding...Jeff got promoted." I give him a half smile when he turns back towards me and I can see the relief in his eyes. "He works out of the LA office now," I tell him and he nods before letting out a breath.

"You could have led with that."

"Sorry, but it was too easy." I giggle.

"Thank you for using this situation against me," he grumbles. "Who's the asshole now?"

I bite my lip at his comment. It was going to be a long three weeks if this is how things were going to be. We move through the streets towards my apartment in SoHo and within forty minutes I'm pulling into the garage at the base of the building. I unbuckle my seatbelt and stare straight ahead as I prepare myself for what I've been practicing in my head for the last twenty minutes. "I'm sorry," I breathe out, "for being insensitive." I look over at him and he gives me a smile.

"I know that I can be a bit of an asshole. I just...I've never been that way with you. You've always seemed to be the one exception to that." He unbuckles his seatbelt and makes a move to get out before he stops and looks at me. "You...and Wren...and my mother, you can all tell me what I did, but I still can't wrap my brain around the fact that it happened. That I hurt you...*in that way*. That being said, I know you have a very different opinion of me than I remember having of you, so it's just going to take some getting used to...that you don't love me anymore." He gives me a sad smile and then he's gone.

I open my mouth to refute his statement when I remember that it's easier for all parties if he just thinks I don't love him.

So, what if I do love him?

Does that change anything?

I hop out and make my way around the car where I see him pulling the bags from the car. I pull them from him. "I got it."

"You sure?" He looks down at me and I'm instantly reminded of the Bennett that rarely let me lift a finger.

"You just worry about keeping yourself upright," I tell him.

Caroline had packed a bag of clothes and brought it over last night as well, which thankfully didn't turn into a whole big thing when she dropped them off. *Thank God for "a six o'clock yogalates class I can NOT be late for."*

We move through the lobby and I see our front desk concierge's face light up when he sees Bennett. "Mr. Clarke!"

I try to hide the irritation from my face as he makes his way over, even though he's one of the kindest men I know. Mr. Kline is old enough to be my grandfather but acts like he's my age or younger and used to tease Bennett endlessly that one day he was going to whisk me away. When Bennett's father passed, he attended the funeral and sent one of the most breathtaking arrangements I'd ever seen. He also took him and got him ridiculously drunk because *"it didn't seem anyone else in his family was too concerned."* He'd sent me flowers the day Bennett officially moved out and took *me* to get drunk the following day.

Needless to say, Bennett and I are fans of Mr. Kline.

"It's so nice to see you two together again." Despite his words, I see the look he gives Bennett before turning his warm gaze to me. "Hi dear, you had a…umm…visitor, while you were gone." He's less than impressed with David Jacobs and has felt the need to let me know, *constantly*. He gives me a pointed look before shifting his gaze to Bennett.

FORGET ME *Not*

I clear my throat and catch a glimpse at Bennett who looks as if he's ready to snap over my visitor. "I see...well, thank you for letting me know," I say nervously. I don't know why I'm nervous. *I haven't done anything wrong. Well, nothing more wrong than Bennett!*

He nods before turning back to Bennett. "Don't fuck it up this time, Clarke," he says looking at him over his round frames.

I roll my eyes. "Oh, for Heaven's sake," I growl as I stomp past them to the elevator. "Come on, Bennett!" I say over my shoulder without another glance at them. I hear the sounds of him behind me and when he enters the elevator, I let out a breath.

"He knows?"

"Yes, you had quite a habit of showing up here drunk after you moved out. If it weren't for Mr. Kline, you'd probably be in jail for public intoxication."

He nods and leans his head back against the elevator. "He hasn't aged a day," he says, ignoring my comment.

"He was worried about you." I don't know why I tell him that. Maybe because I wanted him to know someone cared. That a lot of people cared. That I'd been getting phone calls and emails from countless people from his job wondering how he is. What they could do. If we needed anything.

"You told him?"

"He was working when I got Wren's call. I wasn't...in the best shape when I left." I recall, how he'd offered to drive me before eventually convincing me that I was in no condition to drive and I needed to take an Uber.

The elevator dings, ending our conversation, and as we make our way into the hall, he breathes out what sounds like a sigh of relief. "Fuck it feels good to be here. It's like my body can sense that I'm home." We make our way down the hall and eventually make it to our door. I put my key in the lock as I steel myself to let Bennett back in. Opening this door feels so much bigger than

67

just this physical act and a thought briefly crosses my mind that maybe I'm opening the door to something else entirely.

I cleaned the apartment from top to bottom last night, not that it was particularly messy, but I couldn't sleep and the idea of Bennett being back in my space had me feeling anxious. I toss the keys on the small table next to the door and let Bennett enter behind me. He stands in the doorway and takes in the living room, no doubt remembering it completely differently.

"You redecorated."

"Well, you took the majority of the furniture when you moved out."

A look of shock and almost horror crosses his face. "I did what?"

"No…" I shake my head as I hear how it sounds. "I wanted you to. I wanted new stuff. And you weren't leaving anywhere without your television." I smile as I look at the smaller television mounted on the wall.

"It's…nice." He smiles at me. "It's you." The entire room is made up of light grays and lavenders with flowers on every surface of the room. He moves through the room like he owns it and sits on the couch before looking up at me. "Thank you. For doing this. I'll do my best to stay out of your way." He pulls his jacket off, simultaneously flexing his arm, and I swallow the lump in my throat. He leans back, stretching his long legs underneath the coffee table, reminding me what it felt like to have him here.

"I love it," I squeal as I look out the window at the gorgeous view from the seventh floor window. I turn back to see Bennett moving towards me with a smirk known to make my panties wet and the realtor moving towards the kitchen. "It's a little over our budget though…" Before I can continue, Clarke has me up against the window with my face in his large warm hands staring down at me like he's ready to devour me at any second.

"I can't wait to fuck you against these floor to ceiling windows.

Let everyone down below see you fall apart with my cock inside your sweet little pussy." His voice is gravelly and low and it takes everything out of me not to suggest we go christen the place in the nearest bathroom. I peek around his large frame to look for our realtor, one almost as good as Bennett, when his hands turn me back towards him. "I told him to give us a minute. I also don't like the way he keeps looking at your tits, but I'll consider letting it slide for the sake of this deal I'm about to pose." He lowers his face and presses his lips to the skin behind my ear. "Your eyes didn't light up at any of the other apartments we looked at, but this one..." he nibbles gently on my ear before he pulls back, "you love it, it's yours."

My breath hitches and I feel myself getting emotional at his words, but I shouldn't be surprised. This is how Bennett is; he acts as if it's his job to make me happy. "I love you." I look up at him, and I hope my eyes are conveying just how much.

His emerald colored eyes trace my face before he presses his lips to mine. "I love hearing you say that." His hard body presses against mine as the kiss becomes more intense. I run my hand down his body and slide it between us to palm his dick through his slacks and he growls in my mouth. My hair is pulled to the side in one braid and he yanks on it playfully before letting up. "You'll pay for that later, Mrs. Clarke."

"Promise?" My eyes twinkle with excitement and I swear my panties that were already wet, become soaked the second he runs his tongue over his bottom lip.

"You alright?" Bennett's voice breaks me from my memories and I see him leaning forward, his arms resting on his knees as he stares up at me. "You went away for a second."

"Yeah...I..." I let out a breath. "I made up the master bedroom for you." I swallow as I begin to back away from Bennett and the sudden influx of happy memories I was reliving.

"Wait, what?" I hear him briefly struggle to get up, but when I turn around he's already moving towards me. "I'm not sleeping there. I've already disrupted your life. I'm not going to kick you out of your room." He follows me through the kitchen and down the long hall. He stops and admires some of the pictures on the wall, none of which have him in them. "You look really pretty here." He points at a picture and I turn around to see which one he means. I smile at the picture of Alyssa and me when we'd gone to Miami as a part of my *"I'm Getting Divorced"* tour. "Not a lot of pictures of me here…did you break them all?" he teases and I frown at his joke.

"No. You took most of them when you moved, and the rest are in a box. Breaking pictures of us wouldn't make me feel better over what happened, Bennett," I snap and continue moving down the hall.

"I didn't… I didn't mean anything by that." He sighs and follows me into the master bedroom. When we get to the entrance, I feel his gaze on my face. "Please don't hate me."

"If I did, you wouldn't be here," I say simply, and if that wasn't the fucking truth.

He doesn't respond to my comment but completely changes the subject instead. "I don't want to stay in here."

I wave him off as I move through the room in attempts to put some space between us. "It's fine, Bennett. I moved out of this room when you moved out."

"What?"

"I sleep in the guest room."

"Why?" His eyes scan the room, and I can see the curiosity all over his face as to why I wouldn't be sleeping in the room I'd slept in for years.

I shrug. "It's just too big in here and…sleeping in here alone was just too difficult." I blink the tears out of my eyes as I remember the first night I attempted it. I'd woken up in a panic, my body already anxious and on high alert at the idea of being in the apartment by myself. Bennett had slept in the guest room for the two weeks prior while he looked for a place, but then he was gone and I felt hollow and my chest ached with every breath I took. "If you prefer, I bought a sleeper sofa for what used to be your office, and you can sleep there," I add weakly. "But this bed is still more comfortable."

"I don't know how comfortable it will be without you in it." My head whips to his, and I meet his green eyes that are staring at me hard. I shift nervously under his gaze and he frowns. "I hate that I make you nervous now."

"I'm not," I argue, even though I could sense the mounting tension between us.

He nods, although I know he doesn't believe me. "I can stay in here. This is great, thank you." He makes his way through what used to be our old bedroom and looks around before sitting on the bed. "Looks pretty much the same."

"I still use the ensuite bathroom because..." I look towards it and give him a knowing smile. "Obviously, that bathroom is phenomenal."

"It's a great bathroom, I'll agree. I'm glad we updated it." He agrees before kicking his shoes off.

"You must be exhausted. I'll let you get situated." I point at the suitcase next to the bed. "Your mom brought you some clothes and some of your things. If you're missing something, I can go out and get it or I can drive us to your apartment."

"Livi, stop fussing over me. It's fine, I'll make do with whatever's in there."

"Right." I let out a breath. "Well, you know how the television works and..."

"Liv," he growls and I put my hands up before taking a step back.

"Right, sorry!" I close the door behind me and let out the breath I feel like I've been holding since we stepped foot into the apartment.

I make my way back towards the kitchen and pull off my coat before grabbing my phone from inside my purse. I scroll through the missed calls and texts and decide it might be time to return a few of them.

Which phone call is less likely to drive me to drink?

CHAPTER
Nine

Olivia

AFTER A SHORT YET VERY TEDIOUS CONVERSATION WITH MY mother, where I informed her everything was fine, *and by fine I meant Bennett was alive*, I finally had to fake a headache to get off the phone. It's times like this that I'm grateful my parents live a safe two and a half hours away in Philadelphia. Naturally, they were concerned about Bennett, even if they weren't his biggest fans anymore. But once I told them he was alive, they seemed to calm down and wanted to know more about how *I* was handling everything. Of course, I left out the fact that he's staying with me, knowing that it's the quickest way to get my overprotective parents to the city for a *visit*. I let out a breath and open the door to the guest room to peek my head out into the hallway.

This is ridiculous. This is my house.

I shouldn't feel nervous about leaving my fucking room. I make my way towards the kitchen as I wonder what I should make for dinner. I haven't had much of an appetite the last six months, but I've forced myself to eat, mainly to keep my mother and Alyssa off my back. But I couldn't remember the last time I ate for enjoyment. Bennett and I were big "foodies" and were always trying new restaurants, new cuisines, and took cooking classes together all the time. When we split up, I lost interest in trying new things and found myself barely eating at all. It wasn't until my parents came to visit a month into our separation that my mother became persistent about my eating habits. Cooking for one is depressing, so I've taken to *UberEats* and delivery pizza. Thank God, I picked up working out amidst everything.

I stand in the kitchen momentarily before I decide what I want. I grab the bottle of Malbec I opened last night and pour myself a healthy glass of wine, letting my eyes close as the familiar flavor hit my taste buds. I set the wine on the granite countertop before I lean my head on my forearms and focus on my breathing. *Maybe now is the time to try some of those meditation exercises Dr. Vorges recommended.*

"You alright?" His voice rings through the air and my head snaps up to meet Bennett's gaze. Concerned eyes rove over me and I feel exposed and vulnerable under his stare. He's still in the same white t-shirt but without the jacket, putting his tattoo sleeved left arm on display. The intricate design stops just before his wrist so they wouldn't show when he was dressed for work. I stare at his tattoos just as I always did when he bared them. They're sexy and such a contrast to the straight laced businessman he is during the day. "Can I have some of that?" He reaches for the bottle next to me when I pull it out of reach.

"Not with your medicine."

"Come on, Livi," he pleads.

"No," I tell him as I shake my head. "Don't you want to get better?"

"Not really, no." I narrow my eyes at him wanting clarification when he sighs. "I assume once I'm better, I'm out of here. And depending on when that is, it'll be going against my plan."

I take another large sip of my wine. "What plan is that?"

"Winning you back."

He takes another step towards me.

I take one back. And then another.

I feel the stainless steel refrigerator behind me and try to step to the side away from him when he puts an arm out, effectively blocking me from getting away. "Olivia."

"What?" I ask weakly. He leans down and I immediately hold my breath to not inhale his sexy masculine scent, but I manage to catch a whiff of mint and a hint of his cologne. I shut my eyes, kicking myself for letting my guard down like this. "Please don't do this," I whisper.

His nose grazes mine before he trails it down my face. "You smell just how I remember you," he whispers. "So fucking sweet and sexy."

I let out a breath and press my teeth into my bottom lip, hard. *Snap out of this shit, Olivia.* His hand traces the side of my face, tucking a lock behind my ear and I briefly wonder if he's going to kiss me. My mind races as it battles with my heart over what I want in this moment. "Why the change?" he asks.

My eyes flutter open and I stare up at him, my heart still pounding harder in my chest with each passing moment. "Wh-what?"

"Your hair." He takes a step back but is still very much in my personal space. "It's more curly." He lets his hand fall from my hair after gently fingering the curls.

"Oh…" I look away from his eyes. "When we split up, I wanted something different." I reach up and pull on the ends of my hair.

He closes his eyes and lets his head drop slightly. "Well, regardless of the reason, I like it. A lot."

"You liked my straight hair, if I remember." I cock an eyebrow at him and he chuckles.

"Okay you got me, I like everything on you."

I swallow, not knowing what to say before my eyes move to his arm, zoning in on one particular tattoo just as it always does. Amongst the woven lines and colors painted on his arm are the numbers *10. 13. 12.*

October 13, 2012.

The day Bennett and I got married. I trace each number with my eyes one by one before I follow the trail down his arm to his hand, and I frown slightly when I see the ring on his finger.

My eyes widen in shock seeing it on his finger for the first time in six months. "You're wearing your ring?"

"Well, I am married." I look up at him and he gives me a half smile, half smirk, and I know I need to move before I do something I regret. Something that sets me back months. I move away from him to the other side of the island.

"You can't..."

"Can't what?"

"Do that!"

"Olivia," he begs, "please, can we just talk?"

"Talk about what?" I ask. "How you broke my heart? How *you* destroyed us?" My subconscious, whose voice sounds an awful fucking lot like Wren Hamilton perks up. *You sure it was just his fault?*

"I know but..."

"No buts, Bennett. You cheated. You fucked another woman. I would never cheat on you. No matter what was going on between us."

He's leaning on the island now, assumedly to keep himself steady when his eyes flit up to mine and I can see the question there. "What was going on between us?"

I take another sip of my wine and shake my head as I start to move out of the kitchen. "I'm going to bed."

"No. Olivia. What happened?" His eyes search mine for answers.

"What happened is *you* ran the second things got hard."

"When was anything ever hard between us? We could always talk about everything. *Anything.*"

Until I couldn't.

The wine on top of not eating much today has me feeling warm and fuzzy and all I want is to curl up in bed and sleep until tomorrow despite it only being seven o'clock. "Life happens." I shrug and his eyes blaze with fire.

"Fuck that, Olivia. Don't tell me that shit, what happened between you and me?"

"I—" I start when he's around the island in an instant and standing in front of me.

"Livi, if I'm forced to accept *this*...I need to know why." His eyes are pleading and desperate. "Please."

"I..." I look away from him as tears prickle in my eyes when I feel his hand on my face again, stroking the space beneath my eyes.

"I'm sorry, for whatever it is that made it so you can't talk to me." My lip trembles as his words hit so close to home and resound in my heart. I couldn't talk to him. I couldn't talk about how I felt defective for not being able to protect our babies. I couldn't talk about how much it gutted me when I saw the disappointment on his face every month I wasn't pregnant or when I finally *did* get pregnant but then lost the baby.

"Bennett..." I whisper, shaking my head. *I can't do this. Not now.*

"Whatever it is, you can tell me." His hand is still on my face, and I relish in his touch. His gaze is penetrating, but I can't find the strength to look away. I'm about to suggest we at least move to the couch to talk about this when reality brings me to a screeching halt.

My head snaps to my door and the repetitive knocking. It

takes a second for me to realize someone's at my door when Bennett breaks the silence. "Are you expecting someone?"

"N—no?" I shake my head and move towards the door when I feel a hand around my wrist pulling me slightly. I look up at him and he stares down at me.

"You aren't expecting anyone and it's late. I'll get it," he says and it takes me back to a time when we lived here together. His protectiveness used to be such a turn-on.

Fuck, it's still a turn-on.

But times are different. I shake my head and put my hands on my hips. I meet his gaze with an annoyed one of my own. "You don't live here, Bennett."

"I don't care," he growls, and it's only then that I hear his voice through the door.

"Liv…" The knocks continue and I hear David's voice.

"Fuck!" I whisper yell and press a hand to my forehead as I squeeze my eyes together, begging, praying to wake up from this nightmare. "Can you…go somewhere that's not here?" I ask Bennett while I point to the master bedroom.

"What? Oh, is that your boyfriend?" He nods towards the door and I stamp my foot at him.

"Bennett!"

"No, I'm kinda curious to meet the douche fucking my wife." He makes his way over to the couch and puts his feet up on my coffee table, that puts him in perfect view of the door and I fight the urge to scream. *I cannot handle this.*

I move towards the door and let out a breath. I clear the last bit of tears from both my eyes and the ones clogged in my throat and open the door with a smile. "David." I stand in the doorway, not wanting to let him in, and try to move us into the hallway.

His smile fades and his blue eyes are full of sadness when he realizes I'm not letting him in. "What—" he starts when I hear Bennett's voice ringing through the air.

"Livi!"

David's eyes snap to mine. "Are you serious right now?" He pushes the door behind me to see inside and steps around me and into my apartment.

"David…" I start.

Bennett is sitting on the couch with his arms crossed and a smug grin plastered on his face.

"You must be the guy sleeping with my wife."

"Bennett," I growl.

"Fuck off, Clarke." David takes another step and I put a hand on his bicep, holding him back.

This is probably the time to mention that Bennett has no recollection of ever meeting him before things really get out of hand. "David, can we talk somewhere else?"

"What is he doing here, Olivia?"

"I live here," Bennett snaps.

"Bennett," I implore him with my eyes to be quiet and he furrows his brows before giving me a nod, letting me know he's done talking.

"You haven't answered my question." David stands in front of me, blocking me from looking at Bennett or him looking at me.

"David, there's just…a lot going on right now."

"What kind of bullshit answer is that?" His tone is harsh and biting and I can't remember him ever speaking to me that way.

"Watch your fucking mouth and your tone for that matter," Bennett snaps.

David's eyes look murderous when he looks away from me. "Are you out of your mind? Who do you think you are? Why the fuck are you even here? Olivia threw you out, you fucking prick." He points at my door before taking a step towards him. "And you've got a lot of nerve advising *anyone* on how to treat Olivia."

"David…" I wrap my hand around his arm and try to pull him away from the living room towards my room, but I don't miss the look Bennett is giving him. I ignore it, telling myself I'll deal with him later before I push David into my bedroom.

"Are you back with that asshole?" he asks me.

I shake my head, denying it vehemently. "No! No, definitely not."

"Then what is he doing here, Olivia?"

"It's just…while he gets better—" I start, fully prepared to explain everything when he snaps at me, his blue eyes full of fury.

"He can't recover from the accident somewhere else? Like his apartment? Can't his *girlfriend* take care of him? Why is this shit falling on you?" I think he realizes he's gone too far when he sees the look on my face. "Liv…"

My heart thumps and squeezes painfully in my chest. My bottom lip trembles, and I press my teeth into it. "I can't believe you threw that in my face."

"Olivia, I'm sorry—" His hand rests on my face and I can't ignore how different it feels than when Bennett touched me.

"You should be," I grit out. "I get you're annoyed, but you can't come here and behave like that."

"But *he* can?"

"No! And this isn't a competition between you two. Bennett and I aren't together!" I yell.

"Are we?" he asks as he runs a hand through his hair.

I swallow hard. David and I haven't defined the lines of our relationship, and while he never seemed to pressure me on that, I'm beginning to think my grace period is about to come to an abrupt end.

"David, I'm still married."

"That's not what I asked. He's got a girlfriend, remember? He's moving on. Are you?" If this were anyone else and a different circumstance, I'd say this was coming from a place of tough love or support, but his stance, his tone, the look in his eyes makes me believe this is coming from a place of jealousy and contempt.

"That's not fair."

"What's not fair is your ex-husband being here after everything he's done. Are you that weak that you're just going to let him back in?" *Weak?* I stare at him, my eyes wide as his words sink into my soul. *How could he say that?*

"Weak?" I take a step back. "Is that what you think of me?"

Regret flashes across his face, but it's too late. The very minor progress I'd made post separation seems to evaporate before my eyes. *You're weak, Olivia.* "If you let him use you like this, then yes."

"Well, if that's what you think of me, then I think you should go." *I don't need this.*

"You know if he hurts you again, you'll have no one to blame but yourself." I'm about to tell him that what happens to me will no longer be his problem when Bennett comes through the door.

"Get the fuck out!" he growls and I gasp at the Bennett that I knew very well. The one that would never stand for anyone speaking to me in any way less than respectful. *This is not going to end well.*

"Excuse me?" David snaps.

"Is this how he talks to you?" He looks at me, the anger leaving his eyes when he looks at me. "I've never spoken to you like that... have I?" His brows lower slightly, and I want to tell him that he hasn't because I know he's fearing the worst.

"No, you just fuck other women, while you're married to her," David interjects.

"Okay enough!" I snap. "David, you need to leave."

"Me?"

"Yes, you. You've been nothing but hurtful towards me since you walked in, and I haven't done anything to deserve it."

His eyes soften and I know he's regretting taking his feelings about Bennett out on me. "Because *I'm* your man, Olivia, not him." He points at Bennett.

"Funny, every court in America would say otherwise," Bennett interjects.

I put my hand up towards Bennett, telling him to be quiet, *again*. "You're not anything, anymore." I wrap my arms around myself, my eyes welling up with tears as I "break up" with the man that probably got me through more than he could imagine. "You didn't even let me explain before you exploded."

"Olivia…" he starts. "Is there a reason you're still here?" he snarls at Bennett.

"Baby?" Bennett looks at me and I glare at him for using a term of endearment.

"Baby?" David takes a step towards him and shoots me an angry look. "Are you serious, right now?" He looks at me and shakes his head, a dark chuckle leaving his lips. "You two deserve each other." He takes a step past Bennett before shooting me a glare. "Good luck, Olivia, you're going to need it," he says before he's out the door.

Bennett follows behind him as he storms out. I scurry behind them, hoping that things don't get even more out of hand. "Olivia deserves better than me, I'm fully fucking aware. But she sure as fuck deserves better than you." Bennett barks out just as he slams the door behind David before turning towards me. *"That's* who you've been dating?"

I scowl at him, his chivalrous behavior completely forgotten and my irritation taking over. "Bennett, what the fuck? Was that necessary?"

"Was what necessary? Sticking up for you while he was a complete dick to you?" He puts his hands on his hips.

"I don't need *anyone* to stick up for me! Least of all *you!*"

"I'm never going to let anyone talk to you like that. I don't give a fuck what's going on between us."

"No one asked you to come to my fucking rescue, Bennett." I shake my head and look up at him as I remember all of the good things about David Jacobs. The nights he held me while I cried myself to sleep. The dates where we sat in almost silence while he held my hand. The whispered promises that *one day* I would be fine. "He was there for me."

He moves towards me, wrapping an arm around my waist and pulling me towards him. He tucks a hair behind my ears and stares down at me. "Well, *I'm* here now. You don't need him." I can see the sincerity in his eyes and hear it in his voice, but it's not enough.

Not now.

I remove his hand from around my waist and move back to the island to pick up my glass of wine, suddenly feeling like I need another one. "You're here temporarily."

"No," He argues.

I sigh in exasperation and frustration. "Bennett, why are you so hell-bent on making my life so difficult? Haven't you done enough to me?"

He looks like I've slapped him and shakes his head. "I'm sorry, Livi. I'm sorry I pushed you into the arms of that asshole. All of it."

"Is this all about David?"

"No, but excuse me if it pissed me off to see the woman I love with another man."

I narrow my eyes into slits. "Welcome to my life, Bennett." I grab my glass and the rest of the bottle before moving into my room and slamming the door.

CHAPTER Ten

Olivia

THE SMELL OF BACON WAFTING UNDER MY DOOR PULLS ME OUT of the last few minutes of sleep. I put a hand over my head, trying to will away the slight pounding from all the wine I'd consumed last night all the while cursing myself for drinking so much. I press my face into the pillows before turning to my back and staring up at the ceiling before contemplating going back to sleep. I look at my phone and see I have two missed calls from David and a voicemail and a few text messages from both David and Alyssa. I opt to ignore them both before climbing out of bed, my head pounding with every step I take. I open the door, wishing that a bathroom was connected to this room so I wasn't forced out into the open where I could run into Bennett.

When I don't see him, I dart into the bathroom, close the door behind me and let out a sigh of relief. Staring at my reflection, I'm grateful I had the foresight to bring my things in here last night before I went to bed. I brush my teeth and scrub my face, hoping I can scrub the memory of last night from my skin. I run my fingers through my hair, fluffing it since it had flattened some in the night and shake some of the body back into it before opening the door. Making my way into the kitchen, I see Bennett sitting at the island watching television.

"Hey you." He gives me a timid smile and points at the spread he's laid out. "I made breakfast."

I ignore the thought that a man hasn't made me breakfast in a very long time. *Since the last time he made me breakfast to be exact.* I decide to focus on where all of this food came from. "Where...I didn't have all of this in the fridge."

He sets down his fork and leans forward, cocking a brow and pursing his full lips. "Yeah, about that. What have you been eating? Besides trash?" Worry paints his face and I look away, not wanting to be scolded but also to hide the shame that I know covers mine.

"It's really too early."

"Fair. I used your computer to order groceries. You hardly have anything, Livi."

"I don't eat much at home. It's kind of depressing to eat alone." I shrug sadly and he nods in understanding.

"I get that, but you should still be eating more than take-out."

I swallow when I look at all the food he's prepared. "You made pancakes." My stomach growls instantly, remembering just how good Bennett's pancakes were. They were fluffy and sweet and melted in your mouth underneath the sweet syrup. *Fuck, I've missed his cooking.*

"They're your favorite," he says as if it's the most obvious reason in the world. He gets up and moves towards the stove. "I didn't make your eggs because I didn't want them to get cold. Still over medium?"

"Ummm yes, but you don't have to—"

"Yes, I do." He cuts me off as I pour myself a glass of orange juice. "I made coffee. One of the few things you did have." He chuckles. I pass on the coffee for now and sit at the bar sipping my orange juice slowly.

I watch him prepare my eggs in silence, the only sound in the room coming from ESPN on the television and his spatula against the pan. "You're quiet," he says as he slides the eggs onto a plate for me. I pull a grape from the bowl in front of me and pop it into my mouth.

"I'm hungover," I correct him.

"Ah. I was wondering if you were going to finish that bottle."

"Mama didn't raise a quitter." I chuckle and he smiles.

"How is your mom?"

"Not your biggest fan."

His face falls slightly. "Understandable. Did you tell them what's going on?"

"Yep."

"They know I'm here?"

"Nope," I answer quickly.

"Noted," he says before he takes his place next to me and reaches for the remote, muting the television.

"Oh, you don't have to stop on my account."

"I was just killing time until you woke up." He picks up a piece of bacon and bites into it. I feel his gaze on the side of my face, but I don't meet his eyes. I just focus on cutting the pancakes in front of me.

"Yes?" I finally ask, after what feels like an eternity of his eyes studying me.

"About what you said last night..." he starts. "Was I... flaunting her in your face?"

"No." I shake my head. "I rarely saw her, actually. You were pretty...good at staying on your side of town." I can't read his reaction. He's slightly tense but also seems relieved at my answer.

I take a bite of my pancakes and I can't avoid the moan that escapes my lips. "Fuck, I forgot how well you can cook."

He beams under my praise, despite our prior conversation, and I'm grateful for the change in topic. "All those classes we took."

"You were always better at it than me." I chuckle, remembering how I was usually goofing off in the class and imbibing far too much wine to be absorbing any information.

"You were a good assistant." He smiles and I roll my eyes.

"Thank you for cooking." I nibble on a piece of bacon and eye him nervously. He cocks his head to the side and shakes his head.

"You thank me like I've ever *not* wanted to take care of you." He puts his hand up when I go to respond. "Yes, maybe not recently, but I have no recollection of that. All I know is…*this*." He points at all the food and feelings of warmth flood my bones. I don't respond, not knowing what to say when he speaks again. "So, what else have you been up to?" I look at him before looking around the room, wondering what I should say when he clarifies. "Maybe not in the last six months to avoid giving me a heart attack," he jokes.

"I haven't been…I mean…David was the only…" I snap my lips shut. "I don't owe you an explanation."

His eyes darken and I can tell he's gritting his teeth by how sharp his jaw looks. "No, but I'd prefer not to hear about whatever the fuck you've been doing with that asshole." He leans forward and he smells like syrup and coffee and *Bennett* and it sparks a nostalgia I can't ignore.

Me and Bennett fucking on this bar getting syrup…*everywhere.*

I hop on the island and watch as my sinfully delicious husband makes us breakfast. My eyes rove over his naked chest and my eyes slither down his body to where his sweats hang low on his hips. We'd already had sex this morning after spending the majority of the night making love and even still it wasn't enough. I want more.

I would always want more with Bennett.

I bite my lip, my eyes still planted on where I know his cock is hidden.

"You're biting your lip and staring at my dick. I'm taking that as an invitation." I look up as Bennett makes his way towards me and stands between my legs. "Do you want my fat cock in your pretty little mouth?" He slides his hand up my body to cup my jaw, peppering kisses down the side of my face and I whimper when he squeezes harder. I love this island because his height allows him to grind his cock against my sex when I sit on top. It also allows us to have some of our hottest sex.

He presses his cock into my pussy, which is only covered by a tiny scrap of lace. He pulls away, and I instantly miss his lips on me. "I want to try something first."

My eyes flutter open when he speaks and I nod my head, knowing that whatever he suggests, I'll be up for.

"Strip." His voice is dark and sinful and has a direct line to my clit which pulses in response to his command.

I slide my panties down my legs, tossing them to the floor, followed by his t-shirt leaving me completely nude.

"Lie back," he says and I oblige, propping myself up on my elbows so I can see what he's planning to do. It wouldn't be the first time he ate my pussy on our island, but the look in his eyes lets me know this might be slightly different.

My eyes widen when he grabs the small bowl that he'd heated the syrup in and pours it on my skin from my chest down to the top of my mound. The feeling is warm and sexy and sticky as hell but I can't escape the immediate flood between my legs at the idea of what he's about to do.

Bennett has an obsession with tasting me. He'd told me once that my skin always tasted like vanilla and he wanted to spend the rest of his life with my sweetness on his tongue.

I melted.

His tongue sweeps out as he hovers over me, and rubs his tongue across my lips once. I open my mouth, and my tongue shoots out towards his preparing to welcome him but he shakes his head before pulling back. "Naughty girl."

His lips find my chin and down my neck before I feel the wet muscle at the space between my breasts. I feel his beard rubbing against them as he sucks and licks the syrup from my skin and my body hums with pleasure. I try to press my legs together to relieve some of the ache when his hands find my thighs to hold them down. "I want to smell how wet I make you. I want them spread," he growls.

"Fuck, Clarke." I moan as he continues his trail down my body collecting the syrup but leaving a trail of his saliva in his wake. My body is on fire, desperate for any kind of relief from the pleasurable pain that burns from the outside in. "Please."

He gets to the top of my mound, pressing a kiss there and spreading my lips open in preparation to devour me. "Livi." I watch him stick his fingers in his mouth to wet them. He slides his tongue between his index and middle finger lasciviously as a sign of what I'm in for before shooting me a wink that takes all the air from my lungs.

My husband is walking sex.

"Clarke," I whimper, dying for the feeling of his tongue or fingers or anything rubbing against my clit when I hear him call for me again.

"Livi."

"Mmmm." I let out a moan just as his two fingers make contact with my swollen bundle of nerves. The syrup and his spit and my natural wetness make for a slippery concoction, making my sex slicker than usual.

"Olivia, look at me, baby." I can't even force my eyes open in this moment, I'm too turned on and far gone, my body floating out of my body and hovering above us, watching this sinful display.

"Olivia..." I open my mouth in response, but nothing comes out.

"Olivia?" My eyes pop open but when I look down, he's not there.

"Olivia?"

I blink several times, trying to clear my head of the sexy memory before turning to Bennett. "Sorry…what did you say?" I bite my lip, feeling embarrassed that he caught me having a fantasy about him. *Fuck.*

"Are you okay?" His hand finds my cheek as he turns my face to look at him. "You keep spacing out on me."

"No…I…I was just thinking about something." I clear my throat. "Something I need to do for work." I pull away from his grasp and push my plate away instantly, suddenly not wanting to even think about pancakes or syrup or syrup dripping out of my pussy that Bennett caught with his fucking tongue.

I need to get away from this man.

I get up, deciding now is the best time to get that coffee. I keep my back turned as I make it, my shoulders feeling like they're up around my ears with how tense I am when I feel him at my back. His hands dart out to either side of me, boxing me in and I wish he'd just give me some space because I feel like I can't breathe.

"Were you thinking about the time I licked the whipped cream from the pancakes off of you? Because I was," he growls in my ear before biting it gently. "That time I sprayed it down your body and licked up every bit. Especially between your legs." He presses against me harder. "Although, whipped cream doesn't have anything on the taste of your cunt." Bennett Clarke is a notorious dirty talker. Phone sex with him is undeniably one of the most erotic experiences of my life, and the texts he used to send me when we were apart were some of the dirtiest things I'd ever read.

I spin in his arms. "It wasn't whipped cream it was syrup and…" I bite my bottom lip at the cheeky look he's giving me, having been caught fantasizing about exactly what he thought.

He leans forward and uses his thumb to pull my bottom lip from between my teeth causing a bolt of lightning to shoot through my body. "There was an instance with whipped cream too." He winks before making his way back to the island. My shoulders sag and my heart, which was racing, begins to slow now that he's no longer in my space, but nothing is lessening the dull roar between my legs. I clench, doing my best to stop the pulsing but it seems to only exacerbate the ache.

Holy fuck, I need to come.

I start towards my room when I realize that I can't exactly dart to my room, masturbate, and emerge from my room like nothing happened. I need a reason to be alone in my room and I would have to be quiet. *Which means no vibrator because even the quiet ones make some noise.*

"I'm going to shower," I blurt out.

"Okay…?" He cocks his head to the side, probably confused at the immediate need to shower when I hadn't even taken a sip of the coffee I'd just made.

"I can clean this up when I'm out…" I don't even wait for his response before I'm bolting for the master bedroom, completely forgetting that he'd been staying there.

The second I close the door behind me I almost combust. His scent is everywhere. The bed he'd slept on is unmade, the sheets crumpled and possibly slightly warm with evidence that he'd been there. My eyes dart to the walk-in closet that still houses some of my clothes. I walk to it, peering inside to see that he'd hung his clothes in the space that he'd originally inhabited. Tears well in my eyes at my body being pulled under by this sensory overload.

Bennett is back.

In my house.

In my head.

And evidently, if the throb between my legs is any indication, *in my fantasies.*

I emerge from my bedroom freshly showered, feeling less hungover and more sated than I was forty minutes ago to find Bennett on the couch, the kitchen completely spotless. "I told you I would clean…" I trail off as I take note of his legs propped up on the ottoman. "You should be resting."

He shrugs. "It's fine. How was your shower?"

My mind reels, thinking maybe I wasn't as quiet as I thought and perhaps the shower didn't drown out the sound of me coming. *No way, I wasn't that loud.*

"Fine." I brush a hand down my body as if to brush off the question and look up at him when I see him staring at me.

"You going to come sit with me or…?" He asks as he points at my spacious couch. I swallow and move towards him like a deer fearful of falling into a trap. A very gorgeous trap that has the power to destroy me.

I sit on the opposite side of the L shaped couch and he gives me a sad smile. "Livi…"

"Bennett."

"Tell me what happened between us." He turns off the television. "Tell me why you can't even look at me."

I curse myself for putting on mascara knowing that this conversation would push me to tears when I feel the familiar prickle in my eyes. "Bennett, please."

His eyes furrow. "Are we ever going to talk about it? Or are you just going to let me hate myself forever?" I pry my eyes away from him and his pleading gaze as he continues. "Do you know I didn't sleep last night?"

My eyes shoot away from the spot on the floor I was fixating on and stare into his sad green eyes. "What?"

"I couldn't sleep. I tossed and turned for hours before I gave up and just stared at the ceiling, my brain coming up with all of these scenarios as to why we aren't together. I tried Liv, I tried everything to try and remember. I tried to break into my phone *again*. I think I'm locked out for twenty-four hours." He shakes his head. "What kind of shit is that by the way? Apple is fucked up."

"It's for security since we store so much of our lives in our phone." I shrug.

He closes his eyes and shakes his head. "Look, I know you don't care about me now or the fact that I'm going out of my fucking mind trying to figure out what happened between us... but maybe you care about the old Bennett. I would think you'd care if *he* was hurting."

My eyes well up with tears at the sentiment. He's right. I do care about the Bennett he was before our lives changed forever. The man in front of me is the Bennett I fell in love with. He's the man that had me coming all over my hand not twenty minutes ago. I hate that *he* is hurting.

I guess it's time *this* Bennett knew the truth.

CHAPTER Eleven

Olivia

I SHIFT NERVOUSLY IN MY SEAT AND BEFORE I CAN OPEN MY MOUTH, Bennett has moved closer to sit next to me. He opens his hand and rests it on my thigh, palm up, and I stare down at his offering.

"You look like you're going to burst into tears at any second." I grit my teeth, to try and stop my body from doing just that when his hand moves and laces with mine. I try to pull my hand from his grasp but he just holds it tighter. "Stop."

"We...struggled with..." I clear my throat as I prepare myself for hours of questioning and talking and eventually disclosing what I've learned about myself that I've never told Bennett. "Getting pregnant."

He squeezes my hand and nods solemnly. "I figured," he says sadly. "When you said we didn't have kids."

I lick my lips and let out a slow shaky breath. "I've had two miscarriages...they were...difficult."

Pause.

Take a breath.

"Livi..." My name falls from his lips like a plea as if he's begging for this to not be true. As if somehow, he could change the past. "Baby, I'm sorry." I look up, preparing to correct him for using the term of endearment he just can't seem to shake, when I meet his watery green eyes. I'm not a stranger to Bennett's tears, especially over this, but seeing him this way still guts me.

We'd mourned the loss of both children with more tears than I thought were possible. The second more so than the first.

"How...how far along were we?" he asks.

"I feel like I should back up a second and start from the beginning. It took us a while to get pregnant in the first place. I'm having some trouble placing exactly where your memory loss starts, but it was about two years ago that we started trying." I narrow my eyes, trying to remember exactly when we decided we were going to try for a baby. "As you know, we were always a very sexual couple, so I don't think we necessarily started having more sex, but I went off the pill and we just started trying. In the beginning, we didn't think anything of it. It's common for it to take a while when you've been on birth control for so long. But then the first few months turned to six and nine and every time I took a test, I saw so much disappointment on your face. I felt like such a failure..."

"You're not. I never would have thought that," he interrupts and I nod.

"I know that now, and I probably knew it then, but it's not something I could control. My mind was so messed up during that time. I knew you wanted a baby, and all I felt was self-loathing that I couldn't give it to you. I was scared you'd eventually leave me if I couldn't give you what you wanted." My heart feels like it's about to beat out of my chest as I speak the words I've never spoken to Bennett. I don't know why I'm letting myself be so vulnerable with him. Maybe because this is Bennett pre-miscarriages. The Bennett that believes I walk on water. The one that believes I can do anything. He hasn't seen me when I felt my weakest. When I wondered how it was possible that he still loved me.

"I would never have left you. I can't live without you. I want—*wanted* a baby, yes, but I wanted *your* baby. We would have figured something else out. Did we even see anyone? A specialist?" His brows are furrowed and his lips are fixed into a hard line.

"No, because eventually…" I let out a breath. "Eventually, I got pregnant." A smile ghosts over my lips despite this morbid trip down memory lane, because the memory of peeing on that stick and seeing those two pink lines for the first time in my life was something I'll never forget. "We were so happy. It was like this dark cloud had been lifted and the sun was finally shining. A moment of light after some of my darkest months." My smile fades and the tears rush to my eyes and before I can stop them, they're sliding slowly down my cheeks. My left hand is still encased in Bennett's, and I don't see him letting me go, so I wipe my face with my right hand despite the fact that more tears are quickly forming. "I miscarried the first time at seven weeks." I'm silent for a moment as I let the words settle between us. He doesn't say anything in response so I continue. "They say it happens and there's nothing to be necessarily concerned about and it's common…but there is nothing natural about being pregnant and then just…not. It feels…fuck…inhumane."

He moves closer to me and I fight the urge to move away. There's still space between us, and I'm half expecting him to do what he always does and pull me into his lap, but he doesn't.

I don't know if the thought makes me grateful or disappointed.

"The second time…was worse." He stiffens next to me and his thumb drags slowly over my knuckles. The feeling makes me warm all over, and now I really want to be in his lap. I want comfort and I'm seeking it in what I know to be a warm embrace. I take a breath preparing myself for this part of the story. It's like jumping into an unknown body of water. You're not really sure how deep you'll go, so you dive in. Praying you don't go too deep, and that you reach the surface before you drown.

I don't want to drown in these memories.

"The second time I got pregnant, we made it past the seven week mark. I swear we held our breaths for the entire first two months. We stayed in my OB's office, just to make sure everything was fine. Once we hit eight weeks, and I heard our baby's heartbeat, I allowed myself to get excited. *We* were excited. We started thinking of names and preparing to turn the guest room into a nursery. We told our families. We named Lys and Wren as Godparents." I tuck a curl behind my ear and sigh, my shoulders sinking further down as the pressure of this conversation takes its toll on me. "At eleven weeks, we went back in for a check-up and there was just…no heartbeat." My lip trembles and suddenly I feel a prickle against my hand and I look over to see Bennett dragging his lips across my skin.

"I'm sorry." I'm not sure if he's apologizing for the innocent kiss or what happened but my heart melts at the look he's giving me. He places our hands that are still clasped back on the couch between us and I give him a sad smile.

"I needed to have a surgical procedure to remove…" I trail off. I don't get into the gritty details because, quite frankly, I hate thinking about it or talking about it. The miscarriage is painful enough without thinking of *that* part.

"What did the doctor say after the second time?"

"She said it happens and that two wasn't something to be too concerned about, *yet*." I shrug. "It happens. Three miscarriages is when they'll dive into testing. I could have done it after the second but…" I trail off and my lips form a straight line.

"But…?" he asks, not realizing where I'm going with it.

"I just wanted to wait a few months to heal…but then," I clear my throat, "you slept with someone. And I couldn't deal with that *and* the possibility that something was wrong and that I'd be unable to bear children. I just…I couldn't do it all."

"I slept with someone because of the miscarriage? No…bullshit. It doesn't add up." He pulls his hand out of mine and leans forward, putting his head in his hands. "I would never leave you…to deal with that alone." He turns to look at me, his eyes brimming with unshed tears before he blinks them away. "I loved you so much and…I broke us. I don't know how I've been able to live with myself."

His pain is so evident that I feel it in my chest almost as much as my own. "I pushed you away," I say quietly.

"That's not a fucking excuse," he snaps.

"I know. But my therapist and everyone else who has a goddamn opinion about this, namely Wren Hamilton and my mother," I say with an eye roll, "seem to think that I should have opened up to you about what I was feeling, and allowed you to tell me your feelings. I shut down and couldn't cope with what was happening. I stopped talking. I wasn't eating. I was pretty depressed. You did try, Bennett. I just couldn't. I gave up…and it made you give up."

"I would never give up on you, Olivia. Whatever that shit was with that woman…I don't know if I wanted to feel close to someone or I was just as depressed as you were with no way to express it, but I'd never give us up. I don't give a shit if you did give up first."

"Yeah well…when your wife has two miscarriages and feels inadequate and unsexy and just like the shittiest woman on the planet because she can't give her husband a baby and then said husband comes home after being out all night and confesses to sleeping with someone…" I shrug, "that was you giving up too."

"Livi…" he whispers. "I'm so sorry."

"Me too," I murmur. "I should have been able to talk to you months ago."

"How long ago was all of this?"

"I filed for divorce six months ago. This all happened a little before that." Once I learned he'd been unfaithful, I filed shortly after that. I was hurt and reeling from the miscarriages and probably a little hasty in my decision. He begged to go to counseling or to take a vacation or hell, even move. He'd done everything short of cutting off his manhood and giving it to me and I wasn't having any of it.

I didn't think anyone could fault me for wanting to leave him, but did I regret it?

The jury is still out on that.

"When are we officially divorced?"

"A little over sixty days."

"Is there any chance you'd be willing to try again?" he asks and I frown at his question.

"Please don't ask me that."

"Why?"

"Because it hurts." It hurt every time he'd asked over the past six months, and there has been more than one occasion. This time is no different. I sigh, my body and mind and heart all exhausted from this conversation when I feel his hand slide back into mine.

"I really want to kiss you." His words wash over me and seep into my soul.

"Bennett…"

"I know, I know. It's just you're the love of my life and you're hurting and I can't fix it. Hell, I caused quite a bit of it and I'm sorry and I just want you to know that, alright? I'm really fucking sorry for any pain I've ever caused you, Olivia. You have to know that."

I bite my lip, wanting to give in to the moment of weakness that's begging for him to kiss me. I want to feel his lips on mine, the heat of his body pressed against me. I wanted him so bad I can't breathe. I don't want to be angry anymore. I want the pain to dissipate. I want to be free to fall in love all over again with the man in front of me. One that only knew he loved me and no one else existed. I swallow and pull back slightly, realizing how close I am to Bennett's face.

"I...I just need a second," I whisper before I stand slowly. He nods, finally letting my hand go. It slowly slides out of his as if it's happening in slow motion, and when it hits my side he stares at it, like it's a part of him that he's been forced to part with. Our eyes lock for a moment and I can see the mask he's put up.

He needs you, Olivia, and you're running from him just like you always do.

I squeeze my eyes shut, trying my best to quiet my thoughts and turn away from him making my way towards my bedroom.

This isn't like last time.

I hole up in my room for the next hour alone with my thoughts, my hormones and my heart telling me that I need to check on Bennett. That I'm being selfish *again* by telling him that I need space when it's obvious that he's hurting too.

You're not the only one broken, Olivia.

I open my door prepared to go talk to him when I see him sitting on the floor in front of my room. His elbows are resting on his knees and his silky chestnut hair looks as if he's been running his hand over the strands a dozen times over the past hour.

I clear my throat and his eyes meet mine. "Hey." I lean against the door jamb and stare down at him as his green eyes stare up at me.

"I just wanted to make sure you were okay." He winces

slightly as he stands, towering over me as he moves into my space. I bite my bottom lip when he's close enough for me to breathe in his scent and he lifts my chin to look at him. "I hate that I wasn't there for you…when you needed me." His voice warms me all over and I resist the urge to push myself into his arms and stay there.

"You were, Bennett. What happened between us wasn't because you weren't there. You were." I shrug.

"I've been sitting here thinking…" He leans his arm against the wall and presses his forehead against it. He turns his head slightly to look at me. "I thought it was worse knowing that I hurt you so badly but *not* remembering what possessed me to do it…" He shakes his head and takes a step back. "But I was wrong. This hurts worse. Hearing you spell it out. Hearing what you went through, what *we* went through, and then how I reacted to it."

"Bennett…" I trail off. "Don't be so hard on yourself." *Wait what?* "I mean…I'm much more together than I was six months ago. I could barely talk about it. I could barely talk to *you*."

"And that's an excuse?" he snaps.

"Okay, I'm confused." I put my head in my hands. "I feel like you're me and I'm you." I chuckle to myself, as I realize the absurdity of the points we're arguing.

"It's not funny." When I look up his face is serious and solemn. A scowl finds his full lips as he looks down the hall towards the master bedroom. "I just wanted to make sure you were okay. I'm going to go lay down for a bit since I didn't get any sleep last night."

"Bennett…"

"It's bad enough that I cheated on you and to hear the circumstances around it…" He rubs his jaw and seeing his ring on his hand makes my heart skip a beat. I want to run my finger over the cool metal. "I thought I had a chance at getting you to forgive me. That maybe this situation would bring you back to me..." He shrugs. "But now, I can't see how that's possible." He gives me a smile that doesn't reach his eyes. "You were always the best thing in my life, Olivia Clarke." He rubs his thumb over my chin gently before he backs away towards the master bedroom, and then he's gone, leaving me with the confusing feeling that I want to tell him that just maybe it *is* possible.

CHAPTER
Twelve

Olivia

It's almost seven, which means Bennett has been in his room for most of the day, and while I know he didn't sleep last night, he does need to eat, especially to take the medication to help with his concussion. Maybe he could get away with not taking some of the pain meds, but I knew he needed them. I'm standing in front of his door, willing myself to go in, but not knowing if I want to invade his privacy. "Ummm, Bennett?" I whisper, and I don't hear anything. "Bennett?" I repeat slightly louder and still nothing. I press my hand to the silver French door handle and push slightly peeking my head into the room nervously. The room is dim as he's drawn the shades and it's already getting dark outside. It's fairly quiet, the only noise being the gentle hum from the ceiling fan. "Bennett?"

I pad slowly through the room towards what used to be my side of the bed and turn on the bedside table lamp. I don't miss the fact that he's sleeping on my side, and I wonder if there's more to it or if I'm just reading too much into it. He mumbles and turns his face into the pillow. "Bennett, you should eat something. You have to be hungry," I whisper.

His eyes open when he hears my voice reminding me that I could rarely resist Bennett when he first woke up. Sleepy and lethargically sexy, his dark hair is wild and his eyes are slightly glazed making them look more jade than emerald. His shirt has ridden up slightly giving me a peek at his abs and a glimpse of his happy trail making my sex clench at what I know is underneath. He's wearing basketball shorts instead of sweats, which really does even less to mask the semi hard-on he's sporting, and I find myself getting short of breath. I take a step back when on top of all of that he gives me a lazy smile. "Hey."

My heart races because of that simple word and I try everything to calm the rapid pounding in my chest. "I... umm..." *Why did I come in here? It wasn't just to ogle my estranged husband.* "Food!" I exclaim and I roll my eyes at my outburst. "I mean... are you hungry? You have to be hungry. You should eat something. You've slept most of the day away."

"Shit, sorry." He sits up and rubs his eyes before focusing on me. "I think not sleeping last night caught up with me."

"No reason to be sorry. You should be resting. But I told Wren I'd make sure you'd take your medication, and I'll never hear the end of it if you don't." I smile. It's half true; I do want to make sure he's doing everything he can to get better. But a part of me, a part that is growing steadily by the moment wants to spend more time with him. With *this* Bennett. I'm not sure how he feels about what we discussed earlier and his last comment has been weighing on my mind.

Is it possible for us to reconcile? Is all of this our second chance?

Possibly. My heart answers before my brain has a chance to shoot down the idea.

My heart thumps at the possibilities.

I bite my bottom lip as the ideas take form and bloom in my head.

Counseling. Like a lot of counseling.

"You're staring at me funny." He cocks his head to the

side and I blink away the thoughts as the reality of our situation comes into focus. We can't be anything while he's like this. Because at the end of the day, I still want answers. Answers that could only come from Bennett regaining his memories.

Would I ever be able to truly forgive and move on if Bennett never remembers what he did? How could he really be sorry if he has no recollection of it happening? Maybe he could live like that, but could I?

At this point, he hasn't lived through the darkest part of our marriage...but I had.

"We can order something? Or...I could cook?" I say weakly. I want out of this bedroom and away from our marital bed. My mind is in sensory overload and I can feel my walls flying down over being in this intimate setting with him. "I'll just wait for you in the living room," I murmur before I bolt for the door and down the hall.

"Get a grip, Liv," I whisper to myself as I make my way to the couch. My index finger finds my mouth and I begin to chew on the nail nervously as I wait for Bennett to come out. A part of me hopes that he's slightly more covered up, but clearly the universe is looking to punish me because he's in nothing more than his t-shirt and shorts when he makes his way into the living room.

"Why are you so nervous around me now?" He cocks his head to the side. "You weren't even like this when we first started dating." And it's true; even though Bennett Clarke was older and more experienced and felt like a real adult while I was a fresh college graduate, he never made me feel nervous or intimidated. My mind drifts back to our first date and how effortless things were between us.

"I'm glad we finally did this," Bennett says. He clasps his hand

with mine as we walk through Central Park. We'd gone to breakfast for our first date, something I hadn't anticipated from a man like Bennett, and now we're walking around the empty park, as most people had escaped the New York streets for the Hamptons this particular weekend. There are people here and there, picnicking or bicycling, or touring the infamous park, but for the most part, it's pretty empty.

We begin our walk across the Bow Bridge and as he leans to look over the pond, I stand next to him watching as the water ripples under the warm breeze. "You never did say why you were so insistent on breakfast." I cock my head to the side. "I don't get up before noon on a Saturday for many people, Mr. Clarke." I tease.

"Not a morning person, huh?"

"Not if I can avoid it." I chuckle.

"There's too many connotations with dinner. You have one too many cocktails, your inhibitions are lowered, someone asks someone to come back to someone's place…" He shakes his head. "Your options after dinner are either to end the date because it's late, go get more drunk, or go somewhere and fuck. I wanted more time before any of those decisions needed to be made."

"So, this is you…buying time before you try to fuck me?"

He shoots me a grin. "This is me giving us time to see if there will be more after I fuck you."

My cheeks heat up and I feel his hands on my cheeks. "That doesn't mean I expect anything from you or this."

I lick my lips, unsure of what to say before he nods and lets his hands fall from my face. I tuck a long strand of hair that I'd curled for this date behind my ear and shoot him a lascivious grin. "You know, people do have sex during the day too…" His smile is almost blinding before he leans down and presses his lips to mine. He pushes me against the rail of the bridge, boxing me in as he gives me what would come to be the best first kiss of my life, and in that moment I knew Bennett Clarke was about to change my life.

I'm snapped from my memory by the sound of a knock on my door.

"I'm not nervous, it's just a lot having you here again," I tell him as I make my way to answer it, somewhat shocked that Bennett hadn't tried to answer it for me. It's getting late, and I'm not sure who it could be. I half expect it to be David and I breathe a sigh of relief when I see it's just a teenage kid from the building.

"Hey, Knox." I smile when I see the young kid that often brings deliveries up from the lobby when they can't be buzzed upstairs.

"Mrs. Clarke…" He peeks past me and his blue eyes widen when he sees Bennett. "Mr. Clarke." He waves wildly before turning back to me. "Mr. K, said he was back," he whispers. "Well…is he?"

"Knox, would your mother be happy to know that you're engaging in idle gossip?" I raise an eyebrow at the fifteen-year-old and he gives me a sheepish grin.

"Sorry, Mrs. Clarke." He blushes and I feel heat at my back.

It's then I note the vase of flowers on the floor next to him and I point at the arrangement.

"Are those for me?"

He clears his throat and his eyes shift from me to Bennett. "Yes, ummm, ma'am. They were delivered a while ago. Mr. K wasn't sure if we should bring them up."

"Well, they're mine." I frown.

"Yes but…" He looks at Bennett who I know is behind me and then me again and I hold my hands out.

"Oh, they must be from your boyfriend." Bennett snorts. "Good seeing you, Knox." He turns back inside and I scowl at him behind his back before turning back to Knox.

"Good seeing you too, Mr. Clarke!" he calls after him.

"Thank you so much, and tell your mother I said hello."

"I will. Have a good night, Mrs. Clarke," he says with a wave before he makes his way towards the elevator.

I close the door and Bennett is standing, his arms crossed, looking angry and sexy and like he's about to lose his shit and my sex clenches in response to what I know to be Bennett's jealous and protective side. "He's sending you flowers?"

"Some men send women flowers when they fuck up," I snap as I walk by him.

"That's not the way to your heart though." He quips as he follows me to the kitchen. "Flowers are nice *after* the mind numbing orgasms."

"Excuse me?" I raise an eyebrow at him. I try to ignore the way my body reacts to his mention of orgasms and more importantly the idea of *him* giving *me* orgasms.

"When you're pissed at me, I make you come." *Fuck.*

"Okay first of all, untrue. And secondly, when have I ever *really* been pissed at you? I mean besides the obvious."

"I'm sure there have been times. I'd draw you a bath, give you a glass of wine, and fuck you until you couldn't remember why you were upset." He gives me a crooked smile. "And I'd write you a note."

He was right, that did usually work. *Fucker.*

Bennett bought me flowers all the time, for birthdays and anniversaries and congratulations and for no reason at all, but rarely did he use them to say he was sorry.

He was good with his words and his dick.

What did he need flowers for?

I had shoeboxes full of the notes Bennett had written me over the years, and while Alyssa wanted me to burn them, I couldn't bring myself to do it. He'd poured his heart and soul into some of those notes and some were just plain dirty and sexy and sometimes a girl wants to read those.

Especially when she's going through a divorce and lonely as hell.

"I'm so sorry, Liv. Please call me." Bennett reads aloud and crumples the note. "How unoriginal. Fucking pussy."

"Bennett!" I exclaim as I try and grab the small index card from him.

"What? He should be here apologizing to your face. Not that I think it should matter. He's not right for you, Olivia." He tosses the card in the trash, and in the back of my mind, I make a note to unpack the fact that I don't go in after it.

"Oh, and who is right for me? You?" I don't mean for the words to slip out and definitely not that harshly but I knew we'd be having this argument regardless of who it was.

"Well, yes." He points at me. "But if I'm no longer an option, it definitely shouldn't be that douchebag."

"Well, for your information, I wasn't going to take him back. Not that it's your business, and I'm glad he *didn't* try to come here. You wouldn't know how to act!"

Bennett's response is interrupted by keys in my door and Alyssa coming through it, sporting leggings and an NYU Med School hoodie. "Hiiiiii!" Her face is free from makeup and her black hair is slightly damp, meaning she probably showered at the hospital and came straight here.

"Don't you knock?" Bennett immediately asks, crossing his arms.

"I'm sorry. Don't you *not* live here?" Alyssa quips, just as Wren comes in behind her dressed in jeans and a leather jacket.

"You've been here thirty seconds. Already?" Wren looks at his wife, and tugs on her ponytail. "What did we just talk about in the Uber on the way over?" She makes a face behind his back and gives him her middle finger when he walks by her. "I saw that," he says without looking at her.

She closes the door behind them and bounces her way towards

me before wrapping her arms around me. "We're here to make sure both parties are alive. Well, I don't really care all that much about you." She points at Bennett before she presses her hands to her hips. "You're going out with Wren," she says nodding at Bennett.

He looks at me and Alyssa, eyeing us warily. "And what are you two doing?" I watch in fascination as his muscles tighten when he crosses his hands over his chest. A vein pops out and I turn my gaze away from him, knowing that Alyssa will call me out for eye fucking him.

"Having a girl's night here," she replies.

"You're not leaving?" Bennett asks as his eyes dart back and forth between us searching for the answer of what we're really going to be doing.

"Not that it's any of your business, but no, we're not. I'm getting my girl liquored up." Alyssa does a dance where she stands and looks at Bennett. "Go get dressed and get out."

"Excuse me?" he says.

"Come on, we're going to go watch the game. The Giants are actually decent this year," Wren says and points towards the door. Bennett stares at all three of us, probably figuring that he isn't going to win this argument and pads back to the master just as Wren's blue eyes and Alyssa's brown ones find mine.

"You alright? God, we wanted to come last night, but we both had surgeries," Alyssa says as she pulls me into a hug and kisses my temple. "How has it been?"

"Fine...fine..." I tell her as she lets me go and I can already see Alyssa isn't buying it as she narrows her gaze at me and takes a step back, roving her eyes over me from head to toe. Her eyes widen and her hand goes to her mouth like she's had a sudden realization. "OH for the love of GOD! Did you fuck him?"

"NO!" I shake my head and put my hands up. "No, no...totally did not."

"Oh, but you want to...Jesus, Liv. I leave you alone with him for one day!"

Wren is staring at us with a mischievous smile on his face, his eyes shifting back and forth between us. "I'm really here for this." He slides a hand around Alyssa and I glare at both of them.

"Seriously? Nothing has happened." I resist the urge to snort at my own lie because a fuck ton has happened in the past twenty-four hours. "It's weird having him here and it's fucking with my emotions a little, but I'm fine. It's fine. We're fine."

"Say fine, again," Alyssa says as she pulls out of Wren's grasp and makes her way to the kitchen. "Tell me you have food, I'm fucking starving." She opens the refrigerator and squeals. "Oh! You went shopping."

"Yeah, uh...Bennett ordered groceries."

She slams the refrigerator closed behind her as she pulls a cheese platter out and some crackers from the pantry. "I'm choosing to ignore that for the time being because I haven't eaten anything today, but we are going to talk about that."

I roll my eyes and Wren looks me over. "You sure you're okay."

"No thanks to you and your bright idea."

"Liv...I'm sorry for springing that on you and I'm sorry I was so hard on you yesterday."

I cross my arms and give him a glare, though I don't totally mean it. It's hard to stay mad at Wren. He's like a giant teddy bear with a warm heart and the ability to make you feel better with the best hugs. "You should be; you were a jerk."

"I know and I'm sorry. I had just spent the last three days running on practically no sleep and dealing with my banged up best friend who doesn't remember anything from the last two years other than the fact that he's madly in love with you. We did a lot of talking the night you didn't stay and…I've never seen him like that."

I frown at his choice of words. "Like what?"

"Broken." He shrugs. "That's a broken fucking man in there." I go to protest when he puts his hand up. "I know he hurt you, Liv. I know he crushed you and you were devastated…*are* devastated. But he doesn't remember any of that, and you're so much stronger now. You've moved on and now you have the power to completely destroy him, and despite the anger you feel towards him, I'm just asking you…*begging* that you don't."

Thirty minutes later, Wren and Bennett have left for the night. I had to tear my gaze away from him when he emerged from the bedroom wearing dark jeans and a white button down with his sleeves rolled to his forearms. That was what he wore when he wanted my full attention. When he was trying to seduce me. *And he fucking knew it.* He shot me a wink just as he followed Wren out the door along with the instructions to *"behave ladies."*

Now I was sipping a gin and tonic because *we needed something stronger than wine*, as Alyssa stretches out on my couch with a bowl of popcorn in her lap.

"So, you told him everything and…?

I scoop my hair off my neck and into a ponytail on the top of my head. "And he didn't take it well. I mean better than he could have but I think the whole situation has him thrown."

"Well, it should. It stunned me when you told me he slept with someone." She stuffs a handful of popcorn in her mouth and crunches loudly.

"You and me both." I take a sip of my drink, wondering if I should tell her everything that's been happening between us knowing that she'll probably have a lot to say. I take a long sip, the gin burning my throat all the way down and my eyes water at the strength of the drink. "Jesus, Lys is there *any* tonic in this?"

"A splash." She shrugs as she swirls her straw around her tumbler. "I need honest Liv."

"I need to not be hungover tomorrow," I tell her as I think about the conference call I should probably be on at eight am.

"Why? Aren't you on "taking care of my sick husband" leave or whatever?"

"I'm technically still working, but..."

She scoffs. "God, I want your job."

"No, you don't, you're saving lives and you love your job!"

Her eyes narrow and she shakes her head. "I'd love my job with *your* salary and work-life balance more." She chuckles and rubs her forehead. "I'm off tomorrow and as much as I love you, I wish I was spending tonight sleeping and-or sleeping with my husband."

"I didn't invite you over, Lys." I snort into my drink before scooping a chip around the guacamole that she'd whipped up.

"I'm half kidding. Though I am coming off an eighty-hour work week." She takes another sip and burrows herself into my couch. "But Wren is so worried about Bennett, that asshole."

"Lys..."

"I wasn't in love with the idea of him coming here to live with you, you know." She takes a long sip and I hear her obnoxiously get to the end of her drink.

"Could have fooled me," I reply, sardonically. It only took Wren seven minutes to get Alyssa on board with the idea, and while she was hesitant, she did believe I was the best choice of caretaker while Bennett got better.

She pours more gin in her glass, foregoing the tonic this time. "Wren did make some good points. Everything aside, Bennett doesn't trust many people."

"But I don't trust *him*, Alyssa." I remind her. I'm glad that he felt comfortable here and with me, but what about my feelings?

"You surely still love him." I hate that Alyssa can read my emotions even when I'm desperately trying to hide them.

"Precisely why I don't need him in my house," I blurt out, followed by a sigh when I realize I'll need to explain what I mean. "He's already getting in my head."

She bites her bottom lip and takes another sip before letting out a breath. She stares off into space and purses her lips before looking at me, and it looks as if she's nervous to say whatever it is she's thinking. "Do you miss him?"

I ponder her question as I look down into my drink not wanting to speak the three letter word sitting on the tip of my tongue. The three letter word that welcomed Bennett back into my life.

"Yes." I look up at my best friend, her mocha colored eyes full to the brim with warmth and comfort and I don't see an ounce of the usual sass or snark that I usually see. I just see my best friend, that I've known for years. The woman who was my college roommate for four years, my best friend, my maid of honor, and at times I felt like my true soulmate. I loved her even when I didn't, and I knew she only had my best interest at heart, especially when it came to the man that had broken mine

She moves closer to me, engulfing me in a hug and resting her head on my shoulder. "Wren said he was a wreck when you left the hospital. He kept asking him what happened, but Wren said he needed to talk to you." Her voice is quiet and timid, and unlike how she usually sounds. "I just don't want to see you get hurt again."

"I know, Lys."

She perks her head up and looks at me, sadly. "But I also saw the way you two acted just in the ten minutes I saw tonight.

I saw the spark that's always been between you. The way he looked at you, like you'd disappear if he didn't constantly have his eyes on you. Like you were the most perfect woman in the world and he was lucky to be in your presence." I shift my gaze towards her, wondering where this sudden change of heart has come from.

"You saw all of that in the few minutes you were around us?"

"Your chemistry could stop anyone in their tracks. Watching you two together is like...witnessing magic."

"You're drunk, Alyssa." I knock my shoulder against hers.

"No, I just...I know he hurt you, and it kills me that he did that to you but...I think not being with him hurts you just as deeply."

CHAPTER Thirteen

Olivia

THE FEELING THAT I'M MOVING HAS MY EYES FLUTTERING OPEN. I'm immediately disoriented until I realize I'm being carried. Warm hands are wrapped around my back and under my legs and that smell...*fuck...that smell*. It smells like home. Like being madly in love. It smells like happiness. People always say that your sense of smell is most connected to your memories. It has the power to spark nostalgia instantly, and currently, I'm remembering a particular instance of me and the man carrying me sixty-nineing on the floor of our bedroom.

I let out a whimper, just as he sets me on soft, plush blankets, and I realize in my sleepy, intoxicated haze that I must have fallen asleep on the couch and he's putting me to bed.

"Bennett..." It sounds almost like a moan but also like a whine and I hear a chuckle as my body tries to pull myself out of this in between.

"You have fun getting drunk with Alyssa?" He sits down next to me and I blink my eyes open and sit up slightly. The only light in the room is from the hallway, leaving the room somewhat bathed in darkness.

It's dark.

I'm drunk.

I'm drunk in the dark with my almost ex-husband that's still in love with me.

I bite my bottom lip and look up at him. "Did you have fun with Wren?" I move closer to him, wanting to feel his body heat against me and he nods.

"I did. I couldn't stop thinking about you though." He smiles and my lip finds my way between my teeth as I stare at his mouth. "I know we left things kind of unsettled."

"I'm okay…" I run a strand through my fingers and look up at him in the sexiest way I can when I'm this drunk and he chuckles in response.

"That's right. How could I forget, you get horny when you're drunk?"

I drop my hair from my hands, cursing him for being right…I do play with my hair when I want his attention. "No, I don't. I mean I'm not…" I look away from him towards my nightstand that just happens to have a vibrator that I've spent quite a bit of time with the past six months. *Go for it, Olivia.* "You don't want me?" *Fuck, I might need more alcohol, so I can just forget this embarrassing interaction ever happened.*

His eyes darken and he grabs my hands, squeezing them gently. "More than my next breath. But you're drunk…very drunk, and I don't want you to wake up tomorrow morning and hate me more than you already do."

"I don't hate you…"

"Well, you don't like me very much, and I just don't want you to regret anything. You should get some sleep, Livi." He stands and makes his way towards the door. He's almost out of my door completely, when the words leave my mouth almost on their own.

I snort and roll my eyes. "God, when did you become such a pussy?"

He turns around instantly before he's in front of me, gripping my jaw *hard*. "That was your *one*. So, I hope it felt good." He grits through his teeth. "I actually want *us*, and *you* just want to get off because that piece of shit frat fuck didn't dick you down well enough," he snaps. "Don't take your sexual frustration out on *me* because I'm trying to do the right fucking thing." His tone, the grip on my face, the alcohol coursing through my veins, makes my clit throb painfully and all I want to do is rub it on him. *I don't even care if he's a willing participant.* He lets my chin go turning towards the door and I let out a pained, *"Wait."*

The Bennett I knew—all versions of him, couldn't walk away from me, and certainly not while he's angry so he freezes in the door. His back is tense, his fists are balled, and he turns slightly, so that I can only see his profile. "I'm sorry…that I said that." I let out a breath.

He doesn't say anything at first, and then I see him nod. "You're forgiven. Get some rest, Olivia." He's out of my room, shutting the door behind him and leaving me in the dark.

I manage to drift off to sleep despite the humiliation flaring up in my chest. Despite the alcohol fueling my feelings, telling me that I'd just been rejected, somewhere deep down, I commend Bennett for not letting us go down that road of complicated sex, awkward conversations, and tense interactions.

I wake up the next morning, my head throbbing worse than the day before and I make a mental note that I don't want this to become a habit while Bennett was staying here. I shouldn't need alcohol to deal with him…especially if it's going to lead to what happened last night. I slam my pillow over my head and groan as I think about having to face him after I all but threw myself at him. I peep my head at my phone and notice that it's only seven in the morning and I let out a sigh of relief that I could probably make it to the bathroom and the kitchen and back to my room without running into Bennett. I jump out of bed before I can change my mind and wince at the brief moment of nausea that overtakes me.

I pull my door open, grateful that my apartment is still new enough that there aren't any creaks or noises allowing me to move from my room almost silently. Once out of the bathroom, the Advil slides down my throat as I make my way towards the kitchen. I press a hand to the refrigerator, trying to open it slowly and as quietly as possible, grab a bottle of water and prepare to dart back to my room, moving as quick as I can past his room when I hear my name.

My head snaps towards his door when I hear it again. I go to respond, when I hear it *again.*

"Fuck. *Livi.* Fuck fuck fuuuuuuck."

I yelp, when I realize he's not calling for me, and more importantly what he *is* doing. The bottle slips from my hands and hits the ground, and although it's carpeted, the apartment is silent enough that he definitely heard it, as well as my squeal. I press my hand over my mouth, and reach down, fully prepared to grab it and run when the door opens as I'm huddled on the ground.

I look up, reluctantly, to see Bennett staring down at me in nothing more than a pair of sweats, his erection semi-hard and pressing against the fabric, making me believe that I probably overheard his climax. "Olivia?"

"Hi...I...uh...I just needed...water." I stand up, holding up the water bottle. This is the first time I've seen Bennett Clarke shirtless in months and I have no idea how I'm supposed to string together a coherent sentence. I try to pull my eyes away from the perfectly sculpted body, but I can't stop staring at a tattoo I'd never seen before. I take a step closer, ignoring the look that I'm sure he's giving me as I stare at the black ink tattooed directly over his heart. He didn't have a ton of ink on his chest, most of the tattoos taking up real estate on his arm and a few on his back. I was only aware of the one on his ribcage for his father.

No, this is new.

As in after I left him.

I look up into his eyes that are staring down at me, a smile pulling at his lips. "See something you like?"

"Is that...I mean..." I take a step back, my heart, body, and mind all on the same page that I needed space before I try to mount him in this hallway. "They say it's bad luck to tattoo your lover's name on you."

He looks down, and I think he realizes that I'm not just ogling his body. "I take it this is the first time you've seen this?" he asks and I nod, the words failing me as I take in my initials written over his heart with the words *'forever and ever'* written in neat script underneath it. But not just any script.

My script.

Whenever I'd write Bennett a note or a card, I'd always sign it, *forever and ever.*

He'd tattooed the words in my handwriting. Over his heart.

"Bennett..."

"Well..." he lets out a breath, "if this is the first time you're seeing it, then...it can't really mean bad luck. Certainly not worse luck than getting a divorce." He raises an eyebrow at me.

"How...I...when?" I put a hand over my head, remembering that Bennett would have no recollection of that. "Never mind."

"I was shocked to see it too." He smiles. "And all this." He points at his arm. "Never thought I'd be one for all this ink."

I nod, remembering how he only had a few when we started

dating, but they slowly started to accumulate, and after his father died, tattoos were one of his ways to cope.

"You started getting a lot of them when Senior died." My lip trembles because my father-in-law was truly one of the best men I knew. I don't know how he put up with Caroline some days. *But like Wren said, she'd gotten more insufferable after he died.*

"About five years now?" he asks and when I turn my gaze back to him he's looking off somewhere behind me.

"Yeah."

He clears his throat, nodding, and I can see him closing off that part of himself. I'm not going to push it. Bennett and I had talked about his father in great detail, and he'd told me countless times that I was single-handedly what got him through the hardest time of his life. We'd dropped off the face of the earth together, gone to a Bed and Breakfast in Virginia, and holed up for weeks, ignoring everyone in the outside world with the exception of Caroline, who'd also jetted off to the Bahamas with her girlfriends.

We'd made love for days on end, only resurfacing to eat and sleep. We'd gone hiking in the Blueridge Mountains—which I told him was a one-time deal, and horseback riding which he told *me* was a one-time deal—and fell deeper in love over those few weeks despite the tragedy that had brought us there.

But that was just it; our love had gotten Bennett through that. Having to open that wound without me to shield that pain wasn't going to be easy and I could tell he wasn't prepared to do it.

As if he remembers what brought on this interaction, he speaks. "What are you doing sneaking around at 7 AM? Aren't you hungover?"

"I needed some Advil and some water."

"And to spy on me..." He leans against the door jamb.

"No, no, definitely not!" I exclaim and immediately my mind thinks, *the lady doth protest too much.*

"It's okay, I've got nothing to hide." He smirks and I let my gaze slowly move down his body again. Before I can stare too long, he has me boxed against the wall, his eyes raking over my skin and only now do I remember I'm only wearing a tiny tank top and a pair of silk shorts. I look down and note that my nipples are hard and poking through the low cut cotton tank. "Last night, you were drunk and vulnerable and I wasn't going to take advantage…" he leans down, his voice low and washing over me, "but don't fucking tempt me, Olivia. You're still my wife and I still very much desire you, and what I know to be the best pussy of my life." He licks his lips as his green eyes look down my shirt slightly before backing up. "Put some clothes on and don't listen to me jack off." He moves back into his room and prepares to shut the door. "Unless you're planning to help." He winks before closing the door.

A week later, I'm sitting at the island with my headphones in, a cup of coffee permanently glued to my hand as I sit on the most pointless conference call. My boss has been going on for the past twenty minutes about marketing strategies that I could have explained in a three line email. Bennett walks out completely dressed, his hair still wet from the shower and gives me a smile. I mute the call, pulling a headphone from my ear and look up at him as he slides up next to me, leaning down on the bar.

"Why are you up and dressed so early?"

"Because we're going out."

Both of my eyebrows raise in question. "Are we?" We had been getting along pretty well the past week, moving around like two polite roommates, and thankfully there hadn't been any instances fueled by alcohol. The sexual tension is still there, lurking in almost every interaction, but I'm doing everything I can to ignore it.

Bennett is not.

"Yeah, come on, we can't stay cooped up in the house all day. You need fresh air."

"Well, I'm on a call…" I point at my phone, "and where are we going?"

"To get some food for one." He shrugs and pulls my almost empty cup from my hand and pours me another cup of coffee, before sliding it back into my hand. "And I don't know, it's New York, I'm sure we can find something to do."

I cock my head to the side and raise an eyebrow. "That sounds like a date."

"Call it whatever you want, you're going."

I tune into the last few minutes of my call, grateful that it's finally over and I shut my laptop. "Okay fine, I'll be ready in thirty minutes."

He snorts as I hop up, and I immediately turn around putting my hands on my hips. "Try an hour," he says with a laugh before turning on the television. I make a face at him before darting back to my room, determined to prove him wrong.

CHAPTER
Fourteen

Olivia

An hour and fifteen minutes later, we're walking down the street in almost silence, zig-zagging through other pedestrians as we make our way to a restaurant a few blocks over for breakfast. It's a warmer September day, allowing me to wear only a turtleneck tucked into a short mini skirt and my favorite knee-high boots. I'd watched as Bennett unashamedly ran his eyes up my legs before following me out the door. "Oh," I interrupt our silence as we continue walking, "before I forget, I've been in touch with your assistant. I thought maybe she would have some insight to your cell phone password and she's located your car and it's currently being serviced at Range Rover."

He shrugs and I frown at his lack of gratitude. *I don't see anyone else helping.* "That's an odd way to say thank you."

"I'm just not in a rush to go back to the way things were. Wren said I needed to be taking it easy, so there's no real need for me to go back to work right this second and I'm assuming I'm not pressed for more money than whatever sick leave I'm getting…" He trails off. "I'm not excited at the idea of returning to a life that doesn't have you in it." I look up at him and I wish he wasn't wearing sunglasses so that I could see his eyes.

"But aren't you curious about what's been happening? What you've been doing at work and...I don't know much about what you've been up to these past six months." I frown, as I'm not really sure what he's done. "I think you joined a kickball league or something with the guys at the office?"

"Sounds riveting." He snorts, just as we round the corner to the restaurant.

His hand rests on the small of my back as we move inside, check in with the hostess, and move through the restaurant. It isn't until we sit down and he pulls my chair out for me that he ends the contact. "Thank you." I smile weakly at the hostess. My body is humming with how close Bennett was to me as we maneuvered through the restaurant with his hand resting protectively on my back. I take a sip of water, hoping it cools me down and puts out the fire within.

"Nice place," he says as he looks around. We've been here more than a few times, but I know he doesn't remember that. The restaurant has open air seating, and we have a table almost on the patio, allowing for us to look outside while a fall breeze surrounds us. The restaurant is trendy with a rustic concept and all types of people flock here since it was listed as one of the *It* places in SoHo.

"You like it," I tell him and his eyes move back to mine.

"We've been here?"

"Many times."

He looks down at the menu and then up at me. "What do I like?"

"Everything." I giggle. "But your go to is the chicken and waffles or the eggs benedict or the western omelette... like I said you like all of it."

He looks down at the menu and then back at me. "Why don't you just order for me?" I roll my eyes before I stand up and he follows suit.

"I'm going to the ladies room, I'll be back." He nods and I make my way to the bathroom. I open my purse and unlock my phone only to see a text from Alyssa.

> Lys: What are you doing today? Want to do something later?

My fingers hover over the keys, knowing that I'll be prompted with a slew of questions if I tell her I'm on a date with my future ex-husband, so I avoid it for now.

> Me: Nothing exciting. Will text you about later!

I slide my phone back in my purse and wash my hands before reapplying the bright red lip stain that I told myself I'd put on because it's my favorite. *And not because it's also Bennett's favorite.*

Visions of seeing it all over his cock float across my mind and I let myself relish in the memory instead of trying to push it away. I press my fingertips to my lips as if I can still feel him there. His thick cock pushing through my lips and down my throat as a groan leaves his lips.

"Jesus Christ, Livi," he growls as he grips my chin. It's the first time I've given him head, and I'm nervous to be with someone I know is a bit more experienced than me. I'm not a virgin, but his list is quite a bit longer than mine. "No one has ever sucked my cock like that."

I beam under his praise when he wipes my lips gently and pulls me off the ground and into his arms. "I like seeing your lipstick on me."

"I like it, too." I smile when his lips find my neck. He presses his tongue into the flesh and slides it up the skin until it finds my mouth. He snakes it inside and I can safely say I've never been with a man that kissed me directly after I'd blown him.

FORGET ME *Not*

"Fuck. You taste like me."

"Sorry...I can..." I try to get up when he tightens his grip.

"When did you hear me say that was a bad thing? I love that you taste like me, Olivia. It means you're fucking mine."

The sound of a stall door slamming breaks me out of my thoughts and a woman comes into view in the mirror. She gives me a concerned smile. "You okay?"

"Yeah...ummm...fine," I tell her as I try to control my breathing.

She nods as she turns the water off and grabs a paper towel. "Well, if it's about a guy, fuck him. You're hot as fuck." She giggles, as she puts a hand over her mouth. "In a total straight girl way. I've had a few mimosas." She waves before she's gone and I'm reminded of all the times I've bonded with drunk girls in the bathroom. I shake my head at the intoxicated stranger and make my way out of the bathroom when I hear my name from behind me.

I turn my head and I'm stunned as David moves closer. "Hi Olivia," he says and I almost choke on my words.

"Hi..." I manage to get out despite being stunned over seeing him.

"I'm so glad I saw you." He looks me up and down, pinning his eyes to my legs and my skin prickles for a very different reason than when Bennett did the same earlier.

I immediately look down the long empty hallway extremely grateful that he is nowhere in sight. "Did you follow me here? How did you know I was here?" I'd purposefully never brought him here because it felt like mine and Bennett's place.

It is possible he just found the place on his own, Olivia. Don't be dramatic.

"No. I saw you walking towards the bathroom and I wanted

to see you. I'm here with some guys from work. Who are you here with? Alyssa?" he asks.

"It's not your business who I'm here with, David. We aren't together anymore." I shake my head.

"Because of the other night? I'll admit, I was a little taken aback that you didn't respond to the flowers. Did you get them? You're usually more polite than that." He jokes and I roll my eyes at the passive aggressive comment.

"I got them, and they're lovely, but it doesn't change anything," I say as direct as I can.

"Because of...*him*?" he spits out as he runs a hand through his blonde hair.

"Because of a lot of things, David. You didn't even give me a chance to explain before you jumped all over me and determined that I was weak."

I'm not about to tell him that I had already felt weak. That the walls I'd built around my heart are slowly crumbling under Bennett's eyes and his words. My heart knows Bennett Clarke and is yearning for him on a level that my mind and body are trying to reject.

And failing.

I know there will be obstacles in giving Bennett another chance, and maybe I'll keep him at arm's length until he regains his memories, but I can see the potential for us in the future.

I just don't know how far into the future.

"I was just angry, baby. I'm sorry." His blue eyes don't look quite the same as when I first met him. Blue eyes that were once filled with concern and compassion are now filled with ice and jealousy and betrayal.

But I hadn't betrayed David. I hadn't done anything!

Except fantasize about your ex-husband the few times he tried to fuck you.

I swallow, pushing those thoughts down further. "David, I'm

so sorry. But you knew when you met me that I had baggage and...I was brokenhearted."

"And now he's back..."

"I don't know. He doesn't remember anything. The accident wiped away a lot of his memory and he doesn't remember us being...estranged," I finally confess, hoping that it clears up David thinking that we're just back together.

He sighs and takes a step back. "So, what? How has anything changed on *your* end? So, he doesn't remember? *You* do. How can you two reconcile when he has no idea what the hell he did in the first place?"

"I don't see how that's any of your fucking concern." A voice thunders behind me and I squeeze my eyes shut, sending a silent prayer above that this doesn't become a huge scene when Bennett appears next to me.

"It's my concern because *you* fucked up. You cheated on her and she left you. You don't get a second chance."

I go to interject, that it isn't his choice when Bennett speaks the very words I'm thinking. "Don't you think that's her call to make? Whether she does or does not is none of your goddamn business. And what are you even doing here? Are you following her?" I note his hands are balled into fists and his shoulders are tense as he takes a step closer to David.

"No, he's not," I say in an attempt to ease some of the tension that's boiling between these two. I put my hand on his bicep, trying to pull him back slowly, though he doesn't budge, but I can still tell that just my touch has him less stressed. Bennett has at least five inches and at least thirty pounds of muscle on David, and I know it wouldn't be pretty for David if this came to blows. Bennett is no stranger to putting guys in their place who think that they can talk or even look at me a certain way, and the scene used to make my knees weak and my panties damp.

Not the time, Olivia.

He seems to calm slightly when he turns to look at me and then down at where I'm holding him back and David shakes his head sadly witnessing this small interaction.

"You sure you know what you're doing? You're too sweet and forgiving to see what's happening here. Do you really think he deserves a second chance?"

Bennett snaps his gaze away from me and towards David, the fire returning to his eyes. "You know what? You need to move on because I'm taking my wife back."

I gasp, not expecting him to say that. "Excuse me?!" I squeal as he begins to pull me away when David's voice perks up.

"She doesn't even want you!"

I groan at David's provoking, wishing that this whole altercation could be over when Bennett lets my arm go. "Maybe not," he growls, "but I don't need you in the fucking way while I try."

CHAPTER Fifteen

Olivia

THE REST OF BREAKFAST AND THE WALK HOME IS SILENT, AND AS soon as we get back up to the apartment, I do my best to break the tension. "Are you upset?"

"No," he says without another glance towards me as he heads to his room.

"Wait wait!" I run after him and stand in front of him. "I don't buy that. Are you mad at me?"

His eyes wash over me and the sadness behind them is evident. "I can never be mad at you. Besides, you're the one that's mad at me…"

"I'm not," I whisper and his eyes widen. "I just mean, not because of what happened at the restaurant. David isn't an issue…we're over."

He's silent and I can tell he's mulling over my words. "You're so fucking beautiful." His hand reaches up and pulls the clip from my hair that was holding a few pieces back.

"You know you're still the only man I've ever let play with my hair." I giggle, trying my best to break the tension, but he doesn't smile. He just stares at me, his fingers running through my strands like it's the most fascinating thing in the world.

"I won't back down, Olivia." He leans down, pressing his

forehead against mine. I shut my eyes as he gently pulls away and his lips rest on my forehead. "I might have given you up once but I'm not doing it again." His arms move around me and I'm surrounded by his cologne that used to be permanently ingrained in my skin as he presses me against the wall. "I know I don't deserve you. Your love. Your forgiveness…" He trails off. My heart begins to pound in my chest as the words sit on the tip of my tongue that maybe he doesn't deserve it, but it won't stop me from giving them to him. "But I'm still begging for it."

I don't speak. I just melt in his arms, fully prepared to let him take the lead wherever he wants to take us. "Tell me to stop." He cups my face, forcing me to look up into his eyes. "Tell me to stop," he repeats and I lick my lips in response, unsure of what it is I want next year, or next month or even tomorrow, but I do know I need his lips on mine *now*.

He's breathing heavy and I can almost hear his heart beating in his chest.

"Clarke," I whimper his nickname for the first time in six months aside from that one time at the hospital, but more importantly, for the first time since he woke up, hoping that it serves as the green light.

"Livi." He grazes his nose against mine once, one of his moves that used to drive me crazy. His hands find my mouth, drawing his thumb across my bottom lip. "Did you wear this color for me?"

"Yes," I whisper and I look up to find him biting his lip.

"Fuck." He groans, his lips ghosting over mine gently. I let out a sigh, dying for a taste of his mouth but he doesn't come any closer. We just stand there, breathing the same air, but not making any attempts to close the space between us. It's like we're stuck, neither one of us wanting to make the first move, though I'm surprised that Bennett isn't going for it.

"I remember…" He takes a step back and shuts his eyes. "You came home from work one day. I was already there because I worked from home. You'd gotten your period at work… and you just couldn't stop crying. Nothing I did made you feel better." He opens his eyes and I know mine are glistening with tears threatening to fall. "I felt like such a failure."

I remember that.

"You weren't," I tell him quickly, sliding my hands up his body to his face. "There was nothing you could have done." I pause when I realize when that was. "That was only about a year ago…you remember that?" I smile and he shakes his head.

"It was like a flash." He shakes his head. "Remembering that made me feel like my heart was exploding. Reliving that…seeing how much pain you were in." A tear rolls down my cheek as I start to recall that memory. "God, I'm sorry." I feel his lips at my temple and then dragging down my face, collecting the tear that fell before his lips find mine slowly. A kiss to the corner of my mouth, to the top lip and then to the bottom lip, as if he's re-familiarizing himself with my mouth before he presses his lips to mine gently.

Fuck, I forgot how soft his lips are. I open my mouth wanting more, needing more, and he follows suit. Our tongues meet in the middle before he pushes mine back into my mouth and begins to kiss me with all the same passion that I was used to. An explosive, bruising kiss that tows the line between pleasure and pain.

But also, a line between the past and the present.

His beard scrapes against my cheeks and chin, all the while his teeth nip at my lips. His tongue is forceful, dominant as he kisses me in a way that used to make my knees weak. The kiss he'd plant on me just before he'd fuck me mercilessly. His hands go to my thighs, slowly moving under my skirt that flares out at my hips, allowing him to move underneath with ease. His fingers, warm and soft stroke my inner thighs and I swear I'd give anything for him to touch me. He breaks our kiss and my eyes flutter open to see my lipstick all over his mouth. "I can feel the heat between your thighs. You still get wet for me?"

I nod, remembering all of the nights the past six months when I'd moan his name out in the peak of my climax. "Yes," I whimper as he moves his finger up slightly, grazing over my slit through my panties. I look down at where his hand is under my skirt and I shut my eyes trying to memorize everything about this moment.

"I bet your clit is hard and quivering. Dying for my tongue. Tell me, baby. Is your pussy throbbing?" he whispers in my ear.

"Fuck." A moan escapes my lips just as he slides a finger under my panties and I'm pretty sure I could pass out at any second at the thought of just his hand between my legs when he freezes. His finger traces the seam of my pussy, not pushing inside before his hand slides out.

"You're…bare?" My eyes fly open and I stare at him as the shock takes over his face. "There's no hair."

"Oh…yeah."

He stares at the space between my legs before sliding his gaze upward. "You used to have a tiny thatch of hair…just at the top of your mound. It was so fucking sexy." He grips my hips, pulling my skirt up slowly. "Can I see?"

My throat immediately goes dry at the idea of exposing myself to Bennett. It's a level of vulnerability that's so erotic I feel the wetness dripping into my panties. "Right…now?" I ask weakly.

"I'm almost afraid to touch you…after not being able to for so long." He frowns slightly. "I don't remember us being apart, but my body hasn't forgotten. Every part of me can feel that things are off between us, and it's making me insane, Livi."

"Clarke…"

"Baby," he whispers as he runs his fingers through my slit again. He swallows, and I notice his Adam's apple wobble slightly. He pulls his fingers from me and he holds them under his nose, breathing in my scent and my mouth drops open, remembering just how kinky he always was.

He spins me around to face the wall, pushing his dick into my back. One hand darts out and leans against the wall as his other hand goes between my legs and into my panties. "I'm going to rub this pretty clit until it comes all over my hand and then I'm going to fuck you with my tongue," he whispers in my ear. "How does that sound?"

I nod and he starts rubbing the throbbing bundle hard. He rocks his dick against me, humping me in time with me riding his hand. "Oh my God, baby," I cry out and somewhere in my subconscious I regret my choice of words but Bennett gasps in my ear in response.

"Tell me how good it feels. Tell me everything you're thinking."

Dangerous road, my mind thinks, but I'm too far gone, desperate for the orgasm that's just a beat away. "I'm thinking I miss this. I miss you. I miss us. God, I want you to make me come."

"Fuck." He says in my ear. "I need that. Give it to me. Come all over my fingers. Now." He growls.

And then I do, long and hard after months of pent up frustration. I cry out, the tears flood my eyes as my body explodes with the best orgasm of the past six months. His other hand not in my panties goes to my jaw, pulling my face towards his and he presses his lips to mine. I moan into his mouth as he cups my sex protectively, his finger lazily rubbing my clit even though I flinch every few seconds.

"I need more." He grits out as he pulls me towards the couch. He sits on the coffee table in front of me and pulls my legs around his hips. He lifts my skirt up and stares down at the apex of my thighs like he wants to devour me. I'm wearing a black thong that is completely soaked, and I know he can smell the evidence of my orgasm. "Goddamn, Olivia." He moves off the table, settling on his knees between my legs and immediately presses his face into my sex. I hold my skirt up so I can watch this sexy scene take place as he presses his lips to my covered sex before running his thick tongue over the damp fabric. "You're soaking wet." He presses his lips to me again, sucking the arousal from my panties, all the while grazing my clit with his teeth. I roll my hips hard against his face and he groans. My pussy begins to pulse, a new fire building between my legs that I'm desperate for Bennett to put out.

"Fuck, I'm there, again." I moan as I feel him pulling my panties slowly down my legs before dropping them to the ground. He looks up at me from between my legs then back to my sex. The air hits the wet flesh and I shiver at the meeting of cool air and wet warmth on my clit.

"Your cunt is perfect," he says, breaking the silence. I fully expect for him to dive in and taste me from the source but he stands up, pulling his t-shirt off over his head and unbuckling his jeans. I follow suit pulling my turtleneck off and sliding my skirt down my legs, leaving me only in my bra. His eyes darken when my tits come out even if they are slightly covered by my lacy see through bra. He's still in his briefs, black ones that highlight his hard dick dying to break free, and for a brief moment, time stops as we ogle each other.

He sits next to me on the couch and pulls me into his lap so my pussy is resting directly against his dick. Reaching around me, he pulls off my bra and his eyes devour my breasts like he's never seen them before. "It's too fucking much." He growls as he presses his lips to one of my breasts. He'd always told me how much he loves my tits. He loves how well they fit in his hand and his mouth, and that they are big enough for him to fuck. How my nipples were the prettiest color, not quite pink or brown but a delicious mix between the two. My pussy is literally dripping arousal all over his cock that is nestled between the lips of my sex. His hands find my ass and begin to rock me against him. "You're so wet, you're soaking me through my briefs." He stares at me as he moves me against him.

Up and down

Side to side.

"Take your underwear off," I breathe, wanting to get rid of the only thing stopping him from being inside me.

"Not yet, baby."

"What?" I whine.

"Trust me, I'm going to make you come again. But I don't trust myself going that far."

"Why?"

"Because I think I'd rip you apart, Olivia." His voice is hoarse as his fingertips tighten on my hips. "I can't even put my mouth on your cunt right now. I think I'd lose my fucking mind." He growls and my clit pulses instantly. My insides quiver with need, spurred by him digging his nails into my hips. "I need you so fucking much, Olivia Clarke. You are still mine, aren't you? Your body still knows who it belongs to," he whispers against my neck as his hands palm my ass cheeks. A hand slaps my ass before he grips it as he moves me harder and faster against his dick. Arousal pours out of me as I grind my clit against the hardness between his legs and before I can think I've gripped the waistband of his briefs, pulling it down and exposing his dick.

"Livi," he groans.

"Let me. Please." His cock juts out and bobs between us, standing straight up and rubbing against his abs. "I've missed your cock. It's so smooth and hard and…" I stare at the precum pooling at the tip as I rub my pussy up and down the shaft, my lips stretched around him. "Big."

"Jesus Christ, you're going to make me come all over myself." I bite his bottom lip before sliding my tongue along the seam of his mouth. "Baby, I'm going to come and I don't want to ruin your couch."

"Fuck the couch," I cry out as his thrusts against me get faster and more aggressive. "Mark me."

"Shit."

"You used to love doing that. Coming on me, seeing your seed painting my skin." He pushes me down onto the couch as he begins to jack his cock over my stomach. His eyes are blazing as he hovers over me. "Can't you just fuck me?"

"Not yet." He leans down pressing his lips to mine.

"Why?" I breathe out. I'm completely naked and his cock is out while his briefs are around his knees. It would be so easy for him to impale me.

His hand reaches up and grabs my jaw gently, rubbing his thumb back and forth over my lips. "Once I have a taste, once we cross that line again, that's it. We are calling off our divorce. Once I stick my dick inside of you, it's as good as my ring back on your finger. Is that what you want?"

I sit up on my elbows, the reality of his words serving as a reality check.

"Baby, you don't have to decide right now, while you're high on *this* but it's why I don't want us to go further." His thumb pushes gently inside my mouth pressing the pad of his thumb over my teeth and I bite down gently before I close my mouth around his finger, sucking him slowly, letting my tongue trace his finger.

He licks his lips letting an inaudible *fuck* fall from them and then I feel him moving, coming closer to me. His finger moves from my mouth and it's replaced with his tongue. It all happens so fast that it takes a moment to register that his lips are on mine again.

"I love you so much, Olivia. *Forever and ever.*"

We'd managed to make it off the couch and are now lying in my bed. I've put on one of his old t-shirts and he's put on sweatpants so we aren't *so* tempted, though it hasn't stopped us from dry humping like teenagers again. My head rests on his chest as his hand rubs the back of my head protectively, running his fingers through the strands and playing with my ear every few minutes.

"Are you open to it?"

My head perks up, and I look at him. "Open to what?"

"Trying again?" I freeze, letting his question sink in before I sit up, pulling my hair to one side and straightening my t-shirt as my eyes dart around the room. I move my legs underneath me and tuck a hair behind my ear. "Stop fidgeting, it's okay." He runs his hand up my arm and cups my face. "Come lay back down."

"I just don't know how I'll handle you getting your memory back." I put my hand up. "And that's selfish and I'm sorry—to be concerned about how I'll feel. Of course, I want you to get your memory back...I just don't know what that means for us. Will you still feel the same? Will I?"

He sits up on his elbows. "Nothing will change, Livi."

"You say that now because you can't fathom what we've been through. You've gotten hurt in this marriage too. Despite how you chose to cope with it, we fought and argued and..."

"Did I ever say I wanted out?"

"What?"

"Did I ever tell you I wanted out of our marriage? That what we were dealing with was too much for me and I wanted to move on?"

I don't even have to think about it. I know he's never said it.

"Olivia, baby you have to talk to me." His arms circle around me as he presses a kiss to my temple. I'm going on my second day of sitting on this couch wallowing in my own misery and more fried chicken than could be healthy. "And stop eating this trash. I'll cook you anything you want. Or we can go out. Do you want to go out tonight? Just you and me?" His voice is soft, like how a parent would talk to a child. Loving. Sweet. Compassionate.

I shake my head and bring my knees up to my chest. "Please, just go."

"Olivia."

"Bennett, please."

"You only call me Bennett when you're mad at me." He frowns. "Did I do something?"

"No! You're doing all the right things, and I'm the one that is screwing everything up! Why are you even with me, huh? Go find someone else that can make you happy."

I don't even have to look at his face to see he's angry and then his hand grips my face. "Now you listen to me, Olivia Warren Clarke, do not EVER, and I do mean ever suggest that you and I aren't going to get through this. That you and me aren't forever. Only you can make me happy. You are the love of my life and I'm secure enough in our relationship to know I'm the love of yours, so don't suggest some stupid shit like that again. I'll only go so far with you down this self-deprecating road. Don't do it again." He growls as he lets go of my face. He lets out a sigh when he sees the tears in my eyes, though they're happy tears.

Not sad ones. "*I'm sorry I was harsh, I just love you so much and I want to make it better.*"

"*You do make it better. Just by existing.*" *I climb into his lap, pressing my lips to his.* "*Forever and ever.*"

I thought things would get better after that. But that was the thing about the crippling sadness that comes with miscarriages and facing potential infertility. The happy moments were fleeting and few and far between. The sad moments were severe and constantly lurking in the depths of my mind waiting to rain on those few sunny moments.

"No," I answer finally, "you never said you wanted out."

CHAPTER
Sixteen

Olivia

SOFT LIPS PEPPERING KISSES UP AND DOWN MY NECK PULL ME OUT of the last few moments of sleep and everything comes back to me.

Lips on mine.
Gentle.
Passionate.
Bruising.
Possessive.

I push back, snuggling further into his embrace and he tightens his hold on me. His cock presses into my back and I feel it hardening with each passing second. I move my ass back and forth against him and he chuckles in my ear. "Tease."

I turn in his arms and stare up at him, honestly a little shocked that I'm back in bed with Bennett Clarke. "I can't believe you're here…with me," I whisper, as I feel tears brimming in my eyes and he pulls me harder against him.

"Here with you is the only place I've ever wanted to be." His green eyes are full of sincerity. "From the moment I laid eyes on you, I knew you were the one."

He cups my face and I'm hyper aware of the ring on his finger. *His wedding ring.* And for the first time, I feel the need to have mine.

"I wonder if you still have my rings…" I muse aloud.

"I was wearing mine around my neck, I'm sure I still have your rings…I guess at my apartment? I suppose we should go over there anyway…to maybe get some more of my stuff?"

"You think you're moving back in that easily do you?" I ask cheekily.

"I don't want to be away from you, Livi," he tells me emphatically.

"You want to break your lease?" I raise my eyebrow at the man currently not thinking like a realtor.

"I'll sublet, or fuck it, I'll keep paying for it. I'm not going back there."

I raise an eyebrow at him. "You think I'm giving in that easy? Maybe I want you to court me a little, Mr. Clarke. Make you work for it," I tease as I pull out of his grasp and move off the bed.

"Work for it? Last night you were all but begging to work my dick."

"Rude!" I stomp as I put my hands on my hips and he chuckles. "And you have a good dick. Sue me." I shrug as non-committal as possible and he's off the bed in an instant, pulling me into his arms. His smile has faded from my joke and he looks serious, almost somber. His green eyes are solemn as he studies me.

"Don't make me go back to my apartment, Olivia. I know you don't trust me, but let me earn it while we're under the same roof."

I'm about to respond when my phone begins to buzz on my nightstand. I look towards it before turning back to him. "Give me a second?" I tell him and he nods before sitting back on my bed and I take that to mean he's not granting me any privacy. I wonder if he thinks it's David and is planning to stake his claim *loudly* if necessary. I shake my head at him when I realize who it is and answer the phone. "Olivia Clarke."

His eyes darken at my greeting and then his arms are wrapping around my waist as I try to pull away, stifling the giggle bubbling in my throat as my boss speaks into the phone.

"Olivia?" I hear her voice and I finally succumb to sitting in Bennett's lap.

"Mrs. Clarke," he growls into my neck as he continues to kiss my neck.

"Yes…yes, sorry here!" I swat Bennett away. "Hey Jess, what can I do for you?"

"I know you're still on leave, but I was hoping you could come in for a while today, there's a meeting you need to sit in on."

I look at the man underneath me, who's somewhat behaving and gives me a smile. "Well…." I struggle to answer.

"Please, Olivia, two hours tops."

I purse my lips. "Okay," I nod. It isn't that I think Bennett can't be alone; I know he'll be fine. But I'm enjoying our time in our bubble and I hate the idea of leaving it. I hate the idea of being away from him.

Oh Jesus, I remember what this was like.

It's like when we first started dating all over again. For the first few months, Bennett and I were attached at the hip. We rarely spent any time apart, except when we had to. We fell in love hard and fast, soft and slow. Every day it felt different. Every day felt like an adventure. He became my best friend and my other half and being away from him made me feel incomplete. Bennett felt the same which is how I ended up moving in with him after only seven months.

I get off the phone after I let her know when I'll be making my appearance. "You're leaving?" he asks before pressing his lips to my shoulder. "Work?"

"Yes," I tell him. "But I won't be long." I bite my lip.

"I understand. I'll be fine. I'll survive without you, I think." He chuckles. "Though I do need a taste to hold me over while you're gone." Within seconds, I'm on my back and my legs are wrapped around him.

"I thought you weren't ready to put your mouth on my cunt?" I give him a cheeky smile and he groans at my sinful words.

He grips my thighs spreading them open and rips my panties completely off. I squeal, both over the fact that he just destroyed a ninety dollar thong and that it grazed my clit when he ripped them from me. "Bennett! Those were expensive, you caveman! You couldn't just slide them down nicely?"

"Shut the fuck up, Olivia. Now is not the time for your smart mouth." He growls as he stares down at my bare pussy. He tosses the ruined lace over his shoulder and I swear it's like he's not even breathing. He leans down kissing the top of my right thigh followed by my left before moving his lips inward to kiss the skin right above my sex.

I swallow, my mind, body, and heart completely aware of the intensity of this moment. "Fuck, what was I thinking?" And I don't know if he's talking to himself or me, but I see a fleeting moment of regret and pain cross his face. I run my hand through his hair and cup his face, making him look up at me.

It's okay, I mouth.

He shakes his head as if to say *no, it's not.* Before he presses a kiss to my palm that's still cupping his face. He moves my hand from his cheek to the back of my head and shoots me a grin. "You know what to do."

He drags his nose up my slit, inhaling my scent and my body begins to build. "You smell the same. I know your scent, and it's the same as it was two years ago," he whispers, closing his eyes and taking another deep breath.

The air leaves my lungs as he flattens his tongue and slides it through my sex, stopping at my clit to flick the bundle with the tip of his tongue. *Oh my God, how did I forget what this felt like?* I run my hand through his hair, pulling gently on the strands and he groans against me.

"Let me hear you, baby." He nibbles on my clit as I let my eyes flutter closed, riding the wave of Bennett's mouth. I feel his tongue trace me from base to my clit, working his tongue in and out of my pussy every time he passed over my opening. He licks me hard and fast, like he's desperate for more of my arousal and I feel it pouring out of me, trickling down my crack and marking the sheets underneath me.

"Clarke!" I cry out when he bares his teeth and nibbles gently on my clitoris. "Oh God," I rub the back of his head, pushing him harder against me and locking my legs around his neck. "Fuck fuck fuck." I grit my teeth, knowing that Bennett's tongue can make me say a lot of things when I'm on the edge of my climax and I'm not ready to tell him I love him.

Even if I do.

Even if I have tapped into that part of me that still loves him. I can't tell him that yet.

A hard pinch to my clit has me crying out and I look down to see him looking up at me, his mouth buried between the lips of my sex. He pulls back slightly. "I can hear you thinking."

"I...I am not." I let out a breath, and sit up slightly, putting a pillow behind my back so I can watch Bennett in one of the many ways he used to worship me.

I slide my legs over his shoulder and my feet instantly point on their own, feeling the end nearing. I can see the smile in his eyes, knowing all of my signs when I'm close, and my mouth drops open, but it's as if I'm frozen. Nothing comes out, I don't breathe, I barely even think as Bennett's eyes lock with mine.

"Fuck, eating your pussy still gets me fucking hard as stone." He says and I note him grinding his pelvis into the mattress.

My eyes water slightly, the tingle in my sex spreading throughout my entire body and a lone tear slides down my face. I don't make a move to wipe it, my body paralyzed by the feeling he's inflicting between my legs. He slides two fingers inside my cunt as he continues to lap at my clit and I can feel the metal of his ring inside me. I used to love when he'd fuck me with his ring finger, his metal heating my insides, reminding me that my husband loved me more than anything.

Our eyes stay locked until the very end when I begin to come and my entire body feels like it explodes. My legs snap closed around Bennett's head as my eyes flutter shut, a bright light flashing behind my eyelids as my orgasm seems to go on forever.

"I, Bennett, take you, Olivia, to be my lawful wedded wife.
…To have and to hold
…For richer or poorer
…In sickness and health
…Forever and ever
…this life and the one after."

My eyes pop open and I realize I'm lying on my back, having sent the pillow God knows where, and my entire body feels loose and boneless. I look back down between my legs to see Bennett gazing up at me, the lower half of his face still wet with my arousal, and a smile across his face.

"Holy shit," I whisper.

"Holy shit," he repeats, "did you black out?"

"I…" I'm suddenly freezing, a shiver shooting through my body, and I don't know if it's just because I'm feeling vulnerable after that flashback, but I push my shirt down over my sex and move my legs from around him.

"Hey, what's wrong?" he asks as he moves up the bed and sits next to me. He rubs his mouth before he licks his lips and then I'm in his arms, his hand stroking my back.

"I...I don't know what that was." I grab his left hand, rubbing my finger over his wedding band.

"Let's get your rings later, okay?" He presses his lips to my temple and my sex pulses when I smell my arousal on his face. "When you get home from work, we'll go over to my apartment? I assume you know where it is?"

I nod, not looking up at him, my eyes still fixated on his ring.

"Are you ready to wear them?" he asks me and I press my face into his neck, not wanting to leave this embrace ever.

"I...I don't know. I think I'm confused..." I press my hands to my face. "I'm sorry. I'm not trying to jerk you around," I whisper. "In here...yes. I'm reminded of how things were and I want them again..." I look at the window. "But so much has happened. We're sixty days from our divorce being final..."

"We call it off."

"Your mom still hates me."

"I'll deal with my mother."

"She's a problem, Bennett, and it's not just going to miraculously fix itself because you want me back."

"I said I'll deal with her."

I sigh. "You were with another woman." I look up at him. "That kills me."

"You were with another man. You think that doesn't kill me?" He responds quickly and I can see the pain all over his face.

"That's not even a little bit fair, Bennett." I struggle to get out of his arms and he lets me go. I begin to pace my bedroom. "You left me first."

"What do you want me to say, Olivia? I don't fucking remember that."

"Well, maybe it would be easier if you did."

"Why? What would make me remembering that I cheated on you any better?"

The words make me wince, not because they're particularly harsh, but hearing them just makes for an unbearable pain in my chest. "I'm surprised your girlfriend hasn't tried to track you down." I frown when I remember that he hadn't been able to get into his phone since the accident.

"Ashley is irrelevant," Bennett snaps.

"*Amanda*," I correct him.

"Do you think I give a fuck?" He gets up and stands in front of me. "Do you still love me?"

"Bennett…" I trail off.

"Yes or no." I'm silent and he takes a step back. "Yes or no?" he repeats.

"It's complicated."

"The fuck it is."

"Saying I love you doesn't just make everything better. It doesn't erase the betrayal, Bennett."

"I know there's still something between us, Olivia."

"Sex?" I snort. "Yeah, no shit. You can still make me come, congratulations." I know I'm lashing out, but I'm angry that he thinks that a few orgasms and telling me he loves me makes everything better. That he doesn't understand that lies and betrayal and infidelity are tied up in our marriage, and although he doesn't remember that, I still do.

I remember crying myself to sleep night after night. Drinking myself almost comatose more than once. I remember Alyssa coming over and forcing me into the shower. My mother forcing food down my throat. I remember the fleeting thoughts that maybe things would be easier if I could just not *feel* anymore. I remember the sleeping pills and the Xanax I'd essentially prescribed myself after stealing one of Alyssa's prescription sheets.

The thing about this heartbreak is it consumed my life. Sometimes all I could do was focus on my breathing from one second to the next. And the time between those seconds where I was forced to take another breath felt like an eternity.

I'd been broken in the wake of his betrayal and only in the past month had I started feeling like myself only to potentially be thrust back into our relationship again.

"I'm scared you'll do it to me again. What happens the next time I shut down, or shut you out, or hell, what if I can't ever have children? I take responsibility for my shitty communication skills, but we can't know what the future holds and I can't be panicking that you're going to stick your dick into someone else the second you can't handle your marriage."

"You want to talk about not being fair...?"

I put up my hand, stopping him. "The only reason you say it's not fair is because you can't remember. It doesn't mean shit, Bennett. It was still *you*. You're not a different person. You're still the man that broke my heart."

His shoulders sag and his head lowers in defeat. "So, that's it? I thought..."

"I didn't say no to..." I swallow. "But you backing me into a corner when I'm still trying to get an understanding of my feelings isn't helping."

"I would never cheat on you. I don't...I swear it will never happen again; I know it doesn't mean much. But the idea that I even did in the first place makes me sick." He's in my space, running his hands up my arms. "I love you...so fucking much."

"I know you do."

"Will you ever love me again?" he asks and my heart pounds in my chest as I think about what I should say.

"I do love you," I tell him, and his eyes light up at my words. "But…I love me too, and you don't even want to know what the last six months have been like. I wouldn't survive losing you a second time."

CHAPTER
Seventeen

Olivia

I DROP TO MY CHAIR AFTER PERHAPS THE MOST MIND-NUMBINGLY boring meeting of my life. And after the interaction with Bennett earlier, my head feels like it's about to explode. I became mentally, physically, and emotionally exhausted the second my body came down from the high brought on by Bennett's mouth.

Sex is easy. It's everything else that's complicated.

I'm about to call Alyssa and vent and eventually confess to the fact that Bennett has spent more time between my legs the last twelve hours than not, when my assistant peeks her head in my office. "Hey," she whispers.

Holly is a recent college graduate with a penchant for fashion but also for sleeping with married men, so naturally, I side eye her.

"I'm not here." I groan.

"You sure? Because your sex on a stick boyfriend sure is." My head jerks up, slightly irritated that she referred to Bennett as one, my boyfriend when no one in the office had any idea what had been going on *obviously*, and two, sex on a stick. I can feel the green blaring in my gaze as I narrow my eyes.

What is Bennett even doing here anyways?

Apologize?

Kiss and makeup?

Fuck and makeup?

No, Liv. No sex!

"Fine, send him back."

I'm instantly reminded of all the times Bennett showed up at my office for an afternoon fuck.

My door opens and shuts, and before I can tell my intruder that now really isn't the time, a familiar cologne surrounds me.

"Hey baby." My eyes dart up to see Bennett Clarke, the man I'd been married to for the past two months looking deliciously sexy and moving towards me like he's a jaguar and I'm a gazelle and he's ready to fucking pounce.

"What...what are you doing here?" I let out a breath as he spins me around in my boss' chair. She's currently out on maternity leave and I've been put in charge in her absence, which means I got out of my cubicle and into her swanky office.

"You sent me a picture of your bare cunt and you have the audacity to ask me what I'm doing here? The better question is why aren't you already naked? I walked out of a fucking meeting when I got your message."

"I didn't..."

"Didn't what? Want me to come? Bullshit." He lowers his face to be in line with mine and his tongue darts out to lick my bottom lip. "You rang the alarm the second you sent me a photo with your phone between your legs." I lick my bottom lip, desperate for a taste of his tongue and I watch in fascination as he unbuckles his belt. "Are you still naked under there?"

I nod once.

"And what am I supposed to think about my sexier than sin wife running around exposing the cunt that belongs to me to the entire fucking ninth floor?"

"I… my dress isn't that short and it's tight…" I stammer.

"Hmmm." His eyes are wicked as he raises my dress to my waist revealing my naked pelvis. "Fucking beautiful." He lowers his pants to the ground before he spins me around. "Grip the desk." I do as he says, hoping to God he had the foresight to lock the door but already too far gone to care when he holds his hand out in front of my face. "Spit."

"What?"

"In my hand. Right now."

"I've been wet since you walked in, trust me I'm ready." I chuckle.

"I'm not talking about your pussy," he says, his voice low and sinister.

"Clarke…" I'm not a stranger to anal sex. Bennett and I had explored that pretty early on in our relationship, but I'm not exactly thrilled at the idea of doing it in my boss' office.

"Ah ah ah. You tested the beast, and he came out. So be a good girl and spit in my hand so I can wet my cock. Now."

I bite my bottom lip before I lower my face to his hand and do as he says. Some spit dribbles down my chin and he collects it with his hand before it disappears. "Nasty girl." He growls behind me and I whimper at his words. I look over my shoulder to see him spit into his hand as well, before he slides his hand up and down his cock. "Can you be quiet?"

"While you fuck my ass? Unlikely, Clarke."

His hand lands on my ass making a loud smack bounce off the walls of the quiet room. I bite my lip again to avoid squealing. "I suggest you try to keep it quiet. No one gets to hear you come but me, and I'll be pissed if you let all of Conde Nast know that you're in here letting your husband fuck your ass on your boss' desk." I feel his dick at my hole. "Breathe, baby." I let out a breath as he pushes his way into my ass. It still feels foreign having something so big back there no matter how many times we have done it. I feel so full and I let out another shaky breath as he bottoms out and begins to move. "Jesus Christ, your ass,

Olivia." He runs his hand down my back, his fingertips tapping each vertebra on my spine before reaching the space just above my asshole.

"Don't come in my ass, I'm wearing a thong and it'll take divine intervention for that to keep all your cum in place."

He chuckles before something comes flying over my shoulder. "Good thing I keep a pair of your panties on me at all times."

The sound of the door opening breaks me out of one of the many times Bennett and I had defiled Conde Nast property. I'm fluffing my hair, preparing for his entrance when I realize it's *not* Bennett.

"David?" I blink my eyes several times trying to convince myself that it isn't a big deal that he's popping up *again*. "What... what are you doing here?"

"I came to see you." He smiles, but it doesn't reach his eyes as he pushes a hand through his blond hair. "How are you?" He shuts the door behind him and stands in front of it, seemingly blocking my only exit.

"I'm...good."

"You sure?" His eyes rake down my body and up again, like he's not sure that I'm telling him the truth. He sighs and runs a hand through his hair again. "Listen, Livi, I realize that I was an asshole, and I should have been more understanding of the situation. I just wanted to apologize." He looks at the ground as he shoves his hands into his pockets.

"Olivia, not Livi," I correct him.

Only Bennett calls me Livi. That's his thing.

I can see the hurt in his eyes over my correction. "And that is...big of you," I continue. "But you didn't have to come down here to tell me that. I believe you already apologized, anyway."

He drops to the chair in my office and leans over, resting his forearms on my desk. "I don't want to see you get hurt, Olivia. I do care about you. I know that I've been a dick, but you broke up with me to go back to the man that broke your heart. The man I helped you get over."

Tears prickle in my eyes as I think about refuting his statement that I was back with Bennett. The thump that is still loud between my legs won't exactly allow that. "I know." I bite my lip, the tears forming in my eyes. "I'm so sorry." I wish I knew what to say, but the words are failing me.

"So, what was I...just a substitute until your ex came back? I stroked your hair and held your hand, and made you strong and confident again, all so you could go back to your husband?"

It feels like the wind has been knocked out of me. My stomach is in knots and my throat is suddenly drier than the Sahara. I let out a breath. "No. I never anticipated any of this. I didn't know that he'd lose his memory and forget what happened that made us broken..." I tell him honestly. "I'm working through all of that now." I sniffle back the tears. "But I never meant to hurt you, I swear."

He snorts. "Thanks."

"I'm serious, David. I...can't thank you enough for..."

"Using me?" he interjects.

"No! I..."

His eyes snap to mine, cold and angry and defeated. "Did you fuck him?"

I blanch at his words. "David, you're out of line. That's none of your business."

He stands up and shakes his head. "So, that's a yes. Wow, that took what? A week?" He looks down at his watch before cocking an eyebrow at me. "Classy, Liv."

Fuck this. I really don't need this. I get he's angry, but he doesn't get to slut shame me for being intimate with my own husband. Ex-husband. WHATEVER.

Remembering where I am, and the fact that I'm entirely to

blame for David's feelings, I calmly speak. "I'd like you to leave." It's as if something switches inside of him and he takes a step forward. He reaches his arms out and I flinch away from him.

He frowns. "I'd never hurt you, Olivia. You ran back to the man that broke your heart and you won't let *me* touch you?" he shouts as his eyes widen, and for a moment I think he might put his hands on me. I pick up my phone, wondering if maybe I need someone to get him out.

"I'm calling security."

"For fucking what?" he snarls.

"Because I already asked you to leave, and I'd like you to respect that."

He huffs and narrows his gaze at me before he takes a step back and shakes his head. "You'd think for someone who was hurt as deeply as you've been, you'd be more careful with other people's hearts. Goodbye Olivia."

I push through my door and stop almost dead in my tracks when I see Bennett sitting on my couch—with his mother.

"Caroline." The fake smile that I'd perfected for my mother-in-law, makes its way onto my face just as Bennett jumps to his feet almost guiltily and makes his way towards me.

"Baby…" He can sense my tension, I'm sure, and after the day I've had, the last thing I want is to deal with Caroline.

"Olivia." She nods and takes a sip of her sparkling water, and I glare at Clarke for giving her one of my La Croix.

"To what do I owe the pleasure?" I ask, as I slide my slingbacks off my feet and leave them by the door.

"You just leave them there? What, are we in a barn?" She scrunches her nose and looks at my shoes and then at me.

"Mother," Bennett admonishes and she puts her hands up. I scowl as I pick them up and make my way to my bedroom. I don't even have a chance to shut the door when he's behind me. "I am so sorry."

"Why is your mother here, Bennett?!" I whisper harshly. I want to yell, but a part of me is still scared shitless of Caroline Clarke, and the last thing I need is her hearing the tantrum I'm about to throw. "I'm trying really hard to be respectful because she is your mother. But *we* aren't together, and this is *my* house. And I am this close to telling her to get the fuck out of it. Now what is she doing here?" I hold my index finger and thumb no more than a millimeter apart and hold it in front of his face.

"Okay, first of all, we *are* together." His voice is even and awfully confident for a man I'd yelled at this morning. "Secondly, she showed up and I wanted to call you or text you to warn you but my phone doesn't fucking work."

"You're getting a new phone," I tell him as I put my shoes in my closet and pull off my jacket. "She just showed up?"

"Yes, she wanted to check on me."

"And let me guess, she had something to say about the fact that I wasn't here?"

"No. I made it perfectly clear, you've been the best nurse." He raises an eyebrow at me and I scowl at him as I drop on the bed.

"I don't have it in me for her right now, so can you guys go somewhere else for your mother son bonding or her Olivia bashing. I just can't." My eyes well up with tears, and I'm trying my best not to succumb to the pressures of the day but I feel my heart squeezing in my chest.

Bennett must sense I'm at the end of my rope because he sits next to me on the bed. "We've had a long talk about how she treats you."

"You've had talks with her before. Nothing changes."

"This time is different."

"How?"

"I told her I'd make a choice if she couldn't treat you like the woman her son is in love with."

"A choice?" I'd never given Bennett an ultimatum or asked him to choose between his mother and me. I just grew thicker skin and learned to deal with it the very few times I had to, but to hear him standing up to her so fiercely in protection of me makes me feel like maybe he would do whatever it took to win me back.

"Yes, one she wouldn't love."

"Me?" I say weakly.

"Yeah, you. Who else?" He gives me a half smile. He pulls my hand into his and gives it a kiss. "I'm sorry about this morning. I didn't mean to pressure you."

"Can we talk about it later?" I ask him. "I just want to lay down if that's okay?"

"I think my mom wants to talk to you. Can you just come out for a little?"

"Bennett…" I start knowing the only way to not have another tedious interaction is to confess to him what happened with David.

He's going to lose it.

Four and a half minutes later, my door slams open and Bennett is moving towards the living room with me scurrying behind him.

"Mother, can we finish this another time? Olivia and I actually have somewhere to be."

"Oh, yes of course. I understand prior engagements." She purses her lips and reaches up on her toes to give Bennett a kiss as he lowers his face. She comes face to face with me and gives me a warm-*ish* smile. Though I'm not sure if it's as fake as the one I'm sporting. "Olivia, I'd like for us to have lunch soon. Anywhere you'd like. I'd like a chance to get to know you better."

I nod, not knowing what to say or whether to take her words as genuine, but I suppose only time would tell. It isn't something I'm prepared to deal with tonight.

The sounds of her Prada heels are still resounding through the apartment when Bennett is on the move towards the master bedroom. "I'll kill him."

"Bennett, no!" I run after him and almost slam into the back of him when he stops suddenly and turns around.

"Did he touch you? I swear to God if he touched a hair on your head, I'm going to break his fucking fingers." His eyes are wild and angry, and I know the idea of anyone touching me makes him furious.

"No! No, I'm okay. He's hurt, Bennett. He didn't say anything I didn't already know." His words stung more than I expected and though I never intended to hurt him, I felt an emotion I could only surmise to be guilt was coursing through my veins.

"He has no right to talk to you like that. Fuck that." He growls.

"Is it all that surprising? I hurt him."

"And now he's borderline stalking you."

I shake my head. "We don't know that."

"Well, I'm not waiting until we know for sure. I'm paying him a visit, and then you're getting a restraining order." He says as he moves into the master bedroom.

"For what? He didn't threaten me."

"I don't give a fuck. I know a guy. He'll put it into motion. He needs to leave you alone."

"Fairly certain that's not legal."

"Fairly certain neither is me murdering him. So, you can choose how the law gets broken and by who, Olivia." He pulls off his sweats and replaces them with jeans. It's then I see another suitcase in the room and I wonder if Caroline also brought him more clothes. "Go change."

"I'm going too?" I squeak.

"Someone has to tell me where he lives. Besides, I've seen enough scary movies to know, I go after him and all the while he's camped out here, waiting for me to leave and then he moves in. No. You go where I go."

"You're insane, you know that? Stop with the scary movies. He's not even dangerous! I'm sorry I even told you. You're overreacting." I roll my eyes as I leave his room. I don't make it two steps before I'm pressed against the wall and his lips are on mine. The kiss is warm and wanting and before I can deepen it, he pulls back. My eyes flutter open and meet his piercing gaze and I can see the worry and fear in his eyes. "I just got you back," he whispers. "I'm not letting anyone take you from me. He's unstable and I don't fucking like it."

"He's not unstable, he's hurt. You were too when I left you. You showed up everywhere I went for six straight weeks." He presses off the wall and pinches the bridge of his nose. "Bennett, look at me," I tell him and he does so reluctantly, cocking an eyebrow at me. "Don't look at me like that."

"Like what?" He chuckles.

"Like you're irritated with me. I just don't think it's fair for you to go over there and flaunt that you're...back in the picture." I stand in front of him, running my hands up his chest and to his shoulders which used to be my signal that I wanted to be picked up. He remembers and instantly I'm in his arms with my legs wrapped around his broad waist as he carries me to my bedroom.

"I'll let this go...for now," he says as he sits on the bed with me in his lap. "But if he keeps reaching out, I'm going over there to have a little chat."

I roll my eyes and move out of his arms, pulling off my skirt and pulling on a pair of jeans. Bennett sits on the bed, watching me carefully before he speaks again. "Why are you changing?"

"Did you still want to go to your apartment at least?"

He nods, recalling our conversation from earlier. "If I remember correctly, I have a work phone, I can at least use that for now. Until we get my phone open. You sure we can't just go to Apple?"

"Not without them completely wiping your phone clean."

His eyes widen in shock before his expression switches to confusion. "That is wild, what if a scorned lover changes your code or you do it when you're drunk?"

"Then you're fucked, and just pray you've got everything backed up to the cloud." I shrug.

"The what?"

"The cloud. It's like a virtual storage or something," I say pointing to the sky. "I have no idea what the fuck it is, but I pay like five dollars a month for extra space."

"Apple is literally garbage. I'm going back to a Samsung after this."

I cringe, and scrunch my nose in disgust. "I will never text you with green bubbles."

"Snob," he jokes. "But seriously, I can also grab my laptop, I haven't checked in on the market. I have no idea how it's doing or even where it is after two years. I feel like I've been off the grid for an eternity."

"Yes, I definitely think you should get some of your things. And who knows, maybe something at your apartment will trigger your memory."

CHAPTER
Eighteen

Olivia

"I'M NOT TRYING TO OVERREACT, LIVI. AND MAYBE THIS IS partly due to my own jealousy that there's been someone else." He lets me go and he grabs my hand as we walk down the block towards the corner to hail a cab. "It makes me crazy that he touched you and I know—*I know* I set all of this in motion with my choices, I just…"

I squeeze his hand not exactly knowing what to say as he raises his hand towards the street. "You need to tell me if he bothers you again, alright? I know you want to let this go, but if he keeps bothering you, we're escalating this."

I nod, knowing that he's right. He ushers me into a cab and I give the driver the address to Bennett's apartment. It takes us about twenty minutes to get there, and I'm grateful for the virtual silence we're riding in as I mentally prepare for entering Bennett's apartment. I know where it is, but I'd never been inside, and I'm honestly afraid of what I might find.

Amanda's clothes hanging in the closet?

Her panties in his bed?

Or maybe Amanda hadn't meant as much to him as I thought, and he had a slew of women in and out of his apartment. I bite my bottom lip as we come to a stop in front of

FORGET ME *Not*

Bennett's building. He helps me out and I stare up at it, a knot in my stomach that I wasn't expecting.

"Hey, you alright?"

I let out a breath and nod once. "It'll be weird being in your house. One that's not going to have any signs of...*me*."

He crosses his arms and follows my gaze towards the door where a doorman stands staring at us warily. I don't recognize him, and I'll admit to driving by once or twice...*a week*...early on in our separation. "Do you want to wait in the lobby, and I'll just run up?"

"No." I shake my head. I'm curious and maybe also a glutton for punishment, but a part of me wants to know what he was up to while we were apart. I know if we are going to be together again, I have to let all of these things go, but there might be some things I need to know. Blanks that even Bennett won't be able to fill in at this stage.

"I don't want to make you upset if there's anything up there..."

"Mr. Clarke." The doorman opens the door for us and he looks me over before looking at Bennett.

"Thank you," he responds. "Oh, this is my wife." He points at me and I can see the confusion on the doorman's face before fixing it and I give him a polite nod and wave before Bennett guides me inside.

I wait for him to lead the way, temporarily forgetting that he doesn't know where we're heading so I pull up my American Express app to pull up the credit card statement that we still share so I can confirm his apartment number when I hear a woman's voice. I look up in time to see a woman flying around the counter and towards us. Her red hair flowing behind her long and wild as she pushes her glasses up the bridge of her nose.

"Oh my God, Mr. Clarke! We've been so worried. I've

spoken to your mother and Amanda, and I just..." She looks at me and then back to Bennett. "I...how are you feeling?" There's a pang of jealousy hearing that she knows Amanda well enough to speak with her regarding Bennett. He must feel it because he squeezes my hand.

"Still a little banged up but getting better. My wife has been taking really good care of me." He smiles as he points at me and I'll admit this little game is getting uncomfortable. When it's clear none of these people know who I am, it just adds salt to the wound that I could feel opening the second we pulled up to the building.

"Right." She nods. "Well, it's good to see you, and nice to meet you." She nods at me. We make it to the elevator and I shoot Bennett a glare.

"Can you stop doing that?"

"Doing what?"

"Clearly they're used to seeing Amanda, or whoever else... not me."

"Well, I want it to be clear that I'm with you, just in case anyone's been here. Who even knows what my mother has been telling anyone and what if Amanda has shown up here?"

I sigh, as we reach the fifth floor and Bennett follows me out of the elevator. "Nice building. I wonder what the units are going for?" He runs his hand along the wall and I look up at him. "Not for us, I'm thinking about work." He chuckles. "Although, I think we should look for somewhere new."

The words *us* and *we* blare in my mind. "You want to move out of our apartment?"

His eyes widen and he stops me in my tracks. "What did you say?"

"What?" I repeat what I said in my head and realize my Freudian slip.

He smiles, his eyes light and seductive as he pulls his keys from his pocket. "You said '*our.*'"

I clear my throat and continue walking down the hall. "I meant '*my.*'"

"Too late. You said '*our,*' and I think it's something to think about…a fresh start for us."

I frown when we stop in front of his door. "I love that apartment."

"I just thought we could think about it. If you want to stay, that's fine." He shrugs as he tries a few of the keys to figure out which is correct. "I want to be wherever you want to be." He smiles and stands in front of the door, looking down at me. "Now, before we go in here, you need to promise not to hate me for anything you may find."

I nod reluctantly, knowing I can't be upset over something that happened while we were apart.

He opens the door and leads me inside and I'm assuming he's had the air on this whole time because it's freezing. "Holy shit, it's cold in here!" I shiver as Bennett turns on the lights and I immediately grab a sweatshirt I see sitting on the couch. I frown because Bennett is definitely neater than I am and always kept things in their place. For a second, I panic that it's not his, but I let out a breath when I recognize his football sweatshirt from college. I slide it on over my torso just as Bennett comes back in the main area.

"I turned the air down." He takes in my new appearance and smiles. "You always did look good in my clothes." I pull his hood up over my head and rub my arms. "It's fucking freezing in here, Clarke." I chuckle. "I'm going to raid your closet for more clothes." I chuckle.

But also, to be nosy.

I enter his room, and I'm surprised by how sparse it is.

There's a bed across from the large floor to ceiling window that looks out into the New York night. There's a nightstand on either side and a tall dresser in a corner. A television is mounted on the wall just next to the closet. The room barely looks lived in. Nothing on the walls. No real décor. "I probably didn't want to get comfortable here," Bennett says as he lays across his bed. "Was probably holding onto hope you'd let me come back home." I peek my head in his closet, extremely grateful that I don't see any women's clothes hanging up. When I move back into his room, I go to his drawers in search of a pair of socks as I'd just worn a pair of flats and my feet were cold once I'd removed them.

My heart stops when I see the lace in his top drawer. But...

The lace is familiar. *Really fucking familiar.*

I pull the pink, black, and white pairs of underwear out of the drawer, holding them in my hand. Mixed in with his briefs are my underwear...I peek my head back inside, seeing if he has anything else of mine when I find a picture. I remember this picture. We were lying in bed one morning completely naked when Bennett started taking my picture. I was laughing so hard I could barely speak and then I grabbed the camera from him and tried to take a selfie with him but I completely missed and it was just of me, cheesing obnoxiously hard, my dark hair wild and splayed over his chest. I'd accidentally cut off most of his head, though you can see a sliver of his mouth and a smile. I'm the focal point of the picture, as are the five other pictures I've found.

"What are these?" I hear him approach and I don't even realize that I'm on the brink of tears until I meet his gaze and his face falls. "What's wrong?"

"I just...you have my underwear in your drawer and pictures of me and...why didn't you fight harder for me, Bennett? You should have..." I trail off, wondering what he could have possibly done. I was angry and hurt and I didn't want to hear it at all for the first few months.

He takes a step back, running a hand through his hair. "It sounds like I did, Liv. The only reason you're even talking to me right now is because I don't remember anything. He sits down and I sit next to him and he grabs my panties from my hands. "You can't have these back."

I chuckle and hand him the pictures as well. "Do you remember any of these?"

He cocks his head to the side and points at one a smile ghosting over his lips like he's replaying the memory in his head. "I remember this one." He nods. "Fuck, you're so beautiful, Livi." He sets the pictures and my panties on the bed before he turns to me. "I found your rings. The safe was much easier to crack."

"Really?" He stands up, grabbing my hand and leads me out of the room towards an office. There's a desk with quite a bit of clutter on top as well as his laptop. I make my way around the desk and gasp at the number of pictures of *me* that sit on his desk. "Clarke…" I rub my fingers over the frame of one of our wedding photos and the tears are back in full force. "You never forgot me," I whisper.

"How could I forget you? You're the other half of me." He holds the familiar black box up and I purse my lips as I know what's in it. I look towards the safe that he pulled them out of and I see there's something else inside. I look at him curiously. "Can I see what's in there?"

He nods, pulling the envelope out and handing it to me. My blood runs cold when I realize what it is and my lip trembles as I realize I'm holding Bennett's Last Will and Testament that he'd updated after our separation according to the date listed at the top. I slide it back in the envelope when another envelope falls out. My name is written on top with black sharpie in his handwriting. I run my finger over the letters and I wonder if I shouldn't read it. *But maybe it would give me some insight, or maybe help him remember?*

"Are you going to read it?" He's right next to me, his voice low and gravelly in my ear.

"Should I?" I look up at him and he nods before taking a step back.

"I'll give you some space," he says before he heads out of the room, leaving the door open. I sit down in his chair, not prepared for a letter that Bennett would have meant for me to read after he passes, especially after we'd divorced. My heart thumps in my chest as I slide the handwritten note that is dated two months ago.

Livi,

If you're reading this, that means I'm gone or I'm on life support and you've learned that you're still my power of attorney. Assuming you still hate me, I'm sure you've already pulled the plug. Ha. Look at me, all funny in death.

I don't know exactly where we stand as you're reading this, but I'm assuming I would have drafted another will if I managed to get you back.

I've left you everything, which you know by now. And I'm sorry if I've preceded my mother in death that you'll have to deal with her. But I wanted to make sure you were taken care of, and I knew you'd be fair in doling out everything. Or if you don't want anything from me, feel free to give it all to her. I'm in sound mind, so there should be no worry about her contesting it, but if she does, my lawyer will handle it.

At this point in time, I have no intentions to remarry

or have children, and again if you're reading this, that means I never did. Marrying you is the one thing in this life I've been the most proud of. You're the only person I've truly loved. And I could only see myself being married to you or fathering your children.

I can't believe I let you go.

I know I've said it a million times while I've been alive, but maybe it means something in death. I'm sorry I hurt you. I'm sorry that I broke you. Broke us. I love you so much. Till death do us part, right?

I'm waiting for you on the other side. Maybe we can try this again in the afterlife?

Forever and ever,

Clarke

CHAPTER Nineteen

Olivia

I CAN BARELY SEE THROUGH THE TEARS THAT ARE STREAMING DOWN my face, and a sob bubbles in my throat. I put a hand over my chest, my heart feeling like it could explode from his words.

Take him back, Olivia.

I grab the box he'd left sitting on the desk and open it, revealing the two stunning rings that used to sit proudly on my left ring finger. I hold them in my palm before balling my hand into a fist and almost running from the room. I move into the living room to see Bennett going through a box that he must have found in a closet. He stands up when he sees me enter the room and eats the space between us in three strides. I practically collide with his hard body as I wrap myself around him. He lifts me into his arms as if I weigh less than a feather. One hand slides under me to cup my butt and one hand goes to the back of my head, bringing his lips to mine. He brushes them gently, running his tongue over my lips before catching one of my salty tears cascading down my face. "Why are you crying?" He walks us to the couch and sits down, keeping me in his lap. He wipes under my eyes and kisses me again. "Talk to me." I'm suddenly cold and a shiver moves through me as I'm very aware of the two rings in my hand.

I open my palm, revealing them and slide them into his hand without a word. He frowns, and I realize it's because I haven't explicitly said what I want. "Can I have them back?" I ask, though I already know the answer to my question.

"They haven't belonged anywhere but your finger."

I nod. "I want you to put them on me," I tell him and he reaches for my left hand instantly, probably as desperate as I feel to have them back on. But I stop him. "I want to say something first."

He leans forward rubbing his nose down my face and neck and pressing a kiss to my shoulder. "You can tell me anything."

The smell of him and his sweatshirt I'm wearing is almost too much. I've always been able to get drunk on Bennett, quick, and I know I need a clear head to get this out, so I push him back slightly and move out of his lap to sit next to him on the couch. "Clarke, the day you came home and told me you'd slept with someone else..." He starts to speak up and I put a finger up. "Don't."

He lets out a breath. "This hardly seems fair," he grumbles and his emerald green eyes darken just as a scowl finds his face.

I rub his jaw, loving the feeling of the prickle under my fingers as I try to soothe his annoyance. "I know, you don't know what to say, and it's hard to defend yourself against something you can't remember. But granted you never get your memory back, I need to say this and you need to hear it." He nods, and I bite my lip as I pull at the hem of Bennett's sweatshirt. "I've gone over and over what happened that day in my head for months. There were some nights it played on a loop. It was all I could think of. And I guess in a way, it helped me get through the miscarriages because it allowed me to stop thinking about them. I was in pain every day thinking about losing our babies, but losing *you*? Nothing could have prepared me for that kind of pain. I wasn't prepared for it. And maybe it hurt even more because of everything I'd been going through, but it was the worst."

"You'd been out so late that night," I continue, "but I figured you'd gone out with Wren. I was checked out at that point so I didn't even think to check on you. You got home around six, I remember… 6:17. I'll never forget the time. That's when the door closed. I sat up in bed and called out for you, just in case…"

"Yeah, it's me Liv." His voice sounds pained, almost like he's choked up.

"Are you okay?"

I'm about to climb out of bed when he appears in our bedroom looking completely defeated. He looks down at his feet as he slides his jacket off and tosses it on the end of the bed. He sits down at the end and stares straight ahead.

"What's going on?" I whisper. I don't make a move towards him because I'm not sure if he wants me to touch him. We've been worse than ever this week. We've barely talked or touched. He's kissed me lightly in the mornings before he leaves, but other than that, we've had no physical contact. I know it's weighing on him because of how affectionate and passionate and sexual we've always been, but I feel completely unsexy and even unworthy of his love or affection.

I feel ugly.

Stupid.

Weak.

I know Bennett still desires me, but I can't get out of my own head long enough to let him try. I'm slowly destroying my marriage and I can't stop.

"Baby, I love you so much," he whispers. "I know things have been difficult, and I…I just needed someone to care about my feelings too. You're barely talking to me. My father is gone. God knows talking to

my mother is like trying to put my head through a wall. I tried everything to be there for you, and nothing was enough, Olivia. Why wasn't it enough?"

"It's not you, Clarke. It's...shit, I don't know. Grief." The room has been mostly dark up until this point, as the sun slowly begins to rise on the day so I turn on the Tiffany lamp on my nightstand and crawl over to him. "Are you leaving me?" This is the moment I've been fearing. But now that it's here, I'm not sure I can handle it.

Fight for him, Olivia.

Tell him you want to try.

Tell him you want to go to therapy.

"No, baby. Never." He looks at me and cups my face. "I would do anything for us to work everything out."

"We can go to counseling. I'll go. I just…" I swallow. "I haven't felt great about myself." I let out a sigh. "I'm sorry. So sorry, Clarke. I love you." I wrap my arms around his neck and push my lips to his as I climb into his lap. He tastes like alcohol and mint, like he's brushed his teeth. I pull away, and I see the tears in his eyes, and then they're flowing down his face slowly.

Is this alcohol induced or is something really wrong?

"Livi, I'm so sorry," he chokes out, his eyes shimmering with the devastation that is wracking his body.

"I know. But you didn't do anything. And you tried, I could see you were trying. I just couldn't understand how you could love me or want me since I'm broken…" My lip trembles and he grabs my jaw and squeezes.

"You are not broken. You are perfect. Do you hear me? Never ever let anyone make you feel like you aren't perfect. I will always love you and want you." He presses his forehead to mine. "I want you now, so bad, Olivia."

"Have me," I whimper.

"Now?"

"Yes, make love to me, Bennett, please. We need this," I beg, as I grind down on his dick.

"Livi, I want to. More than anything." I go to pull my top off when he stops me and shakes his head. "But I need to tell you something."

"Tell me later," I breathe out. I'm not sure what it is, but for him to stop us from being intimate it has to be big. In the deepest darkest crevices of my mind, I suspect that he'd been unfaithful based on how he's acting tonight coupled with how I've been acting for the past few months. But I chalk that up to the demons in my mind telling me I'm not good enough and that Bennett has moved on to someone else.

He would never, he loves me. I think, trying to quiet that pesky voice.

"No, Livi. I can't...I need to tell you now." I blink my eyes a few times. He sits me next to him and I immediately hate not being in his lap anymore. I try to climb back to that place of solace when he holds my shoulders, keeping me at arm's length. "Let me get this out."

In this moment, I know, and the tears automatically start flying down my face. I shake my head. "No."

"Baby..."

"Bennett." I get off the bed. "You wouldn't. You couldn't...not to me."

"It was just one time, I swear. I was so drunk... sweetheart, I'm so sorry."

"Honestly, at that point I'm fairly certain I blacked out. Later, you told me I was almost inconsolable and our neighbor came over an hour later to ask if I was okay because I'd been sobbing for that long and that loudly." I bite my bottom lip sadly and look over at Bennett who looks as torn up as I feel.

"Fuck."

"So, you slept with her that night. I guess you'd met her at a bar. You told me you'd been drinking pretty heavily, and she approached you. I don't exactly know what you told her, but I think she knew you were married and were having a rough time." I let out a shaky breath. "The next day, I told you I wanted a divorce. You fought me hard for a few weeks. You wanted us to try and work it out, but I just…I couldn't. I was hurt. I was broken. You devastated me. You'd always looked at me like I was the most perfect woman. You put me on this pedestal, and then to learn that you'd given something to someone else that was only meant for me…" I clear my throat as I remember the weeks of self-loathing that came with the knowledge of his infidelity. "Maybe I just needed space, and in hindsight, I can see that I acted impulsively." I nod, before continuing.

"I loved you so much and so hard, I don't know how I expected that love to just go away. I looked for you everywhere, in everything. I felt you in the most mundane day to day activities. I felt you when I touched myself at night. I was pretty sure that I was never going to get over you. And then this happens. I'm finding out these things about your life. You're wearing your ring, and the letter you left me in your will. My panties and pictures are in your drawers. Wren tells me that your relationship with Amanda only went so far. And even in the past six months, the few times I did see you, I could see how sorry you were…in your eyes, in your body language. In the way you said my name, I could feel how much this hurt you." I fidget nervously. "I could see how much you still loved me too." I flinch. "The only thing I guess I'll never know is why you fooled around with the girl you cheated on me with after the initial time. That fucking stung."

"I'll bet, and I have no idea," he tells me. "Baby, I am so sorry." The look in his eyes matches mine. Green eyes full of pain and sadness. "It sounds like it was a lapse in judgment, and after you left me, I just used her to fill the void. Or, I don't know…I just needed someone there and she was convenient."

He stands up, setting my rings on the table in front of me. "Fuck, I need a drink."

"Not with your medication."

"I don't give a fuck," he says as he pulls some whiskey off the bar cart nestled in the side of the room. He pours two glasses of whiskey and hands one to me. I take a tentative sip, letting the amber liquid burn all the way down. He's still not sitting down as he sips the liquor, his eyes getting angry. "I am so pissed."

"Bennett…"

He puts a hand up and I can see the anger in his body language. His arms are flexing, he's breathing hard and he's pulling at his hair with the hand not holding his drink. He's rolled his sleeves up, revealing his tattoos, and I'm instantly reminded of how easily I'm turned on the second I see my husband like this.

"Come sit down…" I pat the couch, wanting to calm him but also to sate him as soon as possible. "I told you this because I wanted you to know. I needed you to at least hear it even if you can't remember. Even if you can't feel the pain you felt, you need to know this if we're going to have any shot at moving forward. I need you to know that I'm going to try everything to be open and honest with you. To not shut down on you when things get hard. I promise I'm not going to run, but I need you to promise not to run either. You can't turn to someone else just because I can't give you what you need."

"You give me everything I need," he tells me as he sits on the mahogany coffee table in front of me, squeezing my knee. "I love you."

"You can't do this to me again…"

"Never." I bite my lip as I look at the two white gold rings sitting next to him one with a three carat diamond sitting in the center. He follows my gaze and sets his glass down and pulls mine from my hand. "I put these on, and they're never coming off again." His voice is full of conviction and I nod slowly. "You talk to me. Open up to me. We're in this together, baby."

"I know. Forever and ever," I whisper and he smiles before he slides my wedding band on first, slowly, and then my engagement ring after. He presses his lips over them, kissing my ring finger followed by the other four causing a fire to flare between my legs.

I look down at the rings on my finger and then up at my husband and before I can think, our mouths have collided. "Oh God," I moan as I'm in his arms and being carried to his bedroom. "Please fuck me, Clarke." I'd sucked down a good bit of the whiskey, making me warm and horny. Bennett used to say whiskey made me more enthusiastic about his cock.

And I was already pretty in love with it.

"Fuck." He growls in my ear and then I'm on my back and he's on top of me. I want us naked, but I know that would require breaking our kiss, which I'm not interested in. The kiss is passionate and tastes like all of the good parts of our marriage. But it also tastes like *I'm sorry* and *forgive me*. Both of us feeding our apologies to the other for the things done in our marriage.

"I love you." I moan and he pulls away from me, his green eyes bright and shimmering with love for me.

"That's the first time you've said that," he whispers.

I lick my swollen lips and bite my bottom lip gently as my eyes well up with tears, and I remember that it's the first time I've said it in over six months. "I do, Clarke. So much."

He yanks my sweatshirt off from over my head and pops the button on my jeans and slides them down my legs slowly, kissing every inch of skin as it's exposed. "I'm never letting you go."

"Please don't," I murmur as he pulls his jeans down. I undo my blouse, not wanting to waste another second before he's inside of me and pull off my bra as well, leaving me in nothing but my panties. My breasts spring free and he licks his lips as he looks me over.

"Take off your panties." His voice is strong and dominating and it makes my sex slick with arousal. I slide them down my legs and throw them at him and he catches them before bringing them to his nose. I watch in fascination as his tongue darts out, licking the wetness from my panties causing the fire congregating between my thighs to spread throughout my whole body. He tosses them over his shoulder after he's done sucking my juices from the fabric before he grabs me by my ankle and pulls me down the bed.

He yanks his shirt off over his head and slides his boxers down his legs. His cock juts out hard and pointing right at me. "Touch yourself," he tells me.

Frowning, I sit up on my elbows and look at his dick then my pussy, wondering why we're doing anything other than fucking each other's brains out. *"You* touch me."

"I want you to touch your pretty clit until it's nice and hot to the touch, tingling and waiting for me to kiss away the ache." He rubs his hand through my sex, and I moan as he seems to be collecting my arousal. He rubs it on his bare cock and begins to stroke it slowly.

"Are we putting on a show for each other?"

He nods as he pulls at his dick, moving his fist up and down over his thick member and I can already see the precum forming at the head. I sit up, pressing my heels on the edge of the bed and completely opening myself up for him. I can feel myself building as I begin to rub my clit in slow circles, applying just the right amount of pressure and I swear his cock leaks precum every time my sex clenches. "Does that feel good?"

"So fucking good." I groan as my clit begins to pulse under my fingers. I curl my toes as my body succumbs to the pleasure between my legs and I let my eyes flutter closed as I feel myself getting close. My eyes snap open when I feel his tongue against me, and I look down to see him kneeling between my legs. I slide my hand away, wanting, *needing* him to take over when he presses his lips to my sex. "Please don't ever fucking leave me." He grips my thighs hard, digging his nails into the skin as he kisses me hard against my pussy. It's almost how he kisses my lips, with teeth and tongue. He pulls on the lips of my sex every few seconds, sinking his teeth into the sensitive flesh. I look down and see that his eyes are closed and his dark hair has fallen over his face.

"Jesus, Clarke. You're so fucking sexy it drives me insane." I fall back on the bed, the orgasm feeling like a wave preparing to pull me under when the pleasure stops and he's hovering over me.

"Hands and knees." I nod and do as he says knowing how much we have always loved this position. I loved how deep he got, and he loved the view of *"the most perfect ass, I've ever eaten."* A hand comes down on my ass hard and then I feel his teeth sinking into the stinging flesh.

"Ow! Fuck!" Bennett used to love biting me. He'd sink his teeth into my skin so hard at times I was sure he'd break the skin. My tits and the space between my thighs were always riddled with hickeys and I loved the feeling of being marked in such a sexy manner.

"Have you missed my bites? Have you missed looking in the mirror and seeing my teeth marks all over your sexy body?"

"Mmm," I mewl and he smacks my ass again.

"Answer me, Olivia." He grabs my hair and hauls me back against his chest so that my back is resting directly against his chest. He runs his fingers down my body and rubs my clit gently.

"Yes yes yes." I groan when I feel his lips on my neck. "I love the way you mark me. Claim me. Own me. I love being yours."

"When have you not been mine?" He growls as he bites down on my neck. "I know you think that this situation we're in with me not remembering is the only reason we're here now, but it's not. I was coming for you regardless, Olivia. I could only live without you for so long." he tells me as he pushes me down.

And a part of me thinks that he's right.

I feel his cock at my entrance, his blunt tip probing my sensitive sex that is seconds from reaching orgasmic bliss. "Rub your clit on my cock, sweetheart. Just slide your slippery cunt on the top of my dick. I want to feel you dripping all over me and onto the bed." His words are almost my undoing as I rock back on his cock, rubbing my pussy against him. The inferno between my legs is getting more aggressive, and all I want is him inside me.

"Clarke please, stop teasing me. I want this. Please put us back together, baby," I beg. And it's true, sex was a large part of our relationship. Both Bennett and I expressed our love through affection and making love. We were hypersexual people and we'd always had this intense sexual chemistry. And while sex wouldn't fix everything, it is certainly a step in the right direction towards being the old Olivia and Bennett.

"Fuck." He rears back and pushes inside me *hard*. So hard, the bed frame bangs against the wall. "Holy fuck, fuck, fuck. I'm fucking home." He growls and I moan at the same thought as his thick cock stretches me in a way that I haven't felt in months. The familiar tingle in my pussy is already ready to take me over when he pulls back and does it again as a guttural groan leaves him.

"Oh my God, Clarke!" I whine as he pumps inside of me hard. His grip tightens on my hips, his nails digging into to the flesh so hard, I know there will be bruises tomorrow. Bruises I'd rub over gently with a sexy smile on my face as I remember how hard he fucked me. I reach back between my spread legs to cup his balls and squeeze them gently.

"Shit. You always know just what to do, Livi. You were made for me baby. Your tight cunt was made for my cock. Squeeze me, baby."

I cry out both out of the pleasure he's inflicting but also his words that make me feel all kinds of emotions. "Tell me how much you love fucking me," I purr as I clamp down on him.

"Fuck fuck fuck." One hand finds its way into my hair, tangling in my dark tresses and he pulls slightly. The pinch in my scalp sends a message to my clit which pulses in response. "It's the greatest fucking thrill of my life. There's nothing like being inside of you." He continues to thrust, his balls tapping my clit each time he bottoms out inside of me. He hammers into me at a punishing speed, one hand digging into my hips as he fucks me mercilessly. "Fuck. I wish I'd made you come in my mouth. I love fucking you with the taste of your pussy on my tongue." He freezes and I almost think he's going to stop to make me sit on his face, which he's been known to do. "I need my lips on you. I need to fuck your mouth while I fuck your cunt."

I can feel myself getting close, and him for that matter, so I'm surprised when he pulls out of me. I'm about to protest when I'm on my back and he's on top of me, staring down at me. He slides back into me, rocking slowly but it's just as intense as his deep green eyes stare down at me. "I love you." He presses his lips to mine just as I lock my ankles around his back. His thrusts pick up again as his lips find my neck. "Come with me, Livi. Please. I know you're close, I'm waiting for you baby."

"Oh God," I cry out, knowing that the few times Bennett and I have come at the same time, it was intense and I usually bawled my eyes out after.

"I know, I know."

"Bennett, it's just too much!" I squeeze my eyes shut, turning my head to the side, as I raise my hips to meet his thrusts, our pelvises banging together almost painfully.

"It's never too much," he whispers as he brushes the hair out of my eyes. I squeeze down, my body moving with his in perfect harmony and then I freeze as my body goes taut. I feel my clit tingling and my sex quivering and he gasps. "Fuck, there it is." He presses his forehead to mine. "Let go, baby, I'll catch you."

I look up into his eyes, the second before I shatter and all I see is the beautiful man that gave me his heart eight years ago and has never gotten it back. I've had it this whole time and only now do I see he hasn't really been functioning without it. He kisses me hard as he unleashes his seed inside me, sliding his tongue between my lips and coaxing my tongue into his. At some point, I stop coming and he stops thrusting, letting me know he's slowing down as well, but he stays inside of me. I feel him softening but he makes no effort to move, as he stares down at me. We're wrapped up in the most delicious knot, our arms and legs tangled together and deliciously sweaty. We shift slightly, the sweat on our bodies allowing us to glide against each other.

He leans down brushing his nose over mine and his lips across my skin. "Forever and ever," he murmurs against my lips as he slowly slips out of me.

In that moment, I know, and the thought hits me almost as hard as the orgasm:

I am madly in love with my husband and I no longer want to let him go.

CHAPTER Twenty

Bennett

FINGERTIPS GHOSTING LIGHTLY UP MY SPINE ROUSE ME FROM MY LAST few moments of sleep. The smell of vanilla floods my senses and a smile finds my face before I'm even fully awake. I open one eye and see the most beautiful woman I've ever met, the only woman I've ever loved staring at me with the sweetest smile on her face. Her brown eyes are warm and staring adoringly into mine as if I hold the answers to all of life's questions.

Being married to Olivia Clarke has been the greatest adventure of my life and I thank every God there is that she deems me worthy of being her husband. I still remember the look on her face when I slid that ring on her finger. Like I was a prize she couldn't believe she'd won. When in reality, I was the lucky one.

I move from my stomach to my side and pull her against me. "Were you watching me sleep?" I ask her and she nods her head guiltily before a grin breaks out across her face. Olivia's smile is one of the great wonders of my world. She swears up and down that her in that deliciously sinful black dress she was wearing the night we met was what made me fall in love. But before I even got a look at the way that dress hugged her curves, I spotted a woman across the room with the most beautiful smile.

Genuinely breathtaking.

I didn't even know she was friends with Wren's newest girlfriend. All I knew was that I had to know her. I had to be in her presence, and just maybe, one of those smiles would be directed at me.

"I was waiting for you to wake up." She sits up, leaning on her elbow and the sheet falls, revealing her warm brown skin, that is slightly kissed by the sun after this past weekend in the Hampton's.

"And why is that?" My eyes devour her naked chest, wanting to pull one of her pretty nipples into my mouth.

"To fuck me." She giggles and I thank God we are on the same page. Her giggle is like music to my dick that's been awake long before I was. "I'm ovulating." Her teeth find her bottom lip and the thought of impregnating the woman I've been borderline obsessed with the last seven years has me climbing on top of her. She laughs when I tuck my face into her neck inhaling her sweet and sexy scent.

"You want me to get you pregnant, Mrs. Clarke?"

"Please," she whispers as my cock probes her folds that are already wet and ready for me.

"I want that too. Fuck I want that." I press my lips to hers as I begin rocking in and out of her slowly.

I married Olivia when she was fresh out of college, and while I wanted to knock her up the second we said 'I do,' I knew she wanted time to explore her career and adulthood. So, we waited.

Until about two weeks ago, when Olivia came to me and told me she was ready to be a mother.

I'm going to be a dad.

To Olivia's baby.

I can't fucking wait.

My eyes fly open as the memory hits me so hard, I find myself struggling to breathe. I stare at the ceiling as the fan continues to propel above us as memories of the past six months come at me hard, fast and unrelenting.

"Livi, please don't cry." I hold her in arms, stroking her back as she sobs into my shirt, soaking the fabric. Her tears sear my skin, her pain eviscerating me with each choked out plea.

"Why...why can't I get pregnant? It's been months, Clarke." She looks up at me, her big brown eyes full of questions that I don't have the answers to. "What's wrong with me?"

"Nothing!" I tell her immediately. "You're perfect, Olivia. These things take time."

Her lip trembles as she climbs out of my lap and I try not to take it personally that she doesn't want me to comfort her. I can feel her heart hardening in her chest, like it's my own. She's shutting down and shutting me out and I don't know how to stop it.

I sit up, rubbing a hand over my mouth as everything comes back to me. I blink my eyes several times as if it would somehow change what happened between us.

"Olivia...talk to me." She pulls her gaze away from the window. A gaze that used to be full of life and laughter and love, but is now lifeless and cold. I stroke her cheek slowly. "Baby, come on, let's go out."

"I'm tired," she says before turning back to the window.

"I know, but it'll make you feel better."

"Will it?"

"I promise, yes. Or maybe I can call Alyssa and she can come over?"

She

shakes her head. "Can you just...let me be sad in peace please?"

"Olivia..."

"I get it, you want me to feel better. I do, Clarke. But I can't feel

better just because you want me to. That's not how this works. That's not how any of this works." Her lip trembles. *"I don't want to feel like this, but...I don't get a say either."*

"Yes you do, Olivia. We can get through this together. I'm devastated too and I need you just as much as you need me." I move closer and try to wrap my arms around her when she shrinks into herself pushing me away.

"Please, just don't."

My eyes furrow not out of anger, but out of worry. *"Don't what? Touch you? You're my wife, Olivia. We need this."*

"What? Sex? I am really not in the mood."

"Not sex, Olivia. Intimacy. We've never not been able to connect that way."

My eyes move to the woman in bed next to me, her chest moving up and down underneath the thin sheet. The room is quiet except for her gentle breathing and the pounding of my heart that I swear can be heard around New York.

"Olivia, please." I knock on the locked door of our bathroom. She's been in the bathtub for an hour crying. She ran the water for most of the time, trying to drown out the sound but I've been sitting next to the door, trying my best to give her space, but also trying to soothe her broken heart.

"Olivia, we need to talk." I need my wife back. I can't take it another second. I need her and I know without a doubt she needs me.

"About...what?" Her voice wobbles and I regret being so stern with her.

"I just...please?"

"I have nothing to say."

"Well, I do, come out here."

I expect her to ignore me, so I'm surprised when she opens the door and steps out into our bedroom in nothing more than a bathrobe. Her hair is pinned up in a bun to not get it wet and her eyes are glassy and hazy, with bags beneath them. Her skin is blotchy and ashen. Her usual honey glow is gone and the fire in her eyes has long since been extinguished.

"What, Clarke?"

"You have to snap out of this. I've had enough, Olivia. I need my wife back. I know it's been a rocky few months—hell year, but if we're going to get through this, I need you with me. I need you to fight with me. For us."

"I can't fight anymore. I'm tired."

"Too tired for...us?"

"I'm just...hurting, Clarke."

"And you think I'm not?" I snap, the frustrations of being shut out and ignored the last few months finally bubbling over. "Watching you going through that? Through this?" I point at her. "It's destroying me, Olivia. To know that I can't fix this. That I can't help. Goddammit, Olivia, you're my wife. Let me take care of you. Fuck. I need you to take care of me. I need you. I need us." She doesn't respond before I'm out the door, slamming it behind me. I hadn't intended to take that tone with her, but her indifference, the vacant look in her eyes just set me completely off.

I'm tired of feeling like I'm in this marriage alone. I'm tired of feeling like I can't grieve. That my feelings don't matter.

I need a fucking drink.

A lot of them.

I need space.

I'm off the bed before I can think about what I did that night.

No no no, this cannot be happening.

I enter the bathroom, closing it behind me quietly to not disturb Olivia. I grip my hair, cursing my memory for choosing *now* to come back.

Just when I'd gotten Olivia back.

Just when she'd finally let me back in. I stare at my reflection, the heavy feeling in my chest making me feel like I'm having a heart attack.

I don't know what's more aggressive: the pounding in my temples or the nauseous feeling in my stomach. I rub my forehead and groan.

"Fuck." I turn my head into the pillow and immediately my stomach rolls at the smell.

When the hell did Olivia start wearing…what the hell is this, peach? I throw the pillow away from me, the smell making me even more physically ill when I hear a chuckle. Even in my hungover state I know that giggle does not belong to my wife. "I made coffee." I hear the mysterious voice speak and then my eyes fly open. I'm met with blue eyes and a fresh face with long blonde hair pulled over her shoulder. A strange woman wearing a Florida State t-shirt over bare legs is staring at me with a faint smile ghosting across her lips. She holds a mug out for me and my eyes ping-pong back and forth between the cup and her and my naked body underneath the sheet.

"What…what the fuck?" I'm immediately up and off the bed and I note the time on her nightstand reads just after 5 AM. "What… how? Who…?" I look at my left hand, wondering briefly if I'd dreamt Olivia up. If I'd somehow dreamt that I'd married the perfect girl. If I was back to my life of random women and faceless one night stands. Otherwise, my life was about to become a nightmare. My eyes find the platinum ring on my left finger and I fight down the bile rising up my throat. How could I have done this? "I—married." I shake my head. "No. No no no."

"Relax, deep breaths."

"DEEP BREATHS?!" I roar, and immediately regret it when it feels like my head explodes.

"Bennett—"

"Don't say my name. I don't know you. You don't know me," I growl as I pull my briefs and my jeans up over my pelvis.

"Well...we sort of do in the biblical sense." She giggles and the sound is like nails on a chalkboard.

"I didn't fuck you," I snarl. "I would never cheat on my wife," I tell her as I pull on my t-shirt and leather jacket.

"Yes, you said that quite a few times last night." I don't miss the roll of her eyes that makes me want to scream, *you don't know me. You don't know how much I love my wife. I'd never do this. I would never hurt Olivia.*

"And your response to that was to take me home?!" I grab my phone and my heart sinks when I don't see anything from Olivia. She didn't even care that I didn't come home.

"You kissed me." She bites her bottom lip. "You said...you said you were broken."

"What?"

"That you wanted to feel something. So you knew you weren't dead inside."

I shake my head. "I wouldn't cheat on my wife to fucking feel something. Screw you."

Her eyes well up with tears and she takes a step back. "Stop yelling at me."

"I...why did you let things go this far? Clearly you were more sober than I was if you can remember all of this."

"I was pretty drunk. I just didn't black out. And I'm sorry that I didn't do more to protect *your* marriage," she snaps as she shoots daggers out of her eyes.

"Fuck. I'm going to be sick." I rub my forehead. "She's never going to forgive me."

"Livi?"

My eyes snap up to hers and I stalk towards her, backing her into a corner of her room. "Don't you ever fucking say her name. How... how do you even know her name?"

"You..." she clears her throat, "you called her name when you... umm...came."

I take a step back. "What?"

"Yeah...it...wasn't my finest sexual moment." She shrugs sadly.

"Jesus. I have to go." I shake my head. "Look..." I point at her in question and she crosses her arms and shakes her head.

"Amanda."

"Amanda, this never happened."

"If that helps you sleep at night."

I press a hand to the mirror, trying my best to get air into my lungs slowly.

Inhale.

Count to ten.

Exhale.

I'd only cried a handful of times in my life. Losing my father, losing our babies, losing Olivia. All of it was associated with loss. But this is the first time I feel the tears building over something different.

Regaining my memories.

Memories I wanted to forget forever.

"Clarke?" I hear her voice through the door, soft and sensual and calling out to every part of me. I wipe my face and clear my throat.

I'm still madly in love with the woman on the other side of the door. I never stopped loving her. I never stopped wanting her. Losing my memory had granted us a second chance. *Now that I have it back, now what?*

No.

I'm not giving up our second chance.

I need to be certain that we can survive the truth.

"I'll be out in a minute, baby," I tell her as I turn on the water and splash it on my face. I cup my hands under the faucet and bring the water to my mouth to swish out the horrible taste of my memories. I open the medicine cabinet, looking for the Advil and take two before running a hand through my hair.

When I open the door she's staring up at me the same way she used to, full of love and devotion and loyalty.

"Are you okay?" She puts her hand on my face and gives me a smile. "Come back to bed."

I pick her up in my arms before she can take another step. She squeals as I carry her back to bed, depositing her on the plush bedding and hovering over her naked frame.

"Fuck, I've missed you," I whisper as I stare down at her before peppering kisses across her stomach.

"Missed me? You were only gone a few minutes." She giggles as she rubs a hand through my hair.

Get it the fuck together, Bennett.

"I hate being away from you at all. Ever," I tell her. "Promise me, we're done being apart." I part her legs and kiss her inner thigh, just shy of her mound. "I can't take being away from you."

"I hated it too, Clarke." She rubs her hand over my face and pulls my jaw up to look at her. "Every second we were apart felt like an eternity," she whispers. I had fully planned on fucking her with my tongue, but I want to know more. I want to hear how much she missed me while we were apart now that I remember everything.

I have to know if she thought about me.

"Olivia."

"Clarke."

I pull away from that delicious space between her legs and I pull her into my lap. She wraps her legs around my waist making my cock jump between us as it's dying to get inside of her. "Did you think about me when we were apart?"

"Yes," she responds, her eyes staring into mine. I look away in fear that Olivia could see everything I'm trying to hide from her. She runs her hands up my body and cups my face making me look at her. I smile, thinking about how I thought about her every day.

Multiple times a day.

How there were days I couldn't get out of bed. How Wren had to come check in every few days to make sure I had eaten and showered.

There were days I hadn't done either.

"Did you miss me?" My mouth feels dry and it makes my voice hoarse.

"Yes," she whispers and I want to kick myself for making Olivia open up and be vulnerable with me while I'm not being honest with her.

"I'm sure I missed you," I tell her. "I missed you so fucking much."

She smiles, the tears forming in her eyes and sliding slowly down her cheeks. "I know." She rubs her nose against mine. "What's with all this heavy? I thought you were going to make love to me?"

CHAPTER
Twenty-One

Bennett

"NICE PLACE."

I watch as Olivia Warren walks around my apartment, her fingers touching everything and leaving her scent everywhere. Tonight, was our third date and despite the handsy makeout session we had on our first date…and second date, we hadn't gone much further. But the way I'm feeling, I'm ready to take things all the way tonight if she's ready. My eyes follow her around, like if I take them off of her, she might disappear. She's wearing a black dress that comes to just below her knees with heels that make her legs go on for miles. Even with the shoes, she only comes up to my shoulders and I love how short and petite she is. I run my gaze up her legs, wondering how they'd feel wrapped around my waist as I slipped in the space between them.

"I like it." I smile as she takes a sip of the red wine I'd poured her. She sets her glass on the coffee table before taking a seat on my couch, sliding her heels off and putting her feet under her behind.

Shoes off. Good sign.

I move towards the couch and sit next to her, pulling her feet into my lap and rubbing her soles. I note the white polish on her toes and press a kiss to the top of them.

"You have some sort of kinky foot fetish, Clarke?" She pulls her hair over one shoulder and twirls her fingers through it. I smile, because I think it means she's flirting with me.

Remembering her question, I shake my head. "I think I have an Olivia Warren fetish."

She cocks her head to the side. "You must say that to all the women."

"No," I tell her honestly. "Just you." I raise an eyebrow at her and she raises one back.

She studies me, her eyes looking all over me before she speaks again. "Can I ask you something?"

"Anything. I'm an open book." And that's true. I've never been as open and honest this early with someone as I've been with Olivia. I've told her about my childhood, my adolescence, my rocky relationship with my mother. All of it. We've exchanged war stories on our second date, and although she doesn't have much, I had told her about the only woman I'd dated seriously.

"Have you ever been with a black woman before?" she asks, and my eyes widen. I hadn't anticipated that this was where this conversation was going when she sat on this couch. Quite frankly I figured she'd be sitting on my dick.

"Why? Have you ever been with a white man before?" I ask her.

"Maybe." The thought makes me irate. Not that she'd been with a white man, but any man. It pisses me off that anyone has touched her before me. I suddenly feel the need to brand her so she knows...so everyone knows she's fucking off limits from now on.

"Ah, so I won't be your first." I shrug, like I'm not already planning out how I will also be her last.

"I was just curious. I didn't mean to make you uncomfortable," she says as she removes her feet from my hands and moves closer to me.

I pull her hand into mine and run my lips over her knuckles gently. "You didn't, but to your answer your question, no. I have not." I shake my head.

"My mother says that white men date black women to satisfy a deep rooted curiosity." I don't know her well enough to read the look she's giving me, but I feel like she's hiding a painful memory behind her eyes. Like someone had proven her mother correct.

"Is that what you think I'm doing?"

"I don't know yet…" She narrows her eyes at me.

"The guy you potentially dated before me…do you think he was curious?"

"Yes." She rolls her eyes. "And I don't know…when you said you had an Olivia Warren fetish, it just reminded me of something he said."

"I meant because I'm into you, Olivia. I'm thirty-three years old, I'm far past curious. I'm looking for…more than a fuck. Or something to satisfy…some kind of experiment."

She nods. "You're looking for the real thing."

"More or less."

"Someone who sets your soul on fire," she adds. She's not looking at me, she's staring straight ahead, but her hands fidget in her lap.

"What do you think that feels like?"

She turns towards me. "I guess…I guess I'll let you know when I know."

"I can tell you what it feels like," I tell her, my eyes staring at her profile, my heart recognizing the other half of it in the nervous woman next to me.

"Oh?" Her eyes shift towards mine and I can see the question in her eyes.

Who me?

I nod. "It's what happens when you can see your whole future in someone's eyes."

Her lips part and she runs her tongue along her bottom lip. "You… you've felt it?"

"Feeling it."

"Present…tense?" I nod, just before my lips touch hers.

"Fuck. Livi." I press my hand into her hair as she continues to move up and down on my cock, her lips and tongue wrapped around me so snug, I'm ready to explode down her throat. Her eyes look up at me through her thick full lashes as she pushes my dick to the back of her throat. Her eyes water and the tears start to move down her cheek as she gags slightly on the size of my cock. "Swallow, sweetheart."

She does on command, swallowing and forcing my cock down further and I swear for a minute my entire body is paralyzed under her mouth. I push harder, cupping her face. "God, you're fucking beautiful. So fucking beautiful. And mine. You want my cum in your mouth, don't you?"

She nods as she grips my thighs, pressing her nails into the skin as she continues to suck my cock. Spit trickles down my shaft and kisses the base as she pulls me out of her mouth, gripping the base and running her tongue up my length sinfully and giving me a wink before she circles the head. "Jesus, Livi. I'm going to come, put me back in your mouth."

"Beg for it," she says, as she rubs my cock along her mouth, rubbing the precum on her swollen lips like it's lipstick.

I grab her head and our eyes lock. "I should be telling *you* to beg for it. You know you want it as bad as I want to give it to you. Don't deny that you're my little cum slut." She whimpers and shuts her eyes as the filthy words I know she loves circle around her. "You've been addicted to my cock since the first time you sucked me, haven't you?" I grip her jaw as I rub my dick against her tongue and she nods. Even though I'm seconds from blowing, I pull it back out.

"You beg *me* for it." She swallows slowly and digs her nails more into my thighs, causing my cock to twitch. Pre-cum is forming at the head and it feels like my dick is pulsing faster than my heart is racing. "Tell me how bad you want it."

FORGET ME *Not*

"I want it," she whispers. "Please."

"What was that?"

"PLEASE!" She screams as she grips my cock, squeezing hard and just before she puts her mouth back on me, I stop her, putting my hand over her mouth and she looks up at me curiously.

"Tell me you love me first."

I can't see her mouth but I can see her eyes that tell me she's smiling behind my hand. I pull it away from her mouth and sure enough, there's one on her lips. "I love you, Clarke."

She doesn't wait for my reply before her lips are wrapped around me again. I put my hands on either side of her head, pumping into her mouth so she kisses the base of my cock each time I thrust. I'm seconds from exploding when I feel a hand on my testicles. "Fuck, Olivia, I'm going to come." I pull on her hair, tugging it gently as I erupt down her throat. "Fuck fuck fuuuuuuck." I groan as she continues to worship my cock just as she always has. I don't know how long I'm coming, but at some point, I soften and twitch in her mouth as she lets me fall from between her lips. I'm on her in an instant, pulling her up my body and pushing her deep into the blankets. My lips are on hers, tasting me on her tongue and it makes my dick pulse between us despite having just come. "I should have come in your pussy." I growl as I bite down on her neck.

"There will be plenty of time for that." She smiles as she pushes me onto my back and snuggles into my side. "Can we go back to my apartment tonight?"

"Not feeling it here?"

"Well...none of my stuff is here." She sits up and runs a hand through her hair. "I need to do something about this," she says pointing at her hair that looks a little bigger than usual.

"You look beautiful and just fucked." I smirk.

She blinks her eyes at me several times and I chuckle at my wife's very regimented hair care routine. "You were married to me for seven years, and you don't have silk pillowcases?" She points at the head of my bed. "And how do you expect me to shower here without shower caps? Hello?" I chuckle at her rant. "I don't even want to know what kind of hair products you might have in there." She gets up and makes her way over to my closet.

"I didn't want to use anything that smelled like you," I tell her, and I immediately curse myself for saying something that would tell her what I've been feeling the last six months. "I mean I guess," I correct.

She comes out of my closet and I breathe a sigh of relief that maybe she didn't hear me. I note she's wearing one of my button ups covering her gorgeous body and I frown. "Not that it doesn't turn me the fuck on seeing you in my clothes, but why are you getting dressed? I'll be ready to fuck you again in ten minutes."

"Because I'm starving and I was going to see what you had… while I waited for you to be ready to go again." She smirks as she makes her way out of the room. I'm pulling on my briefs just as my doorbell rings. I frown, wondering who it could be as I make my way into the living room behind her. Olivia looks at me and I shrug, just as confused at who would be at my apartment before 9 AM when I haven't even been staying here. I look into the peephole and my blood runs cold at who my visitor is and look down at Olivia who's looking up at me in question.

Who is it? she mouths.

I'm sorry, I mouth back and she pushes me slightly out of the way and stands up on her tiptoes to look out of the peephole. She lands back, flat footed and glares at me before looking down at herself. She looks at me, who's bare chested in only a pair of briefs and I notice her eyes rove over my tattoos, my six pack, and the muscles in my arms. She bites her lip before running her tongue over it. I grip her jaw in response and she looks up at me guiltily having just been caught ogling me. I push her quietly against the door, putting my finger to my lips to warn her to stay quiet. I raise the shirt she's wearing, and stick my hand between her legs, running my fingers between her folds. She watches in fascination as I dip two fingers inside her collecting her juices that have formed from sucking my cock, rubbing my finger over her clit causing her to whimper. I pull my fingers from her cunt and press them to my lips, running my tongue over them and tasting her arousal. When I remove them from my mouth, I tap her bottom lip and push my fingers in her mouth. She sucks, moving her lips up and down my index finger and middle finger like it were my cock and I wink.

"Now," I whisper low in her ear. "I want you to answer the door, in nothing but my shirt, with the taste of my cock and your cunt on your tongue and deal with her." I press a kiss to the space behind her ear and take a step back meeting her wide eyes. "I am *yours*, Olivia Clarke." I back away from her before turning towards my room, I call over my shoulder. "Make sure she's clear on that this time."

CHAPTER
Twenty-Two

Olivia

I FOLLOW BENNETT WITH MY EYES AS HE LEAVES THE ROOM, MY eyes trained on his perfectly sculpted ass and muscular back. The veins on his legs protrude with every step and his arms flex sexily as if he's doing it on purpose. I'm completely turned on by the minor assault on my sex and my heart and mind are completely fucked by his words. He wants *me* to handle Amanda?

I let out a breath, trying to calm myself down and mentally prepare myself for dealing with his mistress.

Ex-mistress.

I press my hand to the lock, turning it shakily before taking a deep breath and opening the door.

Blue eyes widen the second she sees me and I watch with satisfaction as she runs her gaze up the length of my bare legs. I cross my hands in front of my chest and lean against the door jamb. "Is there a reason you're here?" I'm not confrontational. Far from it, and I'd encountered it very few times in my life. I'm well liked and I'm patient and mild-tempered. Until it comes to this woman.

I hate her even though I know *she* didn't cheat on me. I know that Bennett is more to blame and I don't want to be that wife that blames the other woman, but I hate her. I can't help it. She makes me crazy. Maybe a part of it is pure jealousy. She's perfect and gorgeous and blonde and probably could give him a baby that Bennett's mother would love.

She scoffs and narrows her cold hard gaze as she flicks a hair over her shoulder. "I would like to speak with Bennett, *my boyfriend*."

I raise an eyebrow at her. "My *husband* is unavailable; can I take a message? And…furthermore, how did you even know we were here? He's been staying at *our* apartment with *me*." I give her my most saccharine smile and scrunch my nose slightly.

"It's not your business."

My heart rate spikes, as my adrenaline rushes and I feel my patience withering. "Oh, but it is because I'm his wife, and *you're* not."

I can sense her irritation as she presses her hands to her hips. "He's going to remember. He's going to remember *me*."

"And then what? You think he's going to leave me? Oh, you're right because when he remembers, he'll just be reminded that he's spent six months trying to get me back. And you were just…there. You were a mistake, Amanda. A bump in the road. And while the problem in our marriage that this bump has caused may never completely go away," I take a step forward, "*You* will."

Surprisingly, she doesn't take a step back. Instead, her eyes narrow and her jaw clenches before she unleashes the jealous statement I should have been better prepared to hear. "He doesn't love you," she grits out, and I'll admit it stings. It's a pain in my chest that I wasn't expecting. I know she's goading me, but I also know that she had gotten to know Bennett a bit better than I did the past six months.

Had he fallen out of love with me?
No.

He was begging to reconcile and for me to give him another chance even before the accident.

Call her bluff, Liv.

"You don't even believe that." I shake my head and prepare to unleash my feelings on this woman who thought she had a chance with my husband. "This is so sad. Let me guess, how your so-called relationship with Bennett went. You met him at a bar while he was drunk and alone and upset. You had a couple drinks, you professed to know exactly what he was going through. You were a shoulder to cry on. 'I get you, Bennett, *she* doesn't appreciate you.' And while that's not your business, I'll give you that. Because I didn't appreciate him and that's on me. So, while completely hammered on one too many tequila shots. Did you guys have tequila? He blacks out really easily on that." She huffs and I put my hand up. "I digress. You guys hit it off or whatever, you go home and I'm sure he regales you of stories about me, good or bad," I shrug, "but all the while, you're the good friend, that's listening and understanding and blah blah blah." I roll my eyes. "And then you make your move—"

"He kissed me." And the smirk on her face, tells me that not only is she satisfied with the dig, but that it's probably true.

I pause and my pulse quickens in response to the fury building. "Fine. He kissed you. I'm not denying that you fucked my husband. I'm denying that he felt anything more for you than a place to put his dick and someone to stroke his ego. Move on, Amanda, because *this* is embarrassing. If Bennett wanted you, he'd be with you," I snap, much harsher than I've ever spoken to anyone. She looks like she's about to say something in response so I cut her off. "We don't have children and I was more than fair in our divorce settlement, it would be easy for us to proceed with our separation and you two could ride off into the sunset." I lean back against the frame and shrug my shoulders.

"He doesn't want to…and neither do I." I pause. "Now, it would behoove you to stay away from my man and to not ever show your face here again."

She huffs, and I can see the tears forming before she swallows them down. For a brief, and I do mean brief second, I feel bad. I feel bad for the woman who may have been made drunken promises or maybe even sober ones. I know Bennett loves me, but I'd walked away, and maybe he would have kept her around had this accident not happened.

My mind goes to the letter in the safe, the letter he'd written while he was supposedly dating Amanda. To the wedding ring he was wearing around his neck and the shrine to me he still has on his desk. He was never going to want more with her, even if he never got me back. Their relationship had an expiration date one way or the other, and *that* had nothing to do with me.

"It wasn't just sex, Olivia. Would he introduce me to Caroline otherwise?"

I did forget about that little anecdote. Why were her and Caroline so fucking friendly? Caroline didn't like any fucking one except Bennett.

Add that to another question I'll probably never have answered.

"You know I'm right." She takes my silence as defeat, and I am quick to tell her differently.

"No."

"We do yogalates together. She loves me. We have lunch. She says I'm good for Bennett."

It burns, hearing that she's received the approval from my mother-in-law I've spent years yearning for. "I've never been able to understand Caroline's issue with me, but trust me her liking you is just another way for her to stick it to me. You could be literally anyone."

She frowns and I know she's getting frustrated that she's been unable to rile me up. "He's going to do this to you again," she whispers as she shakes her head. "You're stupid to take him back. He'll come running back to me once he remembers how bored he was with you," she bites.

Her words, which sound an awful lot like my subconscious, slither up my spine and burrow into my brain and I wish I could wipe the smug look off her face in the same way I destroyed her car.

Don't let her see you crack.

"I highly doubt that. Because *no one* can fuck that man like I can," I tell her before I back out of the doorway and close the door in her face without another word.

I lean against the door, my body succumbing to the exhaustion of this conversation as I sink to the floor. Hands wrap around my wrist, holding me upright and then I'm in his arms. I note that he's put on sweatpants and I press my face into his bare chest as the tears I've been holding back start to slide down my face. I open my eyes and the first thing I see is the tattoo with our wedding anniversary and it makes me cry even harder.

"I'm sorry. I'm so fucking sorry," he tells me as he sits on the couch with me in his lap. "She's wrong," he whispers into my hair as he rocks me gently. "I'll never do this to you again. I won't take this second chance for granted. Never." He grips my chin and we lock eyes, though I can barely see him through my tears. I do my best to blink them away, but it only causes a fresh batch of them to form. "I love you. I've always loved you, Olivia."

I sniffle and wipe my eyes. "You don't know how you felt the past six months. Maybe you did love her…"

"No. Absolutely not," he says immediately.

"You can't say that for sure…" I trail off and he swallows hard before looking away from me.

"I know but…I can't imagine loving anyone other than you." His eyes are so honest, and I feel like he's been stripped and laid bare for me to see everything. Bennett has always been honest with me and I know he truly believes that I'm the only woman he's ever loved.

"I just...I wish I knew more about your relationship with her. Was it more?" I look up at him knowing he can't answer that question.

He wraps his arms around me and pulls me under his chin allowing his stubble to graze my forehead. "Can you still forgive me, if you never get that answer?"

I pull back. "I'm prepared for that, I just...I wonder if we can really move forward if..."

His brows furrow together. "If...?"

"If we never really work through the past six months."

"Livi...can't we just forget it and try and move on?"

Seriously? Does he think it's that simple? "Forget it? Sure, *you* can. But what about me? How am I supposed to just forget that we broke up?" I move out of his lap and stand up.

"Baby..."

"No, that's not how life works. I can't just sweep it under the rug and pretend it didn't happen. I still don't know why I struggle getting and staying pregnant. Eventually, I'll need those answers. What happens...then?"

"We take things one step at a time. There are other avenues to have children, baby."

"I just think...it'll be hard to navigate if we ever find ourselves in a situation like this again, if we don't work through it now."

"We won't." He stands up and rests his hands on my shoulders squeezing gently. "You and me, remember? There will never be anyone else again." He leans down and his scent surrounds me. The scent that spoke to me on the most primal level. A raw masculinity that has the space between my legs screaming for him. "You promised we would never be apart." His hair falls over his forehead and I push it back, running my hand down his cheek.

"I'm not running," I whisper. "I'm here, I'm not going anywhere." I run my hand down my body and over his shirt I'm wearing, unbuttoning it slowly and letting it slide down my naked body. I feel a surge of confidence as he drinks me in, his eyes devouring me, zeroing in on my sex. The hunger in his eyes is evident and I take a step back.

"You've never looked at anyone the way you look at me." His eyes snap to mine and stare at me curiously. "You used to look at me like I was the center of your world. Like nothing else mattered the second I walked into a room."

"I still look at you that way. You *are* the center of my world."

I run my fingers down his chest and abdomen, grazing his tattoos, and pulling on the waistband of his sweatpants, tugging him towards me. A smirk finds his face when I push his pants to his ankles. "Take them off."

He does as I ask, pulling off his sweats and his briefs and leaving him completely naked. His cock springs free, hard and powerful and my mouth waters at how unbelievably sexy my husband is. "What do you want?" he murmurs and when I look up, he's staring at me like he's ready to break me in half.

"All of you."

"You have me. All of me, Olivia."

I grab his hand, pulling him back towards his bedroom. I feel his hand graze down my back and cup my ass, gripping it gently. "Sit." I point to the bed. He does as he's told and I climb into his lap, staring at him straight on as I slide down agonizingly slow onto his length. "Fuck." I let out a breath when he bottoms out, allowing him to be deeper than usual. My legs are wrapped around his back with his wrapped around mine as he lifts me slowly up and down on his cock.

"So fucking perfect." He groans as he grips my forearms. "I need this."

"Me too."

His hand reaches between us and rubs my clit gently and he chuckles in my ear when I quiver in his arms. "I still can't get over that you're bare. I feel like I'm going to come the second I touch your pussy. You're so smooth, your cunt feels like fucking silk." He growls before he sinks his teeth into my shoulder. "I know you're calling the shots, but I think you want me to take over, don't you?"

I do love when Bennett takes control. He's dominant and aggressive and sexy as hell and I love how he shaped our sex life from the start. He'd made me crave him physically, mentally, and emotionally, and our lovemaking has been some of the most soul shattering experiences of my life. I nod and he grips my jaw. "Use your words," he commands.

"Yes." I breathe out. I don't call him *Sir* or *Master* or *Daddy*, although we have gone down those roads a time or two before, but I loved how he asserted his dominance without making me completely submissive.

I can feel each ridge of his cock sliding out of me as he pushes me slowly to my back, separating my legs. He drags his tongue from the bottom of my pussy to the top, flicking my clit. I cry out, as the feeling sends a jolt of electricity through me. I look down as he continues his trail, licking the top of my mound and dragging up my body. He swirls his tongue around my belly button before giving me a gentle bite and pulling back.

"You're the sweetest thing I've ever tasted."

He kneels between my legs, stroking his cock that's slick and glistening with my arousal. He moves closer to me, sliding his cock through my folds and rubbing against my clit but not penetrating me. He opens me up with one hand, spreading my folds and exposing my sex to him as he continues to rub his cock between my legs. My body begins to build under his assault, as he switches to tapping my clit with his cock.

The throb between my legs is almost too much, and I feel like I can't breathe. "God, Clarke."

I look down and see the trail of cum connecting us each time he pulls away and I watch enthralled as he continues to tap my clit faster. I clench every time his dick touches my clit and my toes begin to curl in preparation of what's to come.

"Are you going to come like this? Is your pretty pussy going to come all over my cock? From it giving your cunt little kisses?" I've noticed his movements have gotten more erratic and his chest heaves with every rub against the swollen muscle between my legs. His cock pulses and I see the precum flowing faster from the tip, making me believe that he's on the precipice of coming as well.

I nod, as my body struggles to take short quick breaths. "I'm there…" I whisper.

As if it were a command, Bennett slides inside of me in one fluid motion just as I begin to fall over the edge. He's still on his knees as he continues to pound into me. Pulling one of my legs over his shoulder he stares down at me with so much intensity it makes my orgasm go on forever. I let my eyes flutter closed as the euphoria takes over. "Fuck, Olivia. You make me feel so fucking good baby. Take everything. All of it," I vaguely hear him say as I feel myself floating away.

I feel his cock swelling inside of me making the fit even tighter than usual and I know he's coming hard and fast. As the high of my orgasm wanes and I begin to float back to Earth, I briefly remember that we haven't been using any type of protection and I'm not on birth control.

I feel his lips a mere inch above mine, breathing against me and when I open my eyes, he's staring into them. I wrap my arms and legs around him, keeping him still and inside of me. "We haven't been using condoms…"

"We're married, why would we?" He freezes and pulls back, cocking his head at me. "Did you not with…"

"Oh!" My eyes widen at his words. "No…Bennett," I grab his face and bring his lips to mine, ghosting my lips across his and giving him a smile. "You're the only man I've ever…not…" He nods before I finish my sentence but the thoughts make my blood runs cold. *Did he use protection with Amanda?* "I guess I don't really know for sure about you…but… I guess I was just thinking it was possible that I could get pregnant." I bite my lip and he pulls back, sliding out of me and sitting on his knees again.

"Pregnant?" he whispers.

"Yes, you know when two people have sex and then…"

He looks away from me and grits his teeth like something is troubling him. I sit up and touch his arm and he swallows hard. "I wasn't thinking…I mean…"

"Hey, what is it?" I press my lips to his shoulder and he wraps an arm around me before pressing his lips to my temple.

"This is what caused so many of our problems before and I'm just wondering if you're ready to go back down this road right away?"

"Well, no…I don't know." I tell him, and I'm honestly not sure. I'd suffered through so much loss already, and I don't want to jump back down this rabbit hole without having the facts about what my body can handle. "But if we're not, then maybe we should consider using condoms or I can go back on the pill…"

"Maybe we need to go see someone?" He pulls me into his lap and I see the sincerity radiating from him as his gaze locks with mine. "I don't want to put us through," he pauses, "whatever we went through. I can't bear to go through it again. I can't lose you again."

CHAPTER
Twenty-Three

Bennett

I AM SUCH A FUCKING ASSHOLE.

It's been a week and I haven't told Olivia that I have my memory back. I've just been pretending that nothing has changed. That everything is fine. Well, better than fine because Olivia and I have been inseparable in every way possible the last few days. I've tried to keep her at arms' length while I figure out how to tell her the truth, but then in my clearer head, I remembered what my wife was doing in our time apart, and I've been feeling possessive ever since.

Fucking David.

I just want some time with her before I tell her the truth. A truth which would lead to having to dig up everything that happened while we were apart. I knew talking about Amanda would hurt her, and it was the last thing I wanted to do. Amanda had truly just been a mistake. A woman I slept with in a weak moment.

More than once, my subconscious sneers.

After the initial time, that set our separation in motion, I was devastated over losing Olivia and Amanda was there. She let me use her to try and fill the void. It was wrong and stupid and pathetic, and it happened way fewer times than I'm sure

Olivia imagines, but I was drowning in self loathing and pity and frustration as well as still mourning our miscarriages and I just wanted a moment where I didn't hate myself or my life.

Amanda did provide that moment of peace.

Before the shame that came with sleeping with her overwhelmed me further.

We weren't dating or living together. I never promised her more. I called her when I was drunk and lonely and she listened to me go on about Olivia. She listened to me cry over being estranged from the other half of me. She let me be sad over everything we'd been through the past year. But I'd been transparent with her, which is why I was furious to hear what she had to say to Olivia. Not to mention saying that I loved her?

And of course, because I'm a pussy, I couldn't refute all of this yet.

I tried to tell her once a few days ago. We'd just made love and she was sleepy and warm and cuddling against my side under the low lighting of our room. The words *"I remember"* were on the tip of my tongue when I heard her whisper my name and then the gentle sound of her breathing.

I thought about waking her up and confessing everything, but I couldn't bring myself to do it. I knew there was so much we had to work through once I told her I remembered everything and after six months of being apart from the other half of me, I was relishing in reconnecting.

I push a hand through my wet hair aggressively as tension builds in my body. I begin rinsing the rest of the shampoo from my hair when I sense that I'm not alone. I open my eyes, blinking them several times and see a figure on the other side of the glass. Instantly I feel the tension leaving my body. I wipe the condensation from the glass, clearing some of the fog to see Olivia leaning against the sink, giving me a sinful smirk. She's still in her clothes from work, a tight pencil skirt that had me rubbing my cock the second she left this morning and a light blue blouse that makes her skin glow. Her lips are nude, but are painted with something glossy that makes me want to shove my cock between them. I open the door slightly and give her a lascivious grin as she does the same to my naked body. I watch as her nipples poke through the silky fabric and I want nothing more than to suck them into my mouth. "Why don't you quit staring and get your gorgeous ass in here?" I ask her as I run my hand up and down my shaft.

She shakes her head as she bites her lip. "We're getting drinks with Lys and Wren, remember?" I groan as I shut off the water and make my way out of the shower. Drops of water fall from my body and I watch as Olivia follows the trails of water slide down and drip down my cock.

"Oh really? Because you're looking at me like you have no intentions of going anywhere tonight." I take a step closer to her and grab her jaw and rub my thumb over her pouty lips. She kisses the pad of my thumb leaving traces of her lipstick and gives me a devilish smile.

"Later, I want that…in my mouth." She reaches down, running her hand up and down my cock once before letting go and gliding out of the room like she hadn't just sent me from six to midnight.

"Tease!" I call after her as I grab a towel from the rack and wrap it around my waist. I follow her back into our bedroom and watch as she slides her skirt down her legs and pulls her blouse over her head leaving her in a tiny thong and a lace bra that she's pulling off her chest and instantly I need my hands on her. It's as if I can't get enough of her after the six months of being apart.

"Olivia." Her name rumbles in my chest and it sounds like a low growl as it leaves my lips. She yelps and turns around and

I'm on her instantly, pulling her into a deep kiss as my hand finds her nipple. "Call Alyssa and tell them we're going to be a little late."

"But..."

"*Now.*"

"So are you ready for the *Hamilton Inquisition*?" Olivia asks as we sit in the back of our Uber.

I chuckle, thinking about our well meaning but very nosy friends that are bound to have a lot of questions about Olivia and me getting back together. *Especially Alyssa.* I sigh thinking about the bodily harm I'm sure she'll threaten if I hurt her best friend again. "If you can handle Alyssa, I can handle Wren."

"Oh God." She laughs as she rubs her forehead. "Alyssa means well, Bennett. She cares about me."

"So do I, baby," I tell her. "No one needs to protect you from me." She twists her mouth and I catch the glistening of her eyes. I pull her closer to me and press a kiss to the back of her ear. "I'll protect your heart better this time, I promise."

She looks up at me and kisses my lips gently, sliding her tongue against mine once before pulling away. "I believe you, Clarke. I trust you."

We beat Alyssa and Wren to the restaurant despite our slight delay because those two were notoriously twenty minutes late for everything where Olivia and I were always five minutes early. I slide her jacket off of her and take a minute to let my eyes rove over her. She was wearing a black dress that falls off her shoulders and comes down just below her knees, with the sexiest pair of heels that I can't stop picturing wrapped around my waist as I fuck her later.

She takes her seat and I move my chair slightly closer to hers so I can touch her. Just like it's always been. If Olivia and I are in the same room we are touching in some way. It's as if our connection is magnetic somehow. I press my lips to the bare skin of her shoulder, letting my tongue dart out to taste her and she squirms in her seat which makes me hard in my slacks. Turning Olivia on does nothing but turn my cock to granite, as if it knows it needs to be inside her. "You are the sexiest woman in this restaurant. Every man in here wants to be me right now." I twirl one of her black wavy strands around my finger before tucking it behind her ear.

I look around the room and sure enough I catch the gaze of a few men raking their eyes appreciatively over my wife. She looked breathtakingly gorgeous and I can't resist the smug grin from sliding across my face telling them, *she's mine.* I'm no stranger to putting men in their place and after being separated, I'm more than ready to stake my claim over my wife if someone looks at her sideways.

She turns towards me and immediately her hand finds her hair. "And you'd do well to remember that," she sasses and pecks my lips. I'm about to respond with a cheeky comment of my own when I hear a gasp. I turn towards the source to see Alyssa staring at us, with her jaw almost on the floor and Wren staring at us with the largest grin on his face.

"Oh My God." She darts around the table and pulls Olivia into her arms. "What? How? When?" Her eyes are wide and I'm fairly certain she hasn't blinked once since she approached the table.

"One question at a time, babe." Wren chuckles as they take the seats across from us.

"You're kissing, you're...clearly fucking," she says as she looks around the restaurant. "Okay, I need a drink." Her eyes find mine and then move back to Olivia. "Liv."

"Lys," She gives her a pointed look, which I know means *now is not the time*, "everything's fine."

"How did this happen? It's been like two weeks."

"We reconnected," I interject. This was what I was afraid of. Alyssa getting in my wife's mind and making her listen to reason. Reason being, I had hurt Olivia. I may not have single handedly ruined our marriage, but I was certainly the final nail in our coffin. Olivia knew that. But I also know that she and I have been shut off from the outside world in this carnal bubble, and Alyssa could be just the person to pop it.

"How can you reconnect when you don't even remember what caused the *disconnect* in the first place?" *And this is where things were about to get messy.*

"Lys, baby, now isn't the time. Let's just be happy that our best friends are working towards reconciling." Wren rubs her back in an attempt to rein in her temper, but I can see she's not prepared to let this go.

She opens her mouth to continue when our server interrupts, and I think a silent thank you for the intrusion. After we've gotten our drinks, the table is tense and quiet as Alyssa stares at us over the rim of her glass of her vodka martini eyeing us. She sets her glass down, and some of the liquid sloshes out with the force.

"Do you know what you did to her?"

"Alyssa..." My arm is still resting on the back of Olivia's chair so I feel her tense next to me.

I clear my throat before setting down the Hendricks and lime I'd ordered much to Wren's irritation over consuming alcohol in my 'condition.' "I do, Alyssa, and I very much appreciate you having Olivia's best interest at heart, but I do need you to back off."

"Easy for you to say, you think everything is perfect between you two."

"Olivia has been very clear on what happened between us." My eyes flit to Wren, urging him to help but he just narrows his gaze slightly at me before turning to Olivia. He puts his drink to his lips and I scowl at the thought that he is literally *no* help.

"Really? Because I doubt she knows why you stayed with that God awful skank." She snorts. "It's certainly not like *you* do."

"Alyssa. Bathroom." Olivia stands, and I reluctantly let her go, though I grab her hand as she tries to leave the table and tug her closer to me as I stand up as well, and press my lips to hers. It's not an obscene kiss, but it's still full of the passion our kisses always have. It still crackles between us when we pull apart. Her eyes flutter open and a dreamy smile floats across her face. "What was that for?" she breathes out.

"I've never needed a reason to kiss you." I hold her chin between my thumb and index finger before pressing another kiss to the corner of her mouth. "Go," I whisper, and she ushers Alyssa away.

Wren raises an eyebrow at me and I raise one back. "What is your problem?"

"Nothing." He shrugs.

"What is it, Hamilton. You've been looking at me weird all night? What the fuck?"

He looks over my shoulder and scans the restaurant before leaning forward slightly. "You're different."

I narrow my gaze, wondering what he's getting at. "Different?"

He shakes his head. "We've been friends for how long now?"

"I don't know, Wren. A hundred years?"

"Right." He chuckles. "I know you almost as well as Liv does. But I certainly knew you better in the six months you guys were apart."

"Okay?"

"It's just funny…" He takes a sip of his drink and points at me. "That you ordered the drink you didn't start drinking until after you and Liv separated."

My heart slams into my chest. "What?"

"I took you out one night, one of the many nights I let you drink yourself into a stupor and all but carried your sorry ass home. You went on and on about how you and Olivia used to make old fashioned drinks together and you couldn't order them anymore. You had to try something new. Under any other circumstances, I may not have remembered something like that. But I was sober, and you proceeded to throw up all over the men's room later that night."

I'm quiet, letting his words sink in because I don't want to confirm the truth, but I'm also unsure how I can deny what he's saying.

"Are you just never going to tell her?" His eyes are hard, and for the first time in months, I can see the disappointment in his eyes. The scolding. The anger. He shakes his head and puts on a smile just as I hear familiar voices just behind me.

"Miss me?" I hear in my ear before she takes her seat and I nod, the words failing me.

"Liv and I think we should go to *Envy*," Alyssa says as she downs her martini.

I look at Olivia, cocking my head to the side. "Now?"

She nods and the second she bursts into giggles, I wonder if they stopped off at the bar on the way from the bathroom. I lean forward and press my lips to hers, sliding my tongue through her lips and instantly taste the tequila that is not on the table. When I pull back, she gives me a sheepish look knowing she's guilty and I shake my head. "Everything okay?" My eyes float to Alyssa and then back to Olivia and they both nod.

"Yes, we just want to dance." Olivia smiles and leans forward, whispering in my ear and slowly sliding her hand up my thigh. "And you know how I get after I drink tequila." Her lips and teeth graze my ear before sliding back in her seat.

Well damn.

CHAPTER
Twenty-Four

Bennett

ENVY IS A NIGHTCLUB LOCATED ON THE UPPER EAST SIDE known for its rooftop that looks over the city with the best view of the Empire State Building. I don't foresee us making our way up with the weather ticking a degree cooler with each passing minute, but I wouldn't be surprised if Alyssa and Olivia have the wild idea to go up there for a photo once they're drunker. We make our way down the long hallway and I don't miss the way Alyssa's eyes flit to me every once in a while, making me wonder if Wren had shared his hypothesis.

His very correct hypothesis.

Or if she's just feeling skeptical for Olivia.

We enter the main bar area, and I smile remembering how many nights the four of us ended up here. The lights are low and my eyes scan the perimeter looking to see if any of the red booths are available, but with it being a Friday night, I see the familiar reserved signs perched on top of all of them. I lean down grazing Olivia's ear and she visibly shivers. "Do you want me to get us a table?"

She turns in my arms and I can see the excitement in her chocolate eyes. *God, she's fucking beautiful.*

"No, I want to dance!" She grabs my hand pulling me

towards the dance floor, moving through the hordes of people. I'm not going to lie, being almost forty I'm not always thrilled about going to these types of bars, but for Olivia, I'd do anything, and the way she's shaking that delectable ass of hers as we move through the crowd makes me more than pleased to be here. "We should have gotten a drink first, but I love this song." I chuckle thinking about my wife's obsession with Beyoncé as I grip her hips, pulling her towards me and holding her ass against my groin, *hard*.

I push her hair to the side exposing her neck and let my tongue dart out to taste the sweat clinging to her skin already. She sways to the seductive beat, pushing harder against me and running her hands up her body and behind my neck. I grip her hips harder, holding her as close as I can to me, my chest pressed directly into her back. I briefly wonder if she had more shots than I initially thought for her to be grinding this obscenely against me, but to be honest, I don't give a fuck.

It has been so long since I've held her like this, since I've felt her soft curves pressed against me as we grind on the dance floor. She drops her hand, bending over, dropping her body completely, her ass never leaving my dick before moving back up. She spins around and puts her hands behind my neck, pressing her body flush against mine and I push my leg between hers, letting her rub her pussy against me and I'm grateful her dress isn't too short. I grab her ass anyway, both in an attempt to keep her dress in place and to keep her pinned to me as she continues to hump my leg. Her eyes are slightly glazed and dilated and staring straight at me as she continues to move to the sultry song.

I lean down, my lips hovering just above hers as my fingers dig into her hips. "You're dancing like a little slut, Olivia. You must want me to fuck you here."

She bites her bottom lip, her eyes dancing with excitement, and I recall all of the times we defiled a bathroom in a club when neither of us could wait to be home after simulating sex on the dance floor and taking too many tequila shots. "What can I say? I'm *drunk in love.*" A wicked smile plays at her lips at the fact that it's the song that's playing and I run my nose down the side of her face, pressing my lips to the base of her throat.

"Are you wet for me?" The song is loud and so is the bar, but it doesn't stop us from having a conversation and she nods like she's heard every word loud and clear.

"Touch me and find out."

I pull back and look down at her, looking at where we're pressed together, knowing that no one would know if I touched her. If I ran my hand along her slit I knew to be dripping for me. I lick my lips, and she grips my jacket with both hands, tightening her hold. "Touch my pussy, Clarke. Feel how my clit pulses. Feel how I tremble when you touch me."

Fuck. Me.

I slide my hand between us and down her body, grazing her full breasts and between her legs feeling the wet satin fabric at the apex of her thighs. I rub her slit and she lets her head fall back as the song blends into another, her hips moving against my fingers in perfect rhythm with the song.

Her sex is wet, soaking my finger and probably my thigh that she's still grinding on. I pull at her panties before letting it snap against her sex and she shivers in my arms. Her eyes fall on mine as she bites her lip, a look that could still bring me to my knees and I debate doing it now in the middle of the club.

"Shit, Olivia." I drop my head into the crook of her neck, inhaling her sweet scent. "Do you want to dance or should I take you to the bathroom?"

"I want to come first."

"Okay." I go to pull my hand away when she holds it in place.

"No, I want to come here." She smiles and I look around, frowning.

"You've lost your mind if you think I'm letting anyone see you fall apart, it's bad enough they can tell you're turned on," I growl, though a part of me is turned on at the idea of making her come so publicly.

"No one is looking at me."

My eyes dart around the room, and while everyone appears to be in their own world, I do meet the gaze of a few men *again*, taking in the woman grinding her body against mine.

Their eyes wanting, their lustful gazes feasting on my woman.

I glare at one in particular before yanking Olivia's hair back and capturing her lips to make a point that she belongs to me. I press my finger to her clit, rubbing the fabric against the pulsing muscle and she groans in my mouth.

She pulls away and nips at my chin. "Close," she mumbles against my skin. My cock is painfully hard, pressing against my slacks trying to break its way out to get inside of Olivia.

"Fuck, I can smell how wet you are."

"And you'll taste it later."

And this is the woman I married. A confident, sexual siren that is vocal about what she wants every time.

"Come now, first," I demand. "Come all over my fingers," I tell her as I slide beneath her panties, rubbing my fingers through her smooth cunt. Her sex clenches, sucking me in deeper and it's taking everything in me not to throw her over my shoulder and run for the nearest bathroom. "That's my girl." I grin as I feel the beginning of her orgasm. The song has sped up, everyone moving faster to the beat, but Olivia and I are still almost frozen in place, moving slowly as I make love to her with my hand.

"Oh my God, Clarke!" she cries out and I run my hand up flicking her clit before giving it a light pinch and she explodes. "Holy shit." Her eyes are squeezed together, her full lips parted and I'm ready to come at the sight of her. Her skin is slick with sweat, her curls, wilder and more untamed and I know she's seconds from putting it up. My eyes dart to my wrist, remembering how I used to wear one of her hair ties around it when we went out in case she needed it. I know one isn't there, and I frown thinking about all the times in the last six months I haven't been able to take care of her.

"Hey, why the face?" She smiles, pressing her hand to my cheek as I slide my fingers out of her. "You just made me come. Pretty hard, I might add."

I push my fingers through my lips, swirling my tongue around them and savoring the taste of her. "I was just thinking about all I've missed this past year." I shake my head. "But this isn't the conversation for the dance floor."

"You won't miss anything else?" Her lips are still parted and I see her tongue peeking through to wet her bottom lip.

"Nothing could keep me away from you," I tell her.

She smiles before something catches her attention behind me because she frowns and instantly I'm wondering what's caused her grief. I go to turn when she grabs my face, pulling my lips down to hers and crushing them together. "Let's go find Lys and Wren and grab a drink?"

Olivia

You have GOT to be kidding me.

Fury runs through my veins, goading the very drunk girl into potentially causing a scene should the opportunity arise. I knew I shouldn't have taken two back to back tequila shots with

Alyssa on top of the whiskey I had, but I knew Alyssa needed to calm down, and alcohol had the power to make her more bubbly and not ask so many fucking questions.

So now I'm drunk and staring down my husband's ex-mistress from across the room. She's not looking at me, but we've locked eyes several times as I dare her to approach us. I down the shot that the four of us take before Bennett hands me a glass of water. I stare up at him in question and he raises an eyebrow at me asking me to test him. "You just came all over my hand in the middle of the dance floor. Drink the water, Olivia, or I'm not fucking you here."

"Good one." I snort and take a sip of the water he handed me. I'm not sure if she's staring at us but I wouldn't put it past her, so I decide to give her something to look at. "You know you love fucking me in clubs. You always have." I take a long sip before setting it on the bar, grateful that Wren and Alyssa had saved some space for us. I run my fingers up his chest and push him against the bar just as another song comes on. I begin moving against him again and his arms wrap around me, spinning me around and pushing me forward so I'm bent almost completely over. I hear Alyssa cheer and I know she's probably only a second from doing the same against Wren and sure enough, when I look over, she's pulling him towards the dance floor.

I want to stay in sight of Amanda, so I continue to grind against him. He pulls me flush against his chest and drops kisses to my bare shoulder. "Fuck, I love you."

I melt under his words. The orgasm. His promise of what's to come. His protective nature. His possessiveness. It's all too much. I'm about to turn around to look at him when she's close. *Much closer.*

She's wearing a bright red dress, her blonde hair pulled into a topknot, her lips painted almost the exact color as her dress with heels almost as high as mine. Her breasts are on display and lifted higher and for a second I wish mine sat as perky as hers do.

Small boobed bitches always have the perkiest tits, I swear.

I ignore my subconscious, knowing my husband loves my breasts. I don't think Bennett has even noticed what's about to happen the way his lips are trailing over my skin. "I'm ready when you are." He groans in my ear. "You're killing me in this damn dress. I'm seconds from sitting you on top of this bar and sticking my head under it."

My knees shake and he tightens his grasp. My body is on the verge of explosion with all of the feelings coursing through me.

Lust. Anger. Jealousy. Possession. Fear.

I'm somewhere between wanting my husband to fuck me and wanting to attack the woman he's also fucked. My heart is racing and I feel a bead of sweat trickle down my neck, that Bennett must notice because I feel his tongue lapping up the moisture. "Clarke…" I start and then she's ten steps away.

Five.

Two.

"Bennett, we need to talk," her voice yells over the music, but she's close enough that we can hear her clearly. His head snaps up away from me, and while I can't see his face, I know it's one of disgust.

"What the fuck?"

"You won't talk to me!" she screeches.

"Some would take that as a sign," I snarl and her blue eyes dart to mine. Hatred floods her features and as much as I'm not proud of it, the look on my face matches.

She swirls her straw around her drink before taking a sip, staring at my husband seductively and I almost lose it. His hands tighten around me and pulls me harder against him, keeping me in place. *Trust me, I'm not moving.*

"I wasn't talking to *you*. I was talking to Bennett. I'd like to talk to him without *you* around." She looks at me and I can't even stop the growl that rumbles in my chest.

"First of all, watch your attitude. Second of all, there's nothing to talk about, Amanda. It's over. We're done. I believe my wife advised you to stay away from me. I believe you should listen to her."

"You told me you were over her. That you loved me and wanted to be with me. She's brainwashing you, and it's not what you want! *I'm* who you want, Bennett."

"False," he grits out. "And I don't know what kind of bullshit fairytale you're living in where you think I ever told you I loved you, or that I was over my wife. You're using my memory loss to your advantage because she doesn't know what happened between us, but you and I both know that I never told you I loved you." He's been leaning against the bar, but he stands straight and moves me slightly to stand next to me, but slides his hand into mine, lacing our fingers. "I fucked you, I don't deny that, and it was the worst mistake I ever made because it cost me the love of my life. But now she's taken me back when I don't fucking deserve her." I gasp and the tears well in my eyes at his words. He must have heard my gasp because he turns to look at me. "I don't deserve you, Olivia, but I'm going to spend the rest of my life trying."

I smile before turning back to Amanda with the smuggest smile on my lips.

"We had sex more than just the one time, Bennett."

He turns back to her and grits his teeth. "Three times." And my eyes blink up at him in shock, as it's the first time I've ever heard a number.

My head is swimming, but even in my fuzzy brain, I wonder how he knows that.

There's no way he has his memory back, he would have told me something like that. Maybe Wren filled him in?

"You were there, Amanda. When I was at my lowest. I shouldn't have used you the way I did, and I'm sorry. But you knew what our relationship was. I never made any kind of promises to you. I was still holding onto hope that I'd get Olivia back, and I know that makes me a shitty person, to sleep with you while I'm still pining after my wife, but I've never professed to be innocent in all of this. You'd show up at my apartment and we'd get drunk and I'd talk about Olivia. Don't you dare try and pretend like it was something else."

Her eyes dart to me and then back to Bennett before she purses her lips. "You don't remember anything."

"Oh? Tell me I'm a liar, then."

I sway slightly, the effects of that last shot starting to kick in.

Wait...he's bluffing? Right?

Definitely bluffing.

But she's not saying much...?

I lift my hair off my neck, suddenly feeling like I'm overheating and I fan myself slightly. The movement attracts Bennett's attention and he frowns as he looks at me. "What's wrong?"

"I just got drunker and really hot all at once," I tell him before looking back at Amanda. "Are we done here?" I bite my bottom lip. "I want you now." My eyes flit to his before I raise an eyebrow at Amanda. "That's right, I want my husband to take me to the bathroom and fuck me against the wall." I flash her a smile and she scoffs.

"Whatever. Bennett, enjoy your boring married life. One day you'll look back and remember how exciting and fun our time was and will regret not choosing me."

I try not to let the tears rush to my eyes but they do and I do everything to try and blink them away but one slides down my face.

I'm surprised to hear Bennett chuckle and when I look up he's staring daggers into Amanda. He takes a step forward and she shakes slightly before taking a step back, stumbling slightly in heels that she clearly can't walk in. "You never meant anything to me. If anything, I resented you. Or you were an extension of the resentment I felt for myself for fucking up the best thing that ever happened to me. I'll admit I enjoyed your company, though seeing this terribly ugly side of you is making me wonder just how much of the *real* you I even knew. But I was never in love with you. We had mediocre *at best* sex a few times. I never even let you spend the night. We weren't together. We weren't dating. I was using you. And I'm sorry. But I'm *not* going to let you take your anger at me out on the only person here who's done nothing wrong. Now, I do believe my wife was very clear that you needed to stay away from me. I suggest, you heed her warnings going forward." His voice is even and sinister and it sets a fire between my legs as Amanda shakes her head and turns around.

She makes it two steps before she spins back around and tosses the remainder of her drink in Bennett's face. "Asshole," she scoffs before she begins to walk away.

My mouth drops open as the remains drip from his face onto the floor and immediately I see red. I lunge after her when I feel arms wrapped around me, and I'm pulled towards a hard chest. "Ah ah ah. Not so fast," he growls in my ear, and I can smell the vodka on his face and feel it dripping onto my skin.

"What a bitch! I'm throwing my drink on her, see how she fucking likes it." I'm fuming. *Is she a fucking child? Who throws their drink in someone's face?*

Probably the same people who key their husband's mistress' car, my subconscious sneers, and I huff indignantly.

"Not worth it." He loosens his hold but still keeps a hand on me as he grabs a few napkins from the bar. I spin in his arms as he wipes his face. "I'm sorry."

"For what? Being so fucking sexy and putting her in her place?" I reach up, grabbing the napkins from him and finish removing the traces of alcohol from his face. "I am burning alive for you."

He groans as I push against him. "Baby, you're killing me."

"Take me to the bathroom," I whisper in his ear.

CHAPTER
Twenty-Five

Olivia

I'M SLAMMED AGAINST THE WALL OF THE STALL IN *Envy* AND Bennett is on me instantly. I drown out the sounds of the catcalls and cheers and chuckles coming from the outside of the stall from the men who saw us stumbling inside in a frenzy. "Clarke," I moan the second his hands find the space between my legs, the space still wet from his earlier assault.

"You drive me so fucking crazy, Livi. Jesus." His teeth nip my ear as he trails his lips down my bare skin, lowering the top of my dress, and pulling my nipple from the lacy cup. He grips my breast hard, circling the nipple with the tip of his tongue before sucking the whole thing inside. "I've been thinking about biting this fucking nipple since we left home." His teeth bite down and I cry out just as his other hand from between my legs slams down over my mouth. "I don't need everyone in this bathroom hearing what I'm doing to you," he growls. I can smell and taste my arousal on his hands and it's all too much. His lips on my breast, the smell of my arousal thick in the air. It all swirls around me like a sensual fog. His hand falls from my mouth just as he drops to his knees in front of me. My eyes flutter open and I look down at him.

"Clarke..." I protest. "I want you to fuck me, you can do this later."

"I just need a taste. One lick to tide me over." He slides my panties down my legs and sticks them into his jacket pocket before he lifts my right leg over his shoulder, opening me up and exposing my glistening pussy to his wanting mouth. He starts at my ankle, kissing the skin and my left leg wobbles slightly with all of my weight resting on it. Like always, he senses my discomfort and grips my ass holding me in place and shoots me a wink. "I've got you."

Words fail me as his lips latch onto my clit and I cry out again, uncaring that he'd previously told me to stay quiet. His tongue swirls around me, tasting my orgasm from earlier and the one forming from his assault. "I lied," he growls against me. "I need you to come on my tongue baby."

"Fuck, me too." I breathe out, wondering in what world we thought either of us would be satisfied with just one lick. I'm already close after the night we've had coupled with the shots I've downed and I feel my orgasm brewing in the base of my spine. I push my hands through his hair as I clench around him, grinding my cunt against his mouth causing the bristles from his beard to pierce my sex. I pull and he groans causing a vibration to shoot through my body. The sound and the feeling causes the orgasm to bloom faster and then I'm exploding. I slam my hand against the wall behind him to keep myself upright as I rock into his mouth, using it for leverage. "Oh my God." A giggle leaves my lips just as he sets my right leg down.

I fall back against the wall and stare down at him and immediately I feel the need to come again. The buzz from the drinks is starting to slowly fade away and the high of my husband and his sinful mouth is now intoxicating me. His hair is sticking up in all different directions from my pulling, his eyes are dark, a forest green, and burning into mine, his brow is slick with a thin layer of sweat and his mouth is covered in my orgasm. His tongue darts out to trace up my thigh and I can see the evidence of my orgasm sitting on his tongue. "Oh my God," I repeat as I squeeze my eyes shut as I try to commit the visual to memory.

He presses his lips to mine, feeding me his tongue and I can taste myself. "I want you to taste how wet I make you." I can hear him unbuckling his pants and the familiar clink of metal hitting the ground makes my sex clench in anticipation of what's to come. He wraps his hands around my ass, lifting me like I weigh less than nothing and immediately my legs wrap around his waist as his thick, hard cock pushes inside of me. He thrusts and I relish in the feeling of him inside of me, taking me hard and I realize how much I've missed our wild uninhibited sex.

He'd once told me that he'd never had this type of sexual chemistry with anyone, that no one ever made him so hard and so often as I did. That he never felt the need to fuck someone in public. Or any of the other kinky things we'd done over the years. He lived and breathed me and *us*.

Take that Amanda...with your mediocre sex. I mentally high five myself at how easily I can bring this man to his knees. How I'm the only woman who can turn him into the savage beast before me. An untamed, uncontrolled man that is currently fucking me so hard against the wall of a bathroom I feel him in my throat.

I'm close, my sex pulsing at the thought of a third orgasm in the span of an hour. I bite down on his neck and he groans. "Fuck fuck fuck. I'm going to come." He sputters and lets out a deep breath as he grips me harder, his nails piercing the flesh of my ass cheeks he's cupping and I fly across the threshold of pain in search of the pleasure that is no more than a thrust away.

"Me too."

"Do it now," he grits out and while he can't make me come on command, he does know when I'm close and uses that to his advantage. "Milk my cock, Olivia. I need you to come and for the juice from your sexy fucking cunt to drip down my cock."

I fucking lose it.

I come so hard for a second I'm not sure I'm even conscious as I slip into what feels like a dark abyss. I can only feel the pleasure between my legs that seems to go on and on. It's hot between my legs, the flesh wet and slick as his cock slips out of my pussy. I watch in fascination as cum drips from the tip onto the floor and I clench at the sexiness of our fucking.

His pants are still around his ankles as he boxes me against the wall, one arm on either side of me. "God, I love you." His nose rubs against mine and I sigh as his lips ghost over mine.

A thought floats across my mind now that the fog of the sex high has lifted slightly and my buzz is lessening and a giggle escapes my lips.

He runs a hand through his hair, pushing it back and shoots me a grin before tucking his dick back into his pants. "What's so funny?"

"I was just thinking," I whisper, "Amanda didn't argue with any parts of your story."

He freezes and kneels back in front of me to help me into my panties. He leans forward in an attempt to kiss my pussy again and I put my hands on his shoulders stopping him. "I'm just surprised…I mean, clearly you nailed what happened between you guys. I'm just shocked she didn't call your bluff?"

He doesn't look at me, just straightens my dress before he stands up. "Olivia, she needed to go and I did what I had to do to get rid of her, alright?" He tucks a hair behind my ear and kisses my lips gently.

I pull back slightly, not wanting to get wrapped up in kissing him. "That…doesn't exactly answer my question." I bite my lip and it's almost as if my mind is screaming at me to connect the dots faster. "Clarke, you had a number. Did Wren tell you it had only been three times? I mean if it were more, she would have called you out on that. It's like as soon as you pretended you had your memory back, she backed off." I smooth my dress down and pull my hair over my shoulder, knowing I'm going to definitely put my hair up as soon as we step out of this stall.

He doesn't say anything again and his silence is starting to trouble me. "Why aren't you saying anything?" I ask him.

"Olivia…I just…" He clears his throat, pushing his hands into his pockets as he looks away from me. "I wanted her to leave us alone."

"Bennett…" My brows furrow as the words sit on the tip of my tongue. Tears are building in my chest as I prepare myself to speak the words that will change everything.

He wouldn't.

There's no way.

"Do you…remember?" I shake my head. "Being with her? Being away from…me?"

Bennett

Fuck.

I knew things were going to get messy the second I lost my shit with Amanda. I just needed her to go away permanently and the only way to do that was to allude that I remembered and to call her on all the bullshit she'd been spewing at Olivia. She wouldn't refute it once I spoke the truth, and I was hoping her silence was enough to corroborate what I was saying. Olivia needed to know we weren't more. We could have never been more. She needed to know I never told her I loved her, that we were nothing more than a few drunken hookups spurred on by losing the love of my life.

But I'd gone too far. I'd gotten too specific and now my very teary eyed wife is putting together the truth.

That once again, I've deceived her.

"Bennett…" She bites her lip to prevent herself from crying but I watch as a tear escapes and trickles down her face.

"Livi." I breathe her name out, like a plea. "Maybe we should go home and talk?" I know she hears the guilt in my voice, I'm just hoping she lets me take her home before she realizes just how guilty I am.

"No." She swallows and I know she's crossing over from sadness into anger as my avoidance is confirming what I know to be her question. "You do, don't you? You fucking remember everything."

"Sweetheart." *Fuck fuck fuck.*

"Don't you sweetheart me," she barks. "Tell me the truth, Bennett. Now."

In a men's room? "It's complicated…baby, let me take you home."

"Oh my God." It's hard for her to move in the tiny stall, but she reaches for the door in an attempt to leave. "I have to get out of here." I press my hand against the door, preventing her from opening it.

"Wait." My voice is pained and barely above a whisper.

She spins around, her eyes full of fury. "Fuck you, Bennett," she growls. "How. HOW?!" The tears are welling in her eyes, her hands are shaking and I note her curling them into fists. "How long? Oh my God, was this all a ploy? To get me back? Was any of this real?! Oh my God, you tricked me!" She puts a hand over her chest and I can only hope she's not trying to shield her heart from me. "How could you do this to me? After everything?!"

"No, Olivia…baby…it was real. All of it was real. I really did lose my memory. This wasn't a ploy. I swear."

Her eyes are hard and I don't see a trace of the woman I know loves me more than anything. "Nothing you say means anything, Bennett…I can't trust anything you say. Now let me go."

"No," I tell her, refusing to let her out of this stall. My voice is low and demanding. I press her against the door. "Listen to me."

Her eyes meet mine and I can see the devastation lurking behind the anger. "Please. Please just stop. You've hurt me so much. I can't take anymore from you."

"I got my memory back a week ago," I tell her honestly. "I swear. The night we slept together at my apartment." I cup her face. "It's like my body knew I was coming back to you…"

She scoffs. "That sounds like a load of bullshit." She pushes me back and removes my hands from her face forcefully. "Were you ever going to tell me?"

"Yes," I tell her immediately.

"WHEN?" she screams. "When were you going to tell me?! When was the right time to tell me if not that exact second you figured it out?"

"I just wanted to make sure *we* were solid before…"

"And you think lying and deceiving me was the way to create something solid?"

"I needed to make sure we could get through getting my memory back and what it would mean. You'd want to know about Amanda. We were going to have a lot to take on and…"

"And you wanted to continue fucking me without having to deal with that," she snaps.

Her words are like a punch in the gut. *Does she think that's all she means to me?* "You know it wasn't about that."

"Oh really? Because that's not what this was?" She points around the stall and between us.

"No. Baby, you know there's so much more to us than sex. I've loved reconnecting with you this week and—"

"But that's the thing! That wasn't us reconnecting! Reconnecting is working through the pain of the past six months, which we haven't done! I've been forced to put that into a box because you couldn't remember, and you were too much of a coward to tell me because you feared what would happen if and when I had to open that box." She points at me. "And I was so caught up in who you *were* that I forgot who you *are* now. And that's a liar." She spits at me. "We are so done, Bennett."

"No. Olivia, listen." My hands shake at her words and I wrap my hands around her forearms, gripping her tightly. "Please."

She shakes her head. "The time to talk has passed. You're only coming clean because I caught you. Who's to say you ever would have told me?"

"I would have!"

"It's easy to say that now."

"We've both had a lot to drink and you have every right to be upset..." I start as she tries to wiggle out of my grasp.

"I have every right?!" she screams. "How fucking dare you tell me about any rights I might have. You lied to me. Right to my face! For A WEEK. I can't even believe we're here again." Her lip trembles. "Let me go, Bennett."

"Livi...I can't."

She's about to respond when there's a knock on the stall door. "Everything okay in there?" the voice booms through the door. "Is she alright? I heard her say to let her go." Olivia looks towards the door with a frown as he continues. "Ma'am, are you okay in there? I can get security for you."

"Back the fuck off," I growl at the door. "I'm her husband and she's fine."

"Frankly pal, that doesn't mean shit. Ma'am, say something please so I know you're alright."

She lets out a shaky breath, knowing she's far from alright but having to pretend that she is so that I'm not potentially at risk of people thinking I've physically hurt my drunk and emotional wife. "I'm okay. We'll be out in a second." Her nostrils flare and she squeezes her eyes shut. "Thank you," she whispers. "It's nice to know there are still good men out there." Her eyes flash to mine angrily and the words are like a pierce to my heart.

"Alright." I can tell his hand hits the stall and then I hear him walking away and the door opens allowing a cacophony of sounds to blast through the room.

CHAPTER
Twenty-Six

Bennett

By the grace of God, I convince Olivia to let me take her home. Olivia hates riding in Ubers or taxis late at night by herself, and despite her anger, she knows she's drunk and doesn't want to be out alone with her sense of awareness drastically lower. Wren and Alyssa had long since texted us while we were fucking in the bathroom, that they were calling it a night and had left. Which also worked in my favor because the last thing I needed was to add Alyssa Hamilton into the mix.

Olivia is silent as we leave the Upper East Side and cross back to our side of town. She's staring out the window, and I stare at her for most of the time. I reach for her hand, and although she whimpers uncomfortably, she doesn't pull away. She doesn't look at me either, but I'm counting the minor contact as a small win.

"Excuse me," she says softly and my head snaps up from staring at our hands to see she's talking to our Uber driver. "It's actually going to be two stops."

"No. It's not," I say immediately and she glares at me.

"Yes, it is."

"I'm her husband," I inform the driver whose eyes are now trained on me through the rearview mirror.

"Stop calling yourself that," she snaps and now it's my turn to glare at her.

"I am. Just because you're angry, it doesn't change the law, now stop being childish." I know my eyes are angry at this point, the thought of her denying me that title making me almost irate.

"Fuck you," she bites out and when I look back towards the driver, I catch him rolling his eyes, realizing that we are clearly just having a fight.

When we pull to the front of our building, she doesn't wait for me to get out to open her door before she's on the move. I'm behind her instantly, my hand at the small of her back, guiding her. We move through the lobby, without a word to the concierge who gives us a polite nod and a warm smile.

The elevator is so tense the air between us is almost stifling. Olivia won't meet my eyes as she keeps hers trained on the floor. "Olivia. Baby, look at me," I tell her and she puts a hand up, shaking her head.

I follow her out of the elevator, towards our apartment and once we're safely inside, I try and talk to her again. "Livi."

She kicks her shoes off, flinging them as if she has doesn't have a care as to where they land and walks toward the kitchen. She opens the refrigerator and stares inside as if she's trying to figure out what to eat, and I move to the other side to look at her. "Are you hungry? I can make you whatever you want? Or I can order something?"

She closes the door and glares at me. "I need you to leave. Go to Wren's. Go to your mother's. I don't care. I don't want you here," she tells me. My apartment is already in the process of being sublet, so I can't go back there, not that I had any intentions of leaving tonight.

"No, Olivia we need to talk tomorrow when we are both sober."

"I'm plenty sober, Bennett." She turns her back, walking towards her bedroom and I follow her. We'd been sleeping mostly in our old bedroom, and I hate the thought that she wants to sleep away from me tonight.

"Do not follow me," she growls over her shoulder before slamming the door in my face. I open it anyway and move inside as she pulls her dress off over her head. "Go away, Bennett, I don't want to see you or talk to you or even be near you right now." She's not yelling or crying and frankly, I wish she was having a more passionate response. This quiet, cold indifference is worse.

"Well, I need to be near you."

She snorts. "And it's always about you and your needs, right? Never mind, that I didn't even fucking want you here in the first place. I knew you'd bulldoze over me. I knew you'd break me down." She pulls one of her t-shirts on and a pair of leggings before moving past me and towards the bathroom. "I just didn't know you'd break my heart again in the process."

I drop to her bed, digging the heel of my palm into my eye as I think about her words. I pull my shoes off, tossing them with more force than I intend into the corner of the room. I yank off my jacket and begin unbuttoning my shirt as the water begins to run in the bathroom.

I grab my phone and pull up my texts with Wren.

> Me: You were right and now Olivia knows. I fucked everything up.

> Wren: Where are you guys?

> Me: Home. She's pissed.

> Wren: You need a place to crash?

Me: God, I hope not. I need to talk to her. I can't lose her again, Wren. I won't survive it next time.

Wren: Tell her that. Make her listen. Grovel.

I'm putting my phone on the nightstand when Olivia comes back into the room. Her face is free from makeup and her hair is piled into a bun on the top of her head. She blinks her eyes several times and shakes her head. "You've lost your mind if you think you're sleeping in here." I had hoped that seeing me shirtless might tip the scale in my favor but she practically looks through me as she makes her way to her side of the bed. "Get out."

"Olivia."

"OUT!" she screams as she points at the door. She climbs into bed and turns the light off on the nightstand before lying down with her back to me. "Go. I mean it."

My shoulders sag and my head lowers in defeat. "I love you," I murmur as I back out of the door slowly. "I've never stopped loving you."

"Why the fuck did you let it come to that?" Wren barks into the phone. It's rounding two-thirty, and I'm not all that surprised he's still awake. He's always a night owl, and I'm sure he fucked Alyssa to sleep and is now sitting up watching Sports Center while eating cold pizza. I'm pacing the length of the living room, too keyed up to sleep and worried about what the morning will bring.

"I needed Amanda to just…go. And I wanted Olivia to be a witness to it."

"And that's all well and good, but you should have told Olivia the truth FIRST. You ratted yourself out!"

"In hindsight, it wasn't my best move, but I was drunk and having to deal with my ex-mistress while my drunk and horny wife who I'd just fingered on the dance floor was standing next to me, excuse me for not thinking clearly."

"Jesus, B, keeping my wife from killing you is becoming a full time job. Can you imagine what's going to happen when Olivia gets her on the phone?"

"That is the fucking least of my worries."

"Well, it's the top of mine. You make it really hard to stay your goddamn friend sometimes."

Fury spikes in my veins. I'm not prepared to lose my wife and my best friend in the same night. I don't want to lose either, but both may actually kill me. "Fuck you, Wren, I don't need this shit from you."

"And Olivia doesn't need this shit from *you*. You destroyed that girl. She was already struggling with trusting you and you think this makes it easier? You know Olivia loves you. Nothing will change that. But if she can't trust you…" He trails off. "She's not going to be with a man she can't trust, you should know her better than that."

"She can! I just…I needed more time."

"With her pussy? Because that's what it seems like you've been doing the last week."

"No! With her. With Olivia…I just missed her."

"And you think she hasn't missed *you*? But you weren't being fair to her. You got to see *her* but she couldn't see you."

I'm silent as his words sink in. I drop to the couch. "She thinks I made the whole thing up to get her back. Well, maybe she doesn't anymore, but she thought I did."

"You don't exactly have a track record of transparency," he says. "Of course she thinks this was all a ruse."

"It wasn't man, I swear."

"I believe that. But I believe I also told you, memory loss usually comes back in a few weeks. I was expecting this to be honest. Of course, I thought you'd tell her the second it happened."

"I just...I knew the second I told her, it would change everything. What if...what if at that point, when we started working through everything she realized she didn't want me anymore?"

"But how is it fair for you to deny me that choice?" Her voice washes over me and I look up to find Olivia standing across the room, her eyes full of tears. Her body language shows me she has her guard all the way up and when I stand up she immediately takes a step back.

"I'll call you tomorrow," I tell Wren, my eyes not leaving Olivia.

"Be honest with her, Bennett. No bullshit," Wren says before hanging up.

I toss my phone behind me, not caring where it lands as I move towards her. She doesn't move away from me and when I'm close enough to touch her, I wrap my arms around her petite frame. She shakes in my arms and I know she's succumbing to the tears she was previously keeping at bay. I lift her into my arms and walk her towards the master bedroom, needing her in our marital bed. I sit her gently on it and she looks up at me. "I just don't see how we can come back from this. This is just another way you've proven that I can't trust you."

"You can," I urge her. "I swear you can." I press my hand to her cheek and rub my thumb across her lip gently. "We can start over, fresh. I'm just asking for a chance."

She nods, her lips forming a straight line, forcing me to drop my hand from her face. "It's always just one more chance. What happens the next time you do something like this? What about the next time you betray me? Or lie to me? Then what? What happens the next time there's a hiccup in our marriage that sends you running into the arms of another woman."

"Not fair."

"Oh? What do you call what happened with Amanda, Bennett? What the fuck was that? I know how I was, believe me. But your response to my depression was you fucking some other girl? If that's your automatic response then we're done here."

"No! That just happened, Olivia. We've talked about this."

"And you continued to spend time with her all the while professing to be in love with me? I call bullshit."

"You heard what I said tonight." I grit out. "I'm not proud of it, but you're telling me you weren't still in love with me while you were banging that douchebag, David?"

She's off the bed in an instant and pushing hard against my chest. "Not the same!"

"Tell me, did you stop loving me while you let him fuck you?" I growl at her. "Did you imagine me when he put his mouth on you? When he put his mouth…here?" I ask as my hand snakes down between her legs.

She gasps when I touch her and then I feel her hand, *hard* against my cheek. In the nine years we've been together, Olivia has never slapped me, and if I didn't feel the tingling on my skin, I wouldn't have believed she did it. Her eyes flare in anger and I know mine match hers when I push her against the wall, *hard*. "Did that feel good?"

"Fuck off, Bennett. We are *not* having sex."

"Why? You're turned on. You want me."

"No," she huffs

"Yes," I argue.

"Maybe my body does, but my heart and mind don't."

"Bullshit."

"Oh?"

"You didn't answer my question either." I look down at her, putting an arm on either side of her. "Did you stop loving me while you were sleeping with David? Were you or were you not using him to get over me?"

"I wasn't using him. I was trying to move on, Bennett."

I pull back. "Did it work? Because I had my mouth between your legs a week after I moved back in."

"You're such an asshole!" She pushes me.

"Admit it," I growl at her. My mind is screaming at me that this is not the way to reconcile. This is *not* the way to win my wife back, but I can't help it. I'm tired of Olivia running from me. I'm tired of feeling like the world's shittiest husband when all I want is to be with her. I'd made a mistake in judgment, but that doesn't mean she isn't my entire fucking world. "I kept this from you to protect us," I tell her when she doesn't answer.

"Bullshit! You didn't want to have to talk to me about your fucking girlfriend."

"She was *not* my girlfriend."

"Are you really arguing semantics with me right now? I had a fucking miscarriage and you dealt with it by sticking your dick in another woman!"

Now I was pissed.

"Are you serious?!" I bellow. "Is that how you saw that go down? You wouldn't talk to me or look at me. I begged you to see someone. I begged you to see someone with *me*. Those babies were just as much mine and I was allowed to be hurt over losing them too. You may have physically felt the loss but I felt it just as much emotionally and it wasn't fucking fair that I wasn't allowed to grieve."

"No one said—"

"No. I wasn't. It was all about you. I was so focused on keeping you going that I had to push my feelings aside, which I could do, *if* you fucking appreciated that. If you fucking appreciated that for months, I kept our marriage going when you checked the fuck out of it," I tell her. "I fucked someone else, and I am sorry, so fucking sorry, you have no idea how much. But you closed your heart off to me. TO ME, Olivia. In sickness and health. Till death do us part. You forgot our fucking vows first, Liv. You turned your back on me when I NEEDED YOU."

"I didn't!" The tears are streaming down her face. I'm not sure what will come out of this argument, but we need to get everything out. There is no holding back if we want to move forward.

And I desperately wanted to move forward from this.

"I'm sick of you running or shutting down on me every time things get hard. Goddammit, you're my wife and I want to take care of you. But fuck, there are two people in this marriage, Olivia."

"So this is all my fault? I'm a shitty wife because of how I dealt with our miscarriages?"

"No," I tell her, my voice calmer than it was before. "I would never say that. You were doing the best you could, but we both made mistakes. You hurt me too, Olivia."

"And that excuses what you did?"

"No," I tell her honestly. "It doesn't. And it's something I'll regret forever. But will you regret leaving me? Because living with regret is tough, Olivia. Trust me when I say that. It's a pain that is so deep in your soul that you can't ever be free from it. You fall asleep with it, wake up with it, and then it haunts your every waking second. It changes the way you see yourself in the mirror. The way you interact with other people. The way you talk to yourself. It's a lonely, self-deprecating feeling that preys on your mind and your heart and it never goes away."

She bites her bottom lip. "I'd rather feel regret than wonder what you're doing or who you're with every time you leave our apartment. That will make me crazy. And I can't spend the rest of my life questioning you."

I shake my head. "You know me, Olivia. You know it wouldn't be like that."

"I thought I did. The fact that you were capable of cheating on me means you're capable of doing it again."

"Don't spew that *once a cheater, always a cheater* bullshit at me, Olivia, because I don't buy it and neither do you. You know how I feel about you and us."

She puts her hands over her eyes. "Oh my God. I'm not denying that you love me, and between the two of us I'm *not* the liar," she sneers. "So I'll admit that I love you too, but it's not enough. I don't trust you, and that's just as important."

"Can't I gain your trust back?"

"That's what I thought you were doing! Despite the fact that you couldn't remember, I was letting you back in. I was learning to trust you again. But as soon as you're tested, you fail! You fall right back into these old behaviors."

"I told you the truth about Amanda from the start, I never lied to you about that. I never tried to hide it."

"Again with the semantics! It's a betrayal of my trust either way."

I cross my arms over my chest and lean against the wall behind me. "Well, it sounds like you've already made up your mind about me and this." I shake my head, not wanting to grovel anymore. I have a headache and a heartache and I just want to sleep this fucking day off. I can feel myself getting frustrated at this maddening woman who I still love with every fiber of my being and the last thing I want to do is say something I can't take back.

"I have."

"Sleep on it," I tell her. "We can talk when you're sober and thinking clearly."

"Drunk words are sober thoughts, Bennett."

"Then you'll have no problem telling me this when you're sober," I tell her as I make my way out of the bedroom and into the room she'd slept alone all those months in. I know she hadn't slept in our marital bed alone since the night I moved out, but I'm going to force her into it tonight.

CHAPTER
Twenty-Seven

Olivia

I BARELY SLEPT ALL NIGHT.

At some point, I sobered up, and with that sobriety brought clarity, pain, and the heartbreak that I was anticipating. After tossing and turning for the majority of the night, I finally get up, preparing myself for this final showdown with Bennett.

There is no denying that I love him. I will always love him and maybe he could eventually earn my trust back. But that day is not today. I need space. And maybe this is why he kept it from me. Maybe he knew all along I would need space.

Maybe I did too.

I'm struggling to make sense of my feelings for Bennett, but that means I can't be around him. I can't let our sexual chemistry or the feelings I have for him cloud my judgment. I can't let the space between my legs control our narrative, and for that I need him gone.

I make my way into the hallway, and when I peek my head into the kitchen and living room, I don't see him. I let out a sigh of relief as I leave the master bedroom and move into the bathroom.

I stare at myself in the reflection, remembering everything

he said last night. Feelings of guilt bloom in my chest and it aches thinking about what I did to the man I love. I left him to deal with everything alone. I was so busy trying to survive the storm, I'd forgotten there was someone else fighting beside me.

I make my way out of the bathroom and just as I expect, Bennett is standing in front of the door, his bare chest on display in nothing more than his briefs. "Can you put some clothes on?" I try my best to appear unfazed by his appearance, but goddamn if he isn't sex on a fucking stick. My eyes rake over his chest and up and down his sleeve of ink before moving towards the kitchen. I hear him moving behind me and I roll my eyes when I know he's not going to oblige my request.

"Olivia, I want to apologize for last night. I said some things that…"

"You didn't mean?"

"No, I meant them, but my execution was off. My emotions were running high, and I snapped when I shouldn't have," he says honestly.

I place a mug under the Keurig. "Do you want some coffee?" I ask, ignoring his apology.

"That'd be great, thanks." He leans against the counter and stares at me as I watch our coffee maker in fascination in an attempt to avoid his gaze or his hard chest and washboard abs. "Look at me," he commands. I do as he asks, and he cocks his head at me. "I want to be able to move past this."

"Of course, you do," I tell him, "but as you so eloquently put it last night, there are two people in this marriage, and it's not just *your* call."

He nods and his arms flex, showcasing the veins, and I avert my eyes quickly. "I…I don't want a divorce, Olivia."

"I also know that," I tell him as I watch the coffee fall into the mug.

"Do you?"

I run my tongue over my teeth and look up at him. "Bennett," I shake my head, "I want space."

He looks relieved that I didn't flat out tell him yes, but he still looks wary of my response. "What kind of space?"

"I would like if you moved out."

His brows furrow as fear flashes in his eyes. "What?"

"I can't work through this with you here."

"What's there to work through?"

"If I can trust you. If I can move on from this…" He doesn't say anything, he just stares at something behind me, as if he's zoning out. His green eyes are dull and not full of the love and passion that he usually has for me.

"Don't do this, baby. If I walk out that door again, it'll break me." His words are so quiet I almost don't hear them, but I feel them so deeply it's as if he screamed them in my ear.

"If you stay, it'll break *me*."

He slouches against the counter. "I never meant to hurt you, Olivia. You have to know that."

"I do," I whisper.

He walks out of the kitchen and I let out a deep sigh. Within moments he's back with a shirt and sweatpants on, much to my relief. I hand him his cup and he sits at the bar, his eyes trained on me. The quiet stretches on between us and I'm not sure what to say. "How long do you think you need this space?"

I shrug because I'm really *not* sure. "I don't know."

"Can I get a ballpark?"

"I can't put a time on healing, Bennett…a month maybe?"

He stares down at his coffee, moving the mug around the counter with his hands, I'm guessing as a way to distract himself. "We can't talk at all?" he asks finally when he meets my gaze. "I can't see you?"

"I think that would be more difficult for both of us."

He snorts. "This is bullshit."

"Excuse me?" I ask.

"I get you're pissed but you know you love me. You know that whatever anger you're feeling doesn't outweigh the pain you'd feel over not being my wife."

"Wow. Someone's full of themselves." I roll my eyes and turn back around to make my coffee when I hear something flung against a wall. I snap my head towards the noise to see he's thrown his stool at the wall and he's stalking around the bar towards me.

"This isn't a fucking joke, Olivia," he snaps. "What we have is fucking real, and you know it hurts not being together."

"If it's so fucking real why did you ruin it?! Why did you break us?!" I snap back. He doesn't say anything and I shake my head. "I can't keep doing this with you. I asked for space so I can clear my head, I'd like for you to respect that. Please. I'm begging you." The tears have started to fall and I can't stop the feeling like my heart is breaking inside my chest. His hands frame my face, wiping the tears and I relish in the contact even if I know it has to be short-lived. His hands are warm and I just want to curl up in his arms and stay there forever. But I know I can't.

I have to be strong.

"I'll give you this space...but you have to promise you'll come back to me," he says.

"Bennett..."

"Promise me." He stares at me, and my heart breaks at the words I have to speak.

"I can't make promises I don't know if I can keep."

Bennett left that day.

It was hard.

Much harder than I thought it would be. Watching him walk out that door felt like someone had kicked me in the stomach and knocked the wind out of me and I struggled to breathe for the first full hour after he left. I sat on the floor of my kitchen, with a glass filled to the brim of pure vodka as I tried to nurse my broken heart.

He told me he was going to his mother's and to call him day or night if I wanted to talk.

I didn't.

As a matter of fact, I didn't talk to anyone for three days. I ignored my mother and Alyssa and work and sat on my couch with fast food and vodka and horror movies because the idea of watching people in love made me want to jump from my seventh floor window.

It isn't until the third day, that I hear keys in my door.

I'm not sure who I expected but Caroline Clarke surely wasn't it.

"Oh Jesus take the wheel." I let my head fall back with a loud groan as I take in my mother-in-law. I hiccup as I pull my drink to my lips and take a long sip. Thank God, I showered today and look somewhat human.

"Jesus is not amused young lady," Caroline says as she pulls off her Chanel jacket and steps into the kitchen.

"Jesus and I aren't exactly on speaking terms at the moment," I tell her as I watch her root through my refrigerator.

"Well, He's listening should you change your mind," she says and I want to ask her where this newfound sense of Christianity came from when she always seemed to be pretty tight with Satan. I roll my eyes and wrap the blanket tighter around myself. "Pizza, Chinese food, wings…honestly, Olivia, how do you keep your figure?"

"I'm not thirty yet." I deadpan and she chuckles.

"Fair, but you should eat better."

"Why? Your son is hellbent on killing me at a young age anyway. Why not clog my arteries?"

She closes the refrigerator and moves into the living room. "You're drunk."

"What was your first clue?" I hold up the glass. I'm not drunk, though I'm not far from it, but maybe a sign of intoxication would get her to leave me alone.

"He would hate to see you like this."

"Well, good thing he's not here." I sigh. "Which reminds me, why are you?"

"I came to pick up some more of his clothes. He didn't think you'd want to see him."

"He would be correct."

She sighs and takes a seat next to me on the couch. I'm instantly on alert and move slightly away, briefly wondering if she plans to hurt me. "Olivia."

"Caroline."

"My son misses you."

"Try to contain your excitement."

"Don't be childish, Olivia. You think I want to see him hurting?"

"I know you don't want to see him with me."

"I want him happy."

"And what makes you think I didn't make him happy?"

"I know you did, Olivia."

"Then why did you hate me so much? Why were you friends with his mistress? Why wasn't I good enough for your son?" The words fly out of my mouth before I can stop them. I have so many questions for his mother, so many why's and how's that I want answered.

"No one was. My relationship with Amanda was superficial. You broke my son's heart and I was angry at you for it. He wanted you back and he was trying so hard to hold onto you."

"He broke my heart first," I snap.

"It was a mistake. People make mistakes, Olivia. You aren't perfect either."

"He slept with another woman. I'm well within my rights to not just look past that like it's nothing."

"And he was wrong for that. We all know that."

"Take Amanda out of the equation for a second. You hated me on sight."

"No, I didn't."

"Really?"

"It's hard letting your only child go, Olivia."

"So you hated me because you wanted him to stay a mama's boy forever? Please." I snort. "I hope you have something better than that because that is weak."

She sighs. "You weren't like the other girls he brought home."

"What? Black?" I raise an eyebrow at her, not in the mood to hear about the parade of Barbie dolls he'd brought home before me.

"No, Olivia. You speak your mind. You are smart and well-spoken and outgoing, but you have a mouth on you and a fiery streak. You have gumption that so many of his past girlfriends lacked and a part of me resented you for being a woman who spoke her mind so freely when I'd been taught to be seen and not heard. My son came alive when he met you. I saw it from the moment he first mentioned you. And then he just… stopped coming around because you became his entire world." She gives me a smile that most would consider warm and genuine, but nine years of interactions have me skeptical.

"So you didn't like me because you felt like I was taking your son away from you?" I roll my eyes. "I never did understand these unhealthy co-dependent relationships between mother and sons. It's strange." I snort as I take a long sip of my vodka water.

She chuckles. "See and that," she points at me, "that's what I'm talking about. You've given as good as you've gotten it over the years, Olivia."

"Hardly. I was taught to respect my elders, and while I might have given you my sarcasm, I've always erred on the side of respect. You however, have not."

"I'm not proud of how I've treated you."

"You shouldn't be."

She nods. "I've been hurtful and rude and inconsiderate and I'm sorry." I stare at her before staring down at my drink. I'm a forgiving person by nature, but I swear these Clarke's love to test my resolve. "Now Amanda…No bullshit?"

My eyes move to hers hearing her swear, having rarely heard her say anything more than *damn* or *hell*. "Sure?"

"I gave my son hell for cheating on you. You may not know that. I knew he loved you, and I was furious at him for taking the coward's way out. Regardless of how I felt about you, I've been there, and it's nothing I'd wish on any woman." My eyes widen. *No way. Bennett's father loved Caroline. Surprisingly.* "Bennett doesn't know, and I'd like to keep it that way." She swallows and dabs at her eyes with a tissue she pulls from her purse.

"Senior?"

She clears her throat. "Don't think he's so perfect now, do you?" She gives me a weak smile and pulls my glass of vodka from my hands and takes a long drink.

"Ummm, when?"

"Bennett was about four." She takes another sip and I watch

as her throat wobbles as she swallows. "So, he won't remember that there was a time when his father wasn't around."

"You separated?"

She nods. "For about two months."

"But you took him back?"

"Because I was twenty-five, with no college degree and a five year gap in my resume. It was the eighties, and I didn't know what to do with a child and all of those very inconvenient characteristics. So I went back. For security and the life I'd grown accustomed to." She sniffles.

"Did he ever...?"

"No, never again." She shakes her head. "At least, not that I know of. Olivia, it took me a very long time to forgive him and I never forgot." She sighs. "But what I'm saying is, you don't have to be me. You have a million choices and options and you have all the tools to make the best decisions. You don't *need* my son to live the life you want," her eyes well up with tears but she swallows them down, "but I think you need him to live the life you love."

I'm silent as her words seep into my soul. Maybe she's full of shit, but her words still ring true. I don't need Bennett in the same way she needed his father. But I need him in ways that I feel deep in my heart. His love courses through me and I feel the absence of him every time I move. Every time my heart beats it feels the loss of the only man I've ever loved. "What if we can't get past it?"

"Have you tried?" she asks. "Or did you just jump ship when it got hard?"

"I didn't..." I start when she pins me with a hard glare.

"Bennett has been fighting so hard for you and for your marriage, and I know he hurt you. Believe me, I know. But I know you love him enough to give him another chance, so I'm just curious what you're afraid of?" I don't answer because really I'm not sure. "I made my relationship with…Amanda so in your face because my son was devastated when he found out you moved on. I was angry at you for leaving him broken."

"What about me? I was broken too."

"Yes. But you left him. So by every rule of life there ever was, it meant *you* were stronger."

"David didn't mean anything," I tell her honestly.

"Neither did Amanda."

"It doesn't change what happened."

"No. Nothing can change the past. But you can change the present. You can do better for the future. There's no room for pride in love, Olivia. Marrying someone is the most humble act. You're promising to put another person first. Sometimes even before yourself. I can't make you do something you don't want to do. But I can empower you to make the choice you want to make but are too afraid to."

CHAPTER Twenty-Eight

Bennett

NINETY-EIGHT
Ninety-nine
One hundred

Sweat trickles down my face and back as I finish the last round of push-ups. I hadn't been working out much and my body felt the difference. I lift my shirt, rubbing it over my brow and down my face. I'm exhausted, mentally and physically. I haven't done much the past week besides wallow in my own misery and ignore the outside world. I haven't gone back to work and I think they are beginning to wonder when their top realtor will return, but I honestly can't be bothered to care. I'd signed the deal of a lifetime before my accident and the commission on the house I'd sold was obscene. I could take the rest of the year off, and still live comfortably.

I stand up on shaky legs, my muscles tired from the workout I had just put them through and grab my mother's yoga mat I'd been using. I opted to work out on her terrace as to not give my mother a heart attack by dripping sweat on her white carpet. My mother still lives in the apartment she shared with my father, as she couldn't bear to move after he passed. I look off the balcony, and over the city. It's officially fall, and the thought chills my bones that I'm going into another season without Olivia.

I wonder what she's doing right now.

Is she thinking about me?

Anxiety zips through my body as I walk back into the apartment just in time for my mother to enter the room. She scrunches her nose, shaking her head. "Go straight to the shower, do not sit on anything."

"I wasn't going to," I tell her as I take long sip from a bottle of water. "Where have you been?" I know she's been out all day and more importantly not seeing any shopping bags in the living room means she actually *wasn't* at Bergdorf Goodman.

"Out." She frowns as she slides her gloves off her hands. "I didn't realize you were the parent here." She raises an eyebrow.

"It was just a question." I shrug, not in the mood to deal with my mother's attitude. I start walking through the apartment towards the guest room where I'm staying when she stops me. "When is the last time you left the house?"

"I don't know." I turn around and give her a shrug.

"You should go out and get some fresh air."

"I got plenty of fresh air on your terrace."

"I'm serious, Bennett. You can't stay cooped up inside. You have to get out and live your life."

I don't say anything. I just stare at this woman who clearly has never had her heart broken, if she thinks I'm in any mood to be around a bunch of people. "You done?"

She shakes her head and crosses her hands across her chest. "She wouldn't want this for you."

I snort. "And you know anything about what Olivia wants." I walk away not wanting to entertain my mother's thoughts about the woman she basically treated like shit. "As a matter of fact," I turn around, "*if* by the grace of God or divine intervention,

Olivia does take me back, you need to deal with whatever issue it is you have with her, because I'm tired of you treating her the way you do. That ends and I mean it, Mother."

She lets out a small puff of air and nods. "I know."

I'm shocked by her response and the fact that she's not putting up a fight. "Okay. Well. Good." I nod. "Olivia will probably never take me back, but…" I shrug. "At least I know you'll make an effort. Thank you."

I turn again, heading down the hall when she calls after me. I turn and she gives me a smile. "You fight for that girl, Bennett. What you two have is special. You do whatever you can to hold onto it. Fight for it. And when you get it back, protect it." Her eyes are hard yet I see so much wisdom in them, like she has firsthand experience.

I can only nod at her words. "I have an appointment at the hospital. They're going to run some tests. It's my last follow-up, and now that my memory is back they just want to make sure everything looks good."

"Of course. Shall I come with you?"

"No." I rub a hand behind my neck as I turn around, surprised to see my mother had followed me. "I'll be fine, but thank you." She presses a hand to my cheek and gives me a smile.

"Give her some time, Bennett."

"She's had six months, Mom," I sigh as the weight of that time apart beats down on me "Either she wants me or she doesn't."

"Your scans look great, B." I nod at Wren as he jots something down on his clipboard. "The swelling is completely gone." He points to the photo scan of my brain.

"Great, I definitely feel better. Physically. The rest of my life is a fucking mess, but at least I'm alive." I do my best to sound optimistic, but to be honest, it hadn't felt all that great to be alive the last week. I lean over, resting my forearms against my knees. "Has Alyssa talked to her?"

He pulls his glasses from his face and slides them across his desk before pressing his hands to his face. "No." He shakes his head. "Olivia has asked for space."

"So no one knows how she is?" I ask. She's by herself, and I was hoping Alyssa would at least be checking in on her.

"Have you talked to her?"

"I called her a few times after that first day, but she's not answering." It's been almost two weeks since I've seen or spoken to Olivia and I'm growing more restless by the day. Olivia and I had spoken with our lawyers during our week of bliss that we no longer wanted a divorce, but I was anticipating a call any day that Olivia had decided to put things in motion again. As sticky as it is, I'm sure we will be in for a fuck ton of red tape after calling it off once, but I fully expect to be served again within the month.

My beard has grown in slightly, making it fuller and less stubble, and my hair is a little longer as well. This isn't a look I usually go for but showering is about all I have the energy for, especially after I put away half a bottle of whiskey.

I'm coming to accept the fact that Olivia and I have gone through too much. Too much has happened that we may never come back from. Our marriage can't withstand everything we've put it through.

Love really isn't enough.

The door opens, interrupting my thoughts and I fully expected a nurse or another doctor to be on the other side, but what I don't expect is my wife. My eyes rake over her and despite the fact that she looks unbelievably gorgeous in jeans and a bomber jacket, I can see the sadness in her eyes. I'd never known Olivia to not wear mascara when she went out, and yet her lashes are bare and the area around her eyes looks red. She bites down on her bottom lip gently and my cock immediately takes notice. Arousal spikes in my veins and she must notice because she lets her lip go and gasps quietly.

Neither of us has said anything, and I'm acutely aware that we aren't alone in the room, but I can't take my eyes off of her. I don't want to even blink for fear that she'll disappear. "I'm going to step out and give you guys a moment," Wren says. I assume he wants out of this tiny office filled with tension, our emotions, and our racing hormones. "Liv." He nods at Olivia and nudges her shoulder gently as he walks by with a smile on his face.

"Hi Wren," she whispers, offering him a smile that I wish she was giving me.

Look at me, baby.

As if she can hear my thoughts, she turns towards me and takes a tentative step into the room. "I knew you had an appointment today…I'm sorry for just showing up. I should have called or let you know I would be here."

"You don't have to call." I shake my head. "You're welcome anywhere I am, anytime."

She swallows and nods towards the paperwork on the desk. "What did Wren say?"

"Oh, well. I'm good as new." I give her my best smile. "Everything looks good."

Her eyes light up. "That's great, Bennett. I'm glad you're better."

I want to tell her that I'm not better. That nothing feels right without her, but I settle for asking her a question, that I'm sure I already know the answer to. "How are you?"

"I'm okay. You?"

I nod. "Fine." I close my eyes for a second, hearing my mother's words in my ear. *Fight for her.* "Terrible," I correct myself.

When I open my eyes, hers are fixed on me. "Same." Her gorgeous waves frame her face and she tucks some of it behind her ear. "I don't know if you're busy or anything, but I was thinking maybe we could take a walk?"

My eyes widen as I hear her request, my mind flashing to weeks down the road where we are back together. *Don't get ahead of yourself, she could be ending it for good.* "Anywhere."

The wind whips around us as we start walking through Central Park, something we'd done hundreds of times when we were married. Olivia and I are one of those couples that never run out of things to talk about. I genuinely enjoy her company and conversation even when we're forced to put on clothes and we'd spend hours in the park talking about everything and nothing. I swear we had so many little moments here that later we realized were big moments.

She'd wrapped a scarf around her neck when we got outside, and I worry she's still cold with how she's got her arms wrapped around her. "Are you cold?"

"No. I'm just…nervous."

"Around me?"

She doesn't respond and we continue walking when she sits on a bench and I follow suit.

"Are you telling me it's over?" I figured if she's about to break my heart, she should just do it now and get it over with.

"Is that…what you want? I mean…have we gone so far down a road we can't come back from?

"You haven't been paying attention if you could possibly think that's what I want. I'm willing to do whatever it takes to keep you. To keep us."

She's quiet for a few moments before she takes a deep breath and looks at me. "I miss you." Her lips form a straight line. "I tried not to. I was hoping that asking you to leave would give me a clear head and it did." The tears have now begun to fall down her face. Slow single tears that I want to lick away. "It made me realize how much I love you and hate being away from you. I don't want a divorce, Clarke. I want to fix our marriage. I know it's been a rough year and things happened that shouldn't have, but I want to leave it in the past and move forward. I want…I want my husband back."

My heart is pounding in my chest hearing her words. I grab her hands, pulling them to my lips and running them over her fingertips. "Baby." I sense her shiver even though I'm not looking at her and when I look up, she's staring at me with a doe-like expression. I press my forehead to hers. "I've been miserable without you. Truly. Living without you has been hell on Earth." I move closer to her and she meets me in the middle so our thighs are touching and I want nothing more than to pull her into my lap, but I know that's the quickest way to get us cited for public indecency because I'm seconds from ravaging her.

"So you'll come home?"

"Fuck yes, and I am never leaving it again. Wherever you are, that's where I need to be."

She must not realize how wound my body is and how desperate it is for her because she lunges for me, wrapping her petite body around mine and squeezing. She's sitting in my lap, her arms wrapped around my neck and her face pressed into it. "I missed you so much," she whispers and I squeeze her to me.

"You have no idea." I rock her gently as she cries into my neck but I pull her back. "Hey hey." She looks up at me and I trace her full pouty lips with my finger before dipping my index finger inside. "Nothing like this ever again, Livi." She nods emphatically. "You and me."

"Forever and ever."

EPILOGUE

Olivia
Two Years Later

MY EYES FLY OPEN AND IMMEDIATELY I FROWN WHEN I realize I'm alone in bed. I've always hated waking up alone. It goes back to those six months Bennett and I were separated. *The Dark Ages,* we called it. It's been two years since then, and if possible I think our marriage is stronger than ever. We are happier than I ever thought we could be after what happened. I sit up in bed, my body still deliciously sore and naked after what Bennett did to me late last night and a smile finds my lips as I rub the chapped skin. My breasts ache slightly after all the attention they received last night and I wince when I slide a t-shirt on over my naked body.

We did move into a bigger apartment, wanting to start over fresh and new as we closed out a chapter of our lives. I tiptoe through the apartment and I can already feel my ovaries exploding as I hear my husband's voice in the room over.

"You are the most perfect baby, you know that?" I hear our son gurgling and I cock my head to the side as I watch my half naked husband talk to our son who's still in his crib. He's leaning against the railing, staring down at him when I see him reach inside. "You want to go see if Mama's awake?"

"Mama!" he cries as Bennett picks him up and cradles him against his bare chest. *Fuck.* I press my thighs together at the visual and when he turns around, the way he rakes his gaze from my feet to my eyes makes me even wetter.

"Good morning, beautiful."

"You weren't in bed when I woke up." I bite my bottom lip and his eyes darken.

"I'm sorry baby, but our little man was talking up a storm." He kisses his temple before smoothing his very curly sandy brown hair back.

"I'm surprised I didn't hear him."

"I'm not. I wore you out last night." He leans forward, letting his lips hover over mine, "and I plan to do it again tonight."

"Mamaaaaa." Bennett pulls back and our son all but lunges for me.

"Well, you are full of energy this morning, aren't you pumpkin?!" Brayden Clarke was the surprise in the second act neither of us saw coming. *Our rainbow baby.*

Imagine my shock when I went to the doctor only three months after Bennett and I had reconciled to find out that we were having a baby. We'd been heavily considering In-Vitro-Fertilization, but Mother Nature beat us to it. We were both scared shitless, but with *a lot* of research and even more trips to the Doctor, I was able to have a pretty normal pregnancy. The doctor's told us this happened all the time, a few miscarriages can often lead to having perfectly safe and normal pregnancies. After that, it was as if everything fell into place. We were both concerned with me having the most low-risk and low-stress pregnancy, so it was as if the problems from before floated away at the promise of new life. Brayden made his entrance into the world, right on time and I've been on cloud nine ever since.

Here's hoping this one will be just as easy. I giggle to myself as I think about telling Bennett, that we are pregnant again when he gives me a look.

"Care to share with the class, Mrs. Clarke?"

"I was just thinking…"

"About…" He raises an eyebrow as we walk towards our bedroom. Brayden is playing with my hair, tugging it gently. I wince, when I feel Bennett, removing it from his hand. "Now Bray, no pulling Mama's hair. Only Dada can do that." He gives me a devilish grin before dropping on the bed and holding his hand out for me to join him. I snuggle against him, holding our baby in my arms just as his eyes flutter closed. I grab one of his pacifiers from my nightstand and slip it into his mouth as he drifts off to sleep.

"So, you were thinking…"

"About maybe trying for another one?" I look up at him and he rubs his chin.

"Hmmm."

Shit. Is he not ready? "No? I mean if you're not ready or you don't think now is a good time…" I begin to panic when I feel his knuckles drifting down my arm gently.

"No, I had just been curious how you were going to tell me you were pregnant." He gives me a cheeky smile and I gasp.

"You knew?!"

A cocky smiles finds his lips as he side eyes me slightly. "Yes, baby. I knew."

"How?!"

"I know when your period is, your boobs are huge, and I know your body better than I know my own. Come on, Livi." He leans back against the bed and I lay our sleeping baby on top of his chest. I press a kiss to his forehead before turning to his father.

"Are you happy?"

"About you giving me another baby? Absolutely. I am so fucking happy."

I glare at him, though the smile threatens to break through. "You know I'm going to kick your…you know what the first time our child says F-U-C-K."

He rolls his eyes. "So, I was thinking of having Alyssa and Wren babysit tonight."

"Why?"

"So, you and I could have a date night."

My eyes light up and a grin finds my face as I think about our date nights of the past year. Essentially, we ate dinner standing up in our kitchen in about ten minutes and then proceeded to fuck over every inch of our apartment and then took a nap before our child returned.

"Really?"

"Well, I was thinking like a real date, where we go out and dress up. Not necessarily one that consists of us sixty-nineing on the couch."

I pout. "I like that, though. I don't have to put on pants."

"Can a guy take his wife out to dinner?"

"Can a guy make his wife come in ten different ways?" I retort and he laughs aloud.

"You're the worst woman ever," he says shaking his head at me.

"You knew that when you married me," I sass. He chuckles, and I lean down and press a kiss to his lips careful not to rouse our sleeping baby. "I will agree to dinner tonight, if you put him back in his crib and we have *my* kind of date night now." I bite my lip for emphasis and his green eyes darken.

He gets up slowly and makes his way to the nursery. He's back in less than a minute and on top of me, pulling me down the bed and wrapping my legs around him. "I love you," he murmurs against my lips.

"I love you too," I whisper back.

"Being with you...being your husband has been the best ride of my life. You. Our babies. I fucking love our life, Olivia."

"Hmmm." I pull my shirt up, revealing my naked body. "And don't you forget it."

The End

Want to read another angsty emotional story surrounding a marriage? Check out *Bittersweet Surrender*.

Preview of *Bittersweet Surrender*

PROLOGUE

I WAS A GOOD WIFE.
   I was loyal to a fault, playing the perfect, doting wife to a man I married at the naive age of twenty-one, when I viewed the world through those rose-colored glasses they warn you about. I loved him, supported him, and I was undeniably faithful to him.

I was a good wife.

Until one day, temptation presented itself in the form of a broken marriage and the beautiful man whose job it was to fix it. I never imagined myself capable of infidelity until the man I married lost all interest in me, just in time for another to take notice.

Now, here I am opening my mind, my heart, and now my body to a man who isn't my husband.

How did I get here?

I feel as if I'm having an out-of-body experience, my soul floating above my physical self as I watch myself in complete fascination. I watch as a man shoves me up against the wall of the large corner office on the fourteenth floor of a building on Clinton Street, in Midtown Atlanta. I watch myself wrap my arms and legs around him as his lips find my neck. I hear the clash of our teeth as our mouths ravage each other, our tongues intertwining furiously. His hands move out of my wavy tresses, down my face to grope my breasts. My hands slide down his torso, my fingertips dancing over every hard ridge hidden beneath his cashmere sweater. I watch as I fumble with his pants, desperate to get them down his legs. My body is on fire for his touch. I'm desperate to feel him inside of me, to feel the connection of our bodies becoming one. The arousal pumping through my veins is something I've never experienced. I've never had this kind of passion with anyone.

Not even my husband.

You may think you know my story, but you have no idea.
I was a good wife…until I wasn't.

Bittersweet Surrender is available now!

ACKOWLEDGEMENTS

This book wouldn't... *couldn't* have happened without some pretty fabulous people. Your input, your love, your support is invaluable to me. As I, (and Carrie Bradshaw) have said probably a million times—sometimes family is the one you're born into, and sometimes it's the one you make for yourself.

Carmel Rhodes, my girl for life. Thank you for everything. For pushing. For mom-aging. For talking every last thing out with me at the most insane hours. For telling me "yes, this is it," but more importantly for telling me "no, this ain't it." The T to my C. Love you!

Melissa Spence, Leslie Middleton, Erica Marselas, Helen Hadjia, Kristene Bernabe, Harlow Layne, Kristina Loaiza my insanely thorough betas, you've been with me for quite a while at this point and I don't think you even understand what it means to me. I love you guys so much for everything you've done and do for me every day. You continue to show up for me and for that I'm so grateful!

Jeanette Piastri, where do I begin? Thank you for helping me bring all of my book babies to life over and over again. I still think this is my favorite cover! I'm so excited to see what you do next!

Kristen Portillo & Stacey Blake, with every book I swear it gets better, and it's because of you both! Your magic never ceases to amaze me!

Kelsey Cheyenne, Danielle James, Gemini Jensen, Rose Croft and Alexis Rae, Thank you for being a sounding board, a safe space and my tribe. I love being on this journey with you guys! So much love.

Denise Reyes, I am so freaking grateful for you. You've taken on so many roles at this point, I don't even know where to start thanking you. For beta reading this. For keeping me going. For talking with me about everything book related and for being in a different time zone which means I can message you at two in the morning and you'll see it! For running my street team. Gah! My love for you is endless! Thank you so much!

My Street Team Babes: What was I doing before you all came along? You guys have changed my writing career for the better and I love you so much! Your enthusiasm, your excitement, your support means everything to me. I don't think I can say that enough. A million thank yous!

All the amazing and super talented authos: I'm so lucky to know so many of you and I can't thank you enough for your friendship and advice and support! I can't wait to meet so many more of you in just a few weeks!

To everyone in the Hive, I love you! Some of you have been with me, what, almost five years? Where does the time go? Thank you for your love and your support and making me feel like I *can.*

And finally, to the readers: Thank you for going on yet another journey with me. You guys rock my world every day!

ALSO BY
Q.B. TYLER

My Best Friend's Sister

Unconditional

BITTERSWEET DUET

Bittersweet Surrender

Bittersweet Addiction

CAMPUS TALES SERIES

First Semester

Second Semester

Spring Semester

ABOUT THE AUTHOR

Hailing from the Nation's Capital, Q.B. Tyler, spends her days constructing her "happily ever afters" with a twist, featuring sassy heroines and the heroes that worship them. But most importantly the love story that develops despite *inconvenient* circumstances.

Sign up for her newsletter to stay in touch!
(eepurl.com/doT8EL)

Qbtyler03@gmail.com

Website: www.authorqbtyler.com

Facebook: facebook.com/author.qbtyler

Reader Group: www.facebook.com/groups/784082448468154

Goodreads: www.goodreads.com/author/show/17506935.Q_B_Tyler

Instagram: www.instagram.com/author.qbtyler

Bookbub: www.bookbub.com/profile/q-b-tyler

Wordpress: qbtyler.wordpress.com

Twitter: twitter.com/qbtyler

Printed in Great Britain
by Amazon